BEAT ME WITH YOUR WORDS

an inspirational story of survival and hope

by Jenny Dee

Beat Me With Your Words

DEDICATION

"He didn't have to hit me to leave a scar."
~Allison M. Rockwell

For every victim and every survivor of emotional abuse. It's time to break the cycle and find the power in our stories. Let no one beat you words ever again.

PROLOGUE

I can't pinpoint the moment I went from a straight-A, clever girl to downright delusional; confident to submissive; loved to abused.

But it happened.

Little by little, the woman that I used to be was chipped away—sculpted into a hermetic shell. Unrecognizable not only to others but to the mirror that reflected every last emotional scar.

How a professionally respected and beloved woman of integrity fell from grace into shell-shocked despair is unknown.

But it happened.

Slowly. Methodically. Almost irreparably. *Almost.*

Years of little white lies and demeaning words metamorphosed into bolder deceptions and a laughable exploitation of desperate gullibility.

Emotional rape.

Violating my heart without consent and pounding away at my sentient vagina until it no longer felt anything but shame.

Shame—and the fear that I would never be the same again.

1. SERENDIPITY

I wasn't always a victim of master manipulation.

I think.

I was born with innate confidence and creativity that kept me reading and exploring all kinds of fascinating subjects. I wanted to know about the diversity of the world's religions and compare how one idea of God was different from the power of another name. I craved an economic understanding of the analysis and predictions behind investments and portfolios.

I begged to learn foreign languages, research our ecosystems like a marine biologist, and taste the exotic cuisines of unexplored cultures. I became self-taught in sewing and costume-making, which became one of my greatest passions (just ask my fabulously dressed Barbie dolls).

I wanted to see the world in all its splendor; from what's left of the seven wonders to ancient sites encased with a magic that defies science.

A fortified nerd, my mind was built to gather information and use it like a *Jeopardy!* champion. It didn't exactly make me popular—the combination of being super smart, yet also painstakingly shy, made friendships, boyfriends, and even peers challenging to come by.

Oh, I had a few friends who accepted my ironically introverted quirkiness—you know, the girl who dared to dream but never left the house. Other than that, only unrequited crushes and being picked last for whatever sport we played in gym class became the story of my life.

Thankfully, I wasn't really bullied. Just not accepted as part of the mainstream crowd. Though the popular kids *did* talk to me. They'd tell me how sweet or funny they thought I was, and they'd often compliment me on my unique twists of those '90s wardrobe trends. I did have style, to my credit.

I guess I was interesting enough to not be made fun of and quiet enough to fly under the radar. I was grateful for this small adolescent miracle.

I survived middle and high school by throwing myself into academia for the chance to matriculate at a good college and make a decent professional life for myself. My confidence came straight from my well-oiled brain, and while it saved me in many ways, it let me down in others.

Like in matters of the heart.

I was raised in middle-class America by two hardworking parents and a younger sister, with aspirations of becoming a world-famous fashion designer. I saw my initials etched on the labels and my designs lining the storefront windows of the most notable boutique stores. Red carpet winners would wear my dresses which, of course, would be *EGD* originals. Paris would be my second home, from which I'd launch my new lines, alongside my close pals, Donatella and Vera.

My life intentions didn't exactly sit well with the elders, who expected much more from me—as in the real-world application of my intellect in exchange for exorbitant amounts of money.

"Emily, you are the first in our family to go to college. Making clothes isn't exactly what we envision for your future!"

"The world right now is all about business. Don't you want to graduate, get a good-paying job, and be able to support yourself?"

"I'm afraid you haven't taken any extracurricular activities in design and fashion, so you may not qualify for the right college entry. Simply liking clothes isn't enough. But I see here that you are at the top of your class in economics—that seems much more suitable for a girl of your intelligence."

Yes, these well-intended talks with my parents, teachers, and counselors taught me from an early age to not dream the impossible. Unless I was a descendant of Coco or Louis, I was assured that fashion success was unlikely for a small-town, Jersey girl. So, I settled on my love of math as my backup plan, with their overwhelming approval.

I rescind my declaration that I was not prone to manipulation.

In my defense, however, I figured maybe one day if I were a successful financial planner, I could afford my overzealous desire to visit all seven continents and appease my heart later in life. I could continue to dabble in Barbie couture—for my younger cousins—to keep that fire burning in my spare time. I'd just make my dreams come true some other way. I would make it so.

It turned out to be a wise choice to listen to the

adults, after all. According to my Macroeconomics college professor, I had a bright, successful future in front of me.

"Miss Davidson, may I have a word with you?" she asked one day as class dismissed. I had two hours before my next class in Statistics, so I was more than happy to give one of my favorite female role models some of my time.

"Yes, Dr. Edelstein?"

"I wanted to speak to you about your plans for an internship. Have you considered where you will be applying yet?"

"Actually, I have a few in mind. Grangers, Carruthers, and Narnians. I was planning on submitting my applications this weekend."

"Those are all decent, entry-level internships. Proper choices," she admitted, but with a bit of dissatisfaction dangling from her words.

"Is something wrong with them?" I inquired, curious to hear her expert opinion on my future.

"Miss Davidson, I have been teaching in this institution for over thirty years, and it is rare that I come across a student who is so naturally gifted in this field—especially one who is a woman. I was rather impressed with your paper on *The Production and Distribution of a Unified Wealth,* which was insightful, innovative, and well-researched," she commended before continuing. "And I have to say, in addition to your intellect, you are poised, respectful, and diplomatic, and I truly believe that great things will come from you."

"Thank you," I blushed, used to academic praise but not compliments on my actual personality.

"That being said, I think you can do much better than Grangers, Carruthers, and Narnians. All respectable, of course. But I have shared your paper with Beckingers, and they are interested in having you come on as their junior intern associate for the fall semester—if you are interested, of course."

I was speechless. Beckingers? *The* Beckingers? It used to be the most sought-after internship in the economics department until they stopped taking applications ten years ago. How was this even possible?

"Miss Davidson?" Dr. Edelstein interrupted; a bit amused that I was mortifyingly shell-shocked but still awaiting my response.

"Oh, Dr. Edelstein, I don't know what to say," I began. "Of course, I would be interested. But how were you able to get them to consider my application? Do you know someone there?"

"I do, yes. However, it was your words and theories that opened the door, not my influence," she cautioned. "Miss Davidson, never doubt your unique abilities or strength. You are an admirable young woman, and this is only the first of many more successes ahead for you."

I smiled, and she softened, seeing as though we were the only two remaining in the room.

"Always stay true to who you are, Emily." And in a rare moment of genuine affection, my esteemed professor hugged me and whispered how proud she was of me.

My future was set. I was going to intern at Beckingers as a sophomore, and that would lead to a solid resumé from which I could land a prestigious position with a firm closer to home. I was going to heed her advice and believe in myself. Believe in my capabilities to be someone important.

I was satisfied with my ambitious plan. I was ready to venture into alpha-female land, confident in the path in front of me. My career would be more than enough for me to build a happy, fulfilling life.

It wasn't like the men were beating down my door anyway, so I convinced myself that love and marriage were not in the cards for this degree-earning diva just yet.

Oh, I dabbled with some kissing and whatnot with a few willing participants who saw my blossoming beauty before my brains, but nothing that ever manifested into a real relationship. I accepted that I was going to be one of those high-powered, female executives who lived an extraordinarily independent existence.

That was before one life-changing summer day when Prince Charming unceremoniously galloped his white horse into my well-thought-out life.

***

It truly began as the real-life fairytale that little girls dream of. That *I* dreamed of.

I grew up on Disney princesses and soap operas, believing in love at first sight. So, I knew it when I felt it.

There I was, Emily Grace Davidson, at my little in-between college semesters, summer convenience store gig minding my own business, when Blake Denton strolled right on up in his signature navy blue uniform polo shirt. He casually sat on the edge of my customer-less cashier counter to purchase a Milky Way bar on his break. Taken aback by the uncontrollable emotional impulses triggered by the visceral shock of this godlike vision before me, my heart thumped in my chest as if it could explode into thunderous pyrotechnics.

Calm yourself, Emily, my mind warned, not completely understanding what was happening inside of me. I had never encountered such an immediate rush of attraction before.

Blake appeared all cool and collected, yet I witnessed him looking me up and down, seemingly surprised at his own reaction. He even needed to clear his throat before speaking, I noticed.

"And who might you be, beautiful?" asked the emerald-eyed stud in front of me, trying to play off some of his own obvious discomposure over our unexpected encounter.

As soon as my brain and heart came back down to join my body on Earth, I pulled myself together to make a quick assessment of the man sitting before me. Assessment was my thing: in money, in decisions, in character.

Oh, he was definitely a smooth talker, I observed critically, who obviously knew he was good-looking—yet, despite my usual resistance to overly suave men, whatever magnetic charges he was sending out, I was being drawn to. I was interested enough to engage, though unsure of myself and the way in which he caught my emotions off-guard. It's like my radar got stuck in this alternate universe.

It's just a conversation, Emily. Just be yourself. I could hear the paraphrase of Dr. Edelstein's wisdom swirling around my head.

"I'm Emily. You must be Blake," I coolly replied, the sweat forming while I nervously fiddled with a loose curl that had fallen out of my pulled-back ponytail. *Why was I feeling so uneasy?*

"Ah, so you've heard of me?" he quizzed with an amused, cocky smile and a tilt of his head that brought a mischievous twinkle to his penetrating eyes. He sure knew how to quickly regain confidence, didn't he? *I see how it is, player,* I thought, gaining my wits back with a smirk.

"No. I read your nametag," I countered, grateful for a clever comeback instead of appearing like a little schoolgirl with a crush. It gave me a rush of pleasure to be able to put his effortless ego in check—and exercise some dignity while I sorted out these raging hormonal urges linked to the sensuality of his deep masculine voice.

Score one for Emily.

"Cute," he responded, acknowledging my ingenuity with a highbrowed inspection.

"Thank you. You're not so bad-looking yourself." Another point. *Yes!*

I couldn't help but default to that innate wit of mine, not knowing how else to control the messy sensations that were bubbling up, courtesy of this electric meet-cute. I could tell I intrigued him—he probably expected fumbled, girly giggles instead of my articulate one-liners.

"You're funny," he acquiesced with a goofy grin. He looked directly at me to continue his first impression investigation. The moment our eyes connected, it was game over for me. The goosebumps popped and the butterflies coursed through me like an out-of-body experience that screamed "soulmate." I shuddered with chills of subconscious recognition.

In that single, unforeseen, destined moment, the universe collided, and I *knew* he was "the one." I couldn't tell you *how* I knew; I just did. He'd be my husband and the father of my children, I surmised dreamily in my head.

I soaked in his tall, basketball-worthy stature, shapely torso, and boyishly blonde preppy cut. His beautiful, deep green eyes lit up, and his side smirk gave me all the validation I needed—that in this very instant, he felt the same spark of kismet I did.

"Well, guess I'll be seeing you around, *Emily*," he hummed, emphasizing my name as he swaggered away back toward the storeroom.

I couldn't believe what had just happened. This kind of thing doesn't happen in real life. Or does it?

I had no doubt that my life was going to forever be changed from that moment on. Years of wondering if I would ever find love evaporated into his jade pools and left me questioning if this was genuinely real.

Did a storybook just jump off the pages and into my life? Could this magical feeling that overcame me truly exist after all?

Yes. Oh, absolutely, yes. I fell for and succumbed to the serendipitous spell.

***

"Emily? Hello? Anyone there?" asked my perturbed co-worker, Marcus, whose classically tall, dark, and handsome Latino looks were disturbed by an uncommon frown as he approached my register.

"What? Oh, yes. Hi, Marc. What's up?" I asked, finally pulling myself out of distraction to give him my undivided attention. After all, he blocked most of my view of Blake's fading backside anyway, so unless I wanted to be obvious, I needed to come back down to reality fast.

"What's up?" he repeated, venturing to turn his head to see where my eyes were recently focused and then rolled his eyes in exaggeration. Too late. I was busted. "We were supposed to meet up for lunch about 15 minutes ago, remember?"

"Oh, right. Sorry. I guess I lost track of time," I responded, fumbling to find my purse.

"Oh no," he moaned, not used to seeing the always-put-together side of me so disheveled. "Please don't tell me you have a thing for that guy."

"What are you talking about? What guy?" I tried to respond innocently. Unfortunately, my dear friend from high school knew me all too well, and I couldn't lie to save my life.

"The one that just walked back into the storeroom. Blake Denton."

"What about him? He seems nice," I defended.

"Oh, Em. You are way too sweet and innocent when it comes to men," he said with half playfulness, half concern. Marcus had always looked out for me since the day we met, and while I liked that in an ally, I didn't need his unrequested opinion when my heart was soaring.

"I'm a big girl, Marcus. I'll be fine," I promised with my hands crossed over my heart.

Luckily, he let it go with a disgruntled grumble,

and off we went to lunch to talk about anything but Blake Denton. And yet, all I could think about was that boy and the enchantment I had just experienced. I felt like I had met that special someone—the one I had been waiting for my entire life—no matter what my overprotective friend might have thought of my innocent instincts. Marcus wouldn't understand. Nobody would. I didn't even understand it myself.

For so many years, I never believed that I was meant to find love; that I was only meant for business. This was potentially a game-changer for me, dispelling every notion I ever had of thinking that the fairytale life was not for me. How could I not be intrigued to walk through that looking glass?

But it took some convincing on my part to hook this hesitant man into my heart's web. Although I was certain Blake felt our connection, he wasn't exactly the romantic and spellbound type at first. He'd weave in and out of interest and was hard to read at times. I couldn't understand his skittishness when he was so naturally flirty.

I thought it was because I might have come on a little too strong in the beginning, persistent in my pursuit of a date—which I later learned can be a turn-off for a man who'd prefer to do the chasing. It was hard for me to consider downplaying my interest when I had been guided all my life to go after everything I wanted; to fight for it.

Thank goodness for friends like Marcus and my bestie, Jessica, who had the experience to steer me in the right direction.

"You're probably scaring him away," Jess warned. "Guys like to be the ones calling the shots."

"But why? What's the big deal? I don't understand why I have to be someone I'm not." This was all counterintuitive to what every elder has ever said to me about being a woman in a modern world.

"I don't know. I think deep down, men are all still cavemen," she said with a giggle. "Just tone down your intensity. Let him come to you."

"Do you think it will really work?"

"Trust me on this. If he's interested, you'll know," she asserted.

Really? *How* would I know? I never had a boyfriend before, so I was entering new territory that my academic brain couldn't give me the map to.

This romance thing was so weird. Not at all like the stories I read.

But just as I was advised, I noticed Blake came around more when I backed off. It was working like a charm.

He started leaving these little notes in my workspace, always signed with *BD* and a mini Milky Way so I'd secretly know who they were from.

"Mr. Horbitz is in a mood this morning. Just dazzle him with your smile and you'll be fine."

"You look adorable today. I like when you curl your hair."

"Lunch break at 1. See you in the café?"

Whenever we did end up having a break at the same time, we'd simply meet up at the next-door café to talk and get to know each other better. The conversations were engaging and enlightening. He was more fascinating than I ever imagined—and more worldly, too. He'd tell me about all the places he visited, and I'd feel like I was living life vicariously through his words.

The strange part for me was how he was actually interested in learning more about *me*—the boring economics girl—and would constantly tell me how I fascinated him by being so real, raw, and genuine. He said it was rare to find a woman who listened with sincere interest and didn't always make the conversations all about her. Refreshing, I believe he called me once.

"I've never met anyone quite like you, Emily Grace. It's like I can just see who you are whenever I look into your eyes. Like I've known you forever," he said, making me swoon while sipping on his fountain lemonade.

"I feel the same way! Weird how I'm so at ease with you," I assured him back, trying to come off casual instead of desperate. Ugh, how difficult it was to find that kind of balance, especially when the wrong words or actions could scare him away. I'm afraid I am much better at negotiating a mock business deal in class than I am at these feeble attempts of romantic connection.

"Cool. I really enjoy spending time with you like this," he responded as he courteously bowed away to return to his shift. I exhaled a sigh of relief that he didn't notice my inept social awkwardness for once.

We continued to have these intriguing conversations whenever we were together—for the short snippets of time I could steal away from him. But whenever I would hint at (or blatantly suggest) a real date—you know, like the ones you would go on *outside* of work—there was always some reason that kept it from happening, even when he finally caved in and committed to a plan.

"Hey, so what movie did you want to see this weekend?" I asked one day after he agreed to catch an evening flick with me.

"Oh, about that," he fumbled nervously. "I'm sorry, but I can't go this weekend. My cousin, Monica, unexpectedly died in a car accident, and we have to travel to Georgia for her funeral this weekend."

"Oh my goodness, I am so sorry! Are you okay? Is there anything I can do?"

"No. You're sweet to ask, though," he replied with a smile. "We weren't really all that close. One of those distant cousins on my mother's side that I hardly saw. It's more of an obligated respect thing that I can't get out of. Raincheck?"

"Absolutely," I agreed with an optimistic grin.

Though, I wasn't quite sure when I would cash in on that raincheck as he had to apologetically cancel a few more times. Like when his brother punched a hole in the living room wall, and he had to help his dad repair the damage. And when he found out that his cat, Spencer, had cancer, and he had to go to the vet with his mom to get the tumor removed.

Talk about a string of mishaps, as if destiny were telling him to stay away from me. I was beginning to think Blake was right when he once claimed that bad luck seemed to follow him wherever he went.

Or maybe I just couldn't take the hint, blinded by my own fixation with fate, and he was trying to let me down easy. Maybe he was seeing someone else, but since I never had the courage to ask, he never offered up that intel. Maybe he was gay, and I didn't have the right signal to read him. Maybe he just simply wasn't interested in me romantically. I did seem to have tunnel vision when it came to this boy, which was very unusual for me. Logic failed me at every turn.

But then, after declining a date, he'd turn around and leave another sweet, flirty note at my cashier post or invite me to lunch, and it would renew my hope that maybe, just maybe, he'd come around in time.

I don't think I was imagining that he seemed to be just as drawn as I was, albeit a man of very little action as the summer months dwindled on. No successful after-work dates, no phone number exchange—what were all those notes and lunch invites if not a show of interest?

I had to sometimes stop and ask myself: *Was I really off track in believing that we were meant to be?*

Time had interrupted my romantic research, and I had to return to William & Mary in Virginia for my fall semester. Blake and I had still not exchanged numbers at this point—he simply hugged me goodbye and told me he couldn't wait to see me again over break—and with that seemingly platonic gesture, I had to let it go.

I guess he enjoyed my company, but only as a friend. Just like so many crushes before him who preferred my friendship to "ruining it with romance." And like Jess lovingly warned, if he were interested, he would have made a move by now.

So, with a heavy heart, I left town, pushed thoughts of Blake aside, and threw myself back into my safe zone: academics.

***

I began my internship at Beckingers and thrived there. I was enamored with everything I learned, soaking up the intricacies of the business world like a sponge. My direct manager, Harold, was a stodgy old man who warmed up to me quickly as I proved my usefulness to him.

"Emily, you are a tremendous asset to the department. I'd like to give you a few more responsibilities, if you don't mind. I think you are capable of handling the workload," said the nearing 60-year-old man with an obvious toupee and yellowed mustache. His frowning wrinkles were prominent, and I wondered if he was ever happy or smiled a day in his life.

"Yes, sir. I am learning so much, and I appreciate your faith in me. I'm happy to take on whatever tasks you need me to."

"It's nice to have someone so eager to learn and pitch in. You will make another company very profitable one day. That is, unless you reconsider my proposal to move to Virginia and stay on with us after graduation."

"We'll see," I responded, feeling grateful for the opportunity. I wouldn't let Harold know, but I was seriously considering his offer. I would be a fool to turn it down, but I wasn't sure I wanted to permanently live so far away from my family. Regardless, I knew that along with an impressive resumé, I'd have an outstanding recommendation from Beckingers that would open almost any door of my choosing when I graduated. That in itself was quite an achievement for a sophomore.

I was back on the right track for my future. Only

two and a half more years, and I'd be ready to take on the world as a badass investment executive (in training).

Well, that vision was clear until I returned back home and found myself face-to-face with Blake Denton once again. All the crazy feels came rushing back, as much as my sensible brain tried to remind me that rekindling an unrequited infatuation would only hurt me again and distract me from my goals.

And yet, it seemed as though it wasn't unrequited after all. Perhaps the break from seeing each other while I was away made him miss me a little; made him realize what he was missing by pushing me away.

Was I imagining that his face lit up at the sight of me walking back into the convenience store that cold December day my winter break began? Was that a sour scowl I saw whenever I would stop and chat with Marcus or other male co-workers? Were those wistful, playful work notes welcoming me home really meant to be just platonic?

Well, if they were meant to be more, I was going to take full advantage of his renewed interest and boyish jealousy. I was ignoring all bestie advice and going for it; it's how I was in business, and I decided, how I'd be in love. And I knew exactly how to get his attention.

After only a few days of another cat and mouse game, I wore him down into submission with my tempting dark chocolate-colored eyes and luscious coffee-highlighted locks that cascaded down to the middle of my backside in curls—exactly the way he liked them. A few more seductive walks, a swivel of my curving hips as I approached, and some hot new ruby red lipstick, and Blake could not deny his attraction any longer.

"Wow. You look, um, pretty hot," he managed to deliver, puffing out air as he ran his hand through his hair in delightful exasperation.

"Blake Denton, are you ready yet to go on a real date with me? I'm tired of waiting around for you to make a move. This is your final offer," I added, not knowing where this feminine confidence was coming from all of a sudden. But it *worked*.

"You are persistent, I'll give you that," he laughed as he relented, finally exchanging phone numbers with me with the promise of a casual dinner date. I had a feeling that it would actually work out this time. I'm pretty sure he caught the vibe that another cancellation would end whatever thing this was between us permanently.

"Just one date. It's all I ask," I requested sweetly. "After that, if you don't want to go back out with me, I will leave you alone forever. Girl Scout honor."

"That's just the problem," Blake yielded, closing part of the gap between us so that our lips were only inches apart. "I already know that once I kiss you, I won't ever be able to walk away."

I'll never forget the sincerity of his eyes as he muttered his vulnerable, solemn truth. Or the way I felt that truth with every fiber of my soul.

2. ROMANCE

Well, Blake was finally true to his word and delivered on his promise of a first date.

My, could that boy clean up nicely. With hair slicked back and a green button-down shirt that matched his eyes, he looked absolutely irresistible. It made me question what a gorgeous guy like him wanted with an average brainiac like me. Though from his wide-eyed reaction, I'm guessing I made the right choice in a hot pink dress that hugged my curves casually and wearing my hair down and curled.

"Well, hello there, gorgeous," he welcomed after composing himself. "Hop in."

His black Ford was an intoxicating mix of an almost-new car smell and his Obsession cologne, a scent my pheromones immediately approved of. I was taken aback by the car's condition, considering every time I went with Marcus somewhere, his car was consumed by gym socks, fast food fries, and other questionable odors. Blake's car was practically pristine, and I felt completely comfortable sliding in beside him.

"Where are we going?" He had my curiosity aroused, refusing to tell me anything ahead of time except to dress nicely—not formal, but not relaxed either. I admit that after being the one to hunt him down to go out on a date, it felt really good that he put so much effort into making our first outing together meaningful.

"You'll see," was all he responded with a look that begged for patience and trust. I reluctantly obliged.

But that patience and trust paid off when we pulled up to the valet at Scampi's, one of the most sophisticated restaurants in town. I remember my parents telling me it was near impossible to get a reservation, and now here I was, about to have dinner with Blake at this coveted couple's hotspot.

Unpredictably a gentleman, he came around to my side of the car to open the door, reaching out his hand to help me out. He gently kissed my hand and then smiled broadly as he looked into my surprised eyes.

"After you, my lady." I had thought the moment we met was like a fairytale, but the exquisite lengths that this man went to for chivalry caught my breath. Never in my entire life had a man ever been this interested, let alone pulled out all the stops to treat me like a princess. My initial reaction was to resist, as if I didn't deserve the royal treatment, but I quickly squelched my brain and decided to indulge in the magic.

The restaurant was ten times more breathtaking inside than out, with dazzling chandeliers and mirrored walls. It was filled with cozy, white-laced tables for two, set elegantly with gold-trimmed plates and candlelit red rose centerpieces. Soft classical music played in the background, setting the stage for the ultimate amorous evening.

Where had he been hiding all this romance?

"Blake, this place is incredible," I mused after we were graciously seated by the host.

"I'm glad you like it," he beamed. "I wanted to make it up to you for canceling so many times over the summer. And now, being with you here in this magnificent place, I realize it was worth the wait. At least, for me it was," he prompted.

"For me, too," I acknowledged, wondering how this night could get any better.

Blake being twenty-one, he was able to order a bottle of champagne for our table, expertly convincing the waiter that I was also of age, even though I was technically two years his junior. I smirked inside as I observed his charm in action—I'm pretty sure whatever Blake Denton wanted, he smooth-talked his way into. He had this coy way of disarming people; I'd seen it sometimes at work with our manager, but tonight I witnessed his true mastery. I had a feeling I'd need to keep my wits about me with this one. Who knows what he'd talk me into (or out of) by the end of the evening if I wasn't careful.

"To having dinner with the most beautiful woman in the world," he said, raising his glass in a toast.

"Thank you, but don't you think you're overdoing it just a little bit?" I giggled, the bubbles instantly rushing to my head. Or was it his compliments and swagger?

"Not at all," he sincerely replied. "You don't see yourself the way I do, do you?"

"I'm not exactly the hot popular girl type, you know," I admitted. "I've always been the nerd in the background, so it's new for me to consider myself as anything else."

"Yeah, but that's what I like about you. You're so sweetly humble. Your wit keeps me on my toes. Your smarts challenge me to think beyond my own perspective. And contrary to what you may believe, you are one hell of an attractive woman, curves and all." I blushed at his sincerity and seized the opportunity to dig deeper.

"Then why did it take you so long to agree to go out with me?"

"It didn't have anything to do with you, I can promise you that," he replied solemnly. "The timing wasn't right, I guess. But that doesn't matter, does it? We're here together now, right?"

"I suppose," I replied hesitantly.

"Oh, no. I can see those wheels turning in your head. Please don't do that thing where you start overthinking everything," he pleaded.

"I'm not—" I started to say, but his raised eyebrows suggested that I was just about to start my analysis of the situation. I stopped my mental chatter to let him finish his thought.

"Listen, I really like you. I like spending time with you. I just want to be here with you—right now. Can we simply start over from this moment and enjoy the evening without looking back? Now is all that ever matters anyway."

How could I resist such a profound and rousing request? I smiled and nodded as I took another sip of bubbly and did as he suggested: put the past behind us and focused only on this amazing night.

The food was more delicious than my tongue had ever experienced. We started with the thinly sliced raw prime sirloin with parmesan and truffle oil, followed by shared plates of veal piccata and shrimp scampi. When we couldn't eat anymore, he rose up from his chair and took my hand unexpectedly.

"Care to dance?"

"Dance? Here? But no one else is dancing," I pointed out as all the other guests were mindfully seated and engaged in conversation.

"Who cares? We make our own rules in life, Emily Grace. Dance with me," he asked again, a little more insistently, and I couldn't refuse. He was full of surprises—surprises I never even imagined, and I loved every bit of it. He was already changing up my routine life, and I was ready to throw some caution to my normally steady wind.

The moment Blake took me into his arms, I thought my insides would burst. Feeling the heat of his body up against mine, his scent enveloping my senses, and the electric softness of his hand entwined with my fingers was an emotional elixir I'd never felt before. Sure, I'd danced with some boys at those cheesy high school dances and with my dad and cousins at weddings, but this—this was different. It was sensual and exhilarating.

Our bodies somehow knew exactly how to sway to the music without ever having touched before, and it was as if no one else was in the room. I leaned my flushed cheek against his, feeling his accelerated breath on my neck and his other hand firm against my back. We spoke no words; we didn't need to. Some communication is stronger than language.

When the song ended and we broke apart, we awkwardly found our way back to our individual seats. We made some small talk after passing on dessert and asking for the check, which Blake insisted on taking care of in its entirety. I wondered if he was as uncomfortable as I was with the heightened tension between us, though he tried to smile it away with a few quips between him and the waiter that had us all laughing.

We moved in silence as we made our way back to the car. But even in the odd stillness of sound, I didn't want the evening to end. I wanted it to last forever. Sensing my reluctance, Blake grabbed my hand and held it tight as we walked, stirring up the same sensations from dancing. With just a single touch, I felt the serendipity I swore existed the moment we met.

When we arrived at the car, he stopped me for a moment to gently lift my chin up and sweep a loose tendril away from my eyes. We locked on each other for what seemed like an eternity before he leaned in cautiously, uncertain about how I would respond.

"I would *really* love to kiss you right now."

"Please do," I answered breathlessly.

When his lips met mine, it was delicately tender and inviting. I yielded, begging him for more, and he gave it to me, taking my breath along with my heart. His tongue found mine as he pressed his body against mine, his mere touch igniting the dormant passion yet to be accessed within the depths of my being.

Our first kiss was the most powerful connection I had ever experienced in my entire life. The cliché of fireworks really did burst all around us in that most exquisite moment. Time stood still, and life as I knew it would never be the same.

One date was all it took for us to realize we had

zero say in what destiny intended for us. From that very first evening, he had me wrapped around his beguiling finger.

***

There was no going back after that night; it instantly turned into a mutual desire to spend as much time as we could together before my winter break ended. Lunch breaks, dates, endless phone calls. Love notes, flowers, stolen kisses. The romance between us simply flourished beyond my wildest imagination.

And as much as the physical chemistry was clearly there, we were so much more than that. The conversations—oh, the conversations!—were just so enthralling. We'd talk about everything and anything. I'd come to realize that we were both sapiosexuals and stimulated by intellectual discussions of all kinds— travel, world events, spirituality. He could even keep up and was interesting in having conversations about economics.

The more I talked to Blake, the more I realized he wasn't just a captivating, pretty face; he was deep and smart and full of wisdom. He told me he had always been afraid to show this side of himself to people because then they would expect too much of him. But he said I was different, that I'd never make him be something he wasn't, and I accepted him for who he was.

"You know, my parents think I'm setting myself up for failure by wanting to pursue a career in photography. They said if I didn't go to college, I'd amount to nothing. But college just isn't for me."

"It's not for everyone, Blake," I agreed. "Besides, you took some trade school classes. You have an education in your field. Isn't that enough?"

"Apparently not," he huffed under his breath. "They expected more from me."

"I know how that feels," relating to his pain as I remembered how I sold out my dreams to become the business-minded major everyone expected me to be.

"You didn't want to go to college either?"

"Oh, I did. I just thought my path would be taking a different direction, that's all," I admitted.

"Yeah? So, what made you major in economics then?"

"I was good at math and analytics. It was a sensible choice."

"Being sensible sucks," he quipped, and I couldn't help but laugh at his bluntness. "Why don't you just change it now? They got what they wanted. You're in college. People change majors all the time. Can't you do whatever you want?"

"I guess I could," I reflected for a moment. "But I'm good at economics. I have an amazing internship opportunity that students in my position would kill for, and its pay grade is high once I'm out of entry-level. It's not what I imagined, but I'm happy enough with how things are working out."

"If you say so," he said, leaning in to give me a sweet cheek kiss. "All I know is that no one can make me give up my dream. It's full speed ahead for me! No matter where the road twists and turns."

I admired Blake's fearlessness. The way he was so

sure and confident about what he wanted. The way he was willing to risk it all, despite what his parents or anyone else thought. I wish I had that kind of courage to say, "fuck it" and follow my passion back to fashion design.

But we all have our choices to make, and where Blake was innately audacious, I was habitually prudent. I think that's what made us such a great match; the yin and yang of our very natures created a harmonious balance.

That harmonious balance, however, seemed to be put to the test whenever we were physically alone together. Not long after our first date, he had invited me over to his apartment to watch a movie. When I showed up at his door, he greeted me with a stunning array of pink lilies—one of my most favorite flowers. I instantly melted. A girl could get used to this kind of spoiling!

We settled onto his worn, plush couch, sitting uncomfortably distanced from each other as if we were some kind of new acquaintances. Thankfully, it didn't take long into the movie for him to gesture for me to come closer, where I nuzzled right into the space between his arm and chest contentedly. I inhaled his scent deeply—not of cologne this time, but merely of freshly washed, natural masculinity, and it was just as arousing.

Cool it, Emily, I warned myself. I was in new territory, and I needed to take things slow. I watched Jess jump into bed with too many guys before the relationship took off, and it either ended immediately with her in tears or became the basis of her relationship until they finally realized they didn't like each other outside of the bedroom. I wanted better for myself, and so, I knew I had to control my urges, no matter how strong they pulled me toward Blake.

But it was the normally restrained Blake who surprised me with an over-the-sweater rub of my breasts, trying coyly to be respectful about it. I counted on him to continue being a gentleman to spare myself from crossing a line, so now I knew I was in trouble.

"I'm sorry, I just couldn't resist," he apologized half-heartedly. "I've been wanting to be with you ever since I first laid eyes on your beautiful face. And I can't stop thinking about that kiss the other night. Now that you are here alone with me, it's hard for me to behave myself. I'll stop if you want me to," he offered.

Stop if I want him to? Hell, no!

My body craved him the second I not-so-innocently laid back to cuddle into his inviting arms. I instantly felt his heat—our heat—and it spurred tingling sensations that I had never felt in the presence of another man before.

"I don't mind at all," I voiced hoarsely, relaxing into him as I permissively allowed his hand to travel under my sweater and into my bra cup to feel the tautness of my bare nipple.

I was completely comfortable with taking it to second base, and only partially relieved that he didn't push for more. A moan escaped as he fondled me exquisitely yet delicately. How could a simple brush of my skin make me feel so wonderfully helpless and uninhibited?

"Be careful what you wish for, Princess. I'm not

sure you realize what you are getting yourself into," he teasingly forewarned, finally moving my body so that he had access to softly and passionately draw me in for a deep mystical kiss that liquified me from head to toe. His masterful tongue found mine, and we symbiotically forged an explorative union that drove our senses into the electric heavens.

"I never knew I could feel like this," he continued, gently groaning while nibbling my ear and neck, still massaging my breasts and resisting going any further. How he resisted, I couldn't tell you, because I was on the verge of succumbing to whatever he wanted in that very moment—well-thought-out intentions to take it slow be damned. Instead, he just seemed mesmerized by my lips and breasts until I found him deeply gazing into my eyes with intensity.

"I think you cast a spell on me, Emily Grace." Oh, how he made my heart smile and my soul playful.

"Didn't you know that was my plan all along? Welcome to my secret lair, Mr. Denton," I sensually joked before leaning in for another kiss.

Once I had him exactly where I wanted him, he acquiesced that he was under my spell forevermore.

***

After that night, I knew that if I was to sanely make it back to college with my innocence intact, I'd have to avoid clandestine movie nights on his couch. But as I'd soon find out, anywhere I was with Blake created temptation. There was no muting this growing feeling, especially when he was so damn charming and irresistible. No man had made me feel as attractive, as special, as he had in just a few short weeks.

He seemed to love planning these interesting dates that kept me guessing. One of my favorites, admittedly, was when he staged a photo shoot for me. He was still trying to make it in the photography business, and while his specialty was landscapes, he wanted to do something special for me while introducing me to his passion.

"Blake, what is all this?" I asked in a daze, admiring the racks of designer clothes that awakened my inner fashion diva. Chanel, Gucci, Prada—I was afraid to ask how he had gotten ahold of this dream wardrobe collection.

"Do you like it?"

"Like it? I feel like I've died and gone to Heaven! These gowns are exquisite—and these shoes? You have got to be kidding me. I saw them in a catalog the other day and envied the women of the world who were able to afford such glamour."

"Try them on," he gestured.

"I couldn't!" I gasped, appalled at the thought of rummaging through a gallery that belonged to someone else. Though it didn't stop me from running my fingers over those suede Jimmy Choos with longing.

"Emily, I organized all of this for *you*," he laughed. "There is nothing here that you cannot touch or try on." I looked at him in wonder and amazement. Surely, he was joking. But he wasn't.

"How—why—" I just couldn't find the words to express the marvelous disbelief I was feeling.

"I know some people," he smirked mischievously.

When I eyed him curiously to tell me more, he conceded. "I once helped a Vogue editor's nephew at the hospital I volunteer at, and she said if I ever needed anything, to call in the favor. She was more than happy to help me set this all up."

"I can't believe you did all of this for me," I barely whispered before I hugged and kissed him tenderly. It was the sweetest gesture anyone could have ever done for me. It's like Blake knew the doorway to the deepest part of my heart, and this was the key to open up what had been previously locked up.

"I want you to see yourself as I see you," he cryptically revealed as he left me with the coordinator, Gloria, to do my hair and makeup while he went to check on the "crew."

I was no model, but I felt like I could be on the cover of the magazine that day. He had all kinds of scenarios lined up for me—cowgirl (complete with hats and boots), over-the-top crinoline prom queen, sexy songstress in a revealing black dress, skimpy swimsuit model—you name it, he tried to dress me up as her.

Even though fashion was my dream, it wasn't easy for me to step outside of my personality comfort zone. But Blake had a way of easing my tension and convincing me to let my guard down. He made me feel so pretty and worth photographing. In every outfit, in every scene, he would encourage me to open up to the role currently on display, urging me to look deep within to find my hidden personas.

"Relax, girl. Pretend you are singing one of your favorite songs in your head—you know, the old Crystal Gayle one your mom always played that you secretly love," he taunted, tongue-in-cheek.

"Emily, you are riding a horse! Giddy up, girl! Make me believe you can control that steed!" Of course, that made me blush, but I believe that was the look he was going for.

"You are a queen. Wave to your crowd, madam," he mocked in his spot-on English gentleman imitation, and all I could do was laugh at his ridiculousness.

It was so easy to laugh with Blake, as if the weight of the world of school, my less-than-perfect home life, and other stressors didn't exist. He took me away to another dimension altogether. I became uninhibited, completely letting my uptight, serious side fade and go with the flow, falling into character effortlessly as the cameras flashed and the fans blew and the lighting brought me into a spotlight.

When all was said and done, I couldn't recognize the woman in those still photos.

"Wow," was all I could manage to say. "Is that really me?"

"It is," he whispered, coming up behind me and wrapping his hands around my waist. "This is who I see when I look at you. Everything you are and can be. This is my Emily."

I smiled warmly from the inside out at him calling me his, though I couldn't just let him take me without permission. I turned to him with questioning eyes.

"*Your* Emily, huh? Is that so?"

"Oh, it's so," he replied and drew me into a heated kiss without warning. There was no resisting his touch or his charm. He was right; I was his—hook, line, and sinker. With the building now empty of all his assistants, the heat rose, hands exploring, moans escaping, to the point where we almost lost control. As much as I didn't want to, I remembered my promise to myself and managed somehow to pull away breathlessly.

"I'm sorry," I mumbled, ashamed that after all he had done for me, I couldn't give him yet what I thought he expected. What I thought I wanted and was ready for. What was wrong with me?

"It's okay, Em," he reassured me. "Truth be told, this is happening faster than I expected it to myself."

"Really? So, you're not mad?"

"Not at all," he smiled, pushing back a few loose wisps of hair from my heated face. "I understand completely. If it makes you feel any better, my grandmother had always taught me to wait for marriage anyway. She says some things are meant to be sacred."

That single comment put my soul at ease. I didn't need to feel pressured in any way. He wasn't looking for sex from me; I wasn't Jess in one of her entanglements. I had found myself a respectful, chaste man who was willing to take things slow.

This relationship was an absolute dream come true.

3. CHARMED

Yes, Blake was everything I never knew I dreamed about: a budding traveling photographer who went on grand adventures with oodles of charisma and a wicked sense of humor that made my serious side melt into a pool of butter.

We had a spark that could not be denied even if I wanted to defy the universe. He was hot and sexy, and his gemstone eyes burned right through me. Our kisses were full-blown fire, and his touch set every ounce of my essence ablaze.

But it was his charming mannerisms and way of speaking that completely captivated me, as if I were the only woman who existed in his world.

"You dance like an angel. So graceful and light as a feather. How did you learn to dance like that?" he asked one day as we turned the car radio on and moved under the moonlight in an abandoned town parking lot. I loved moments like this where we were alone with nothing but the starry skies above.

"I took ballet as a little girl, plus I've studied every Disney princess waltz," I informed him.

"Well, you definitely have the princess thing down," he replied. "But the question is—am I good enough to be your prince?"

"Let's see," I teased. "You do have charm and a

gentlemanly elegance when you walk into a room."

"Okay, that's a good start, right?"

"It is. And you can dance—not as good as I can, of course—but you can keep up, so you have potential."

"Ah, so I'm allowed at your ball?"

"Hmm, perhaps. But I'm not sure about that wicked smile or those tempting lips of yours. I don't think you're wholesome enough to be princely."

"That's too bad," he mused, inching closer to where I could feel his sweet, hot breath tangling with mine. "I'll just have to work on being worthy of your virtue, Princess."

"Not if it means that I can't kiss you like this," I declared, inviting him deeper into my royal heart with my lips. He surprised me with a gentle, loving, closed-mouth graze before adorably stepping back, bowing gracefully, and winking to let me know that he indeed wanted to earn his way into my kingdom.

His romantic gestures continued, from the occasional bouquet or corny mixtape to an impromptu champagne brunch and wild sledding adventure that ended with hot chocolate and snuggles by the fireplace. Every moment was magical, and I found myself whisked into a storybook world that I never knew could exist. We declared our exclusivity and simply couldn't get enough of each other.

He made a habit out of photographing me everywhere we went and then surprised me on Valentine's Day with an entire photo album of my modeling poses. He admitted that he also made a book for himself so that when I was away at college, he could see me any time he wanted. I couldn't believe how genuinely sweet and sentimental this guy was—so different than the first impression smooth, tough guy I met only a few short months ago. He was nothing like I anticipated, in the best of ways.

I was enamored by how freely and generously he expressed his feelings for me, which developed rather quickly. Sometimes it was a full-on poem attributed to my eyes or heart, and other times, it was a romantic stringing of lyrical phrases left in those signature notes and texts of his that continued to appeal to my inner princess.

"You make my heart smile."

"I am completely mesmerized by you."

"Just a short little note to let you know you are in my thoughts and in my heart. Sweet dreams, baby."

Sigh. Romance was but a dream, and I was living it. Enraptured.

***

I was also charmed by his dramatic manner of storytelling. The fervor with which he spoke about life—the good and the bad—was one of his most attractive traits.

He had a way with words, creating a visual as if you were there with him like a verbal virtual reality experience. He was a magnet for my student-of-life kind of mind. I had so much to learn from him and I'd listen intently, hanging on his every last word.

So much so that I felt like I was on the photo shoot with him in China as he was up close and personal with pandas during his 4-day intensive hike at the Wolong Panda Center. I could feel the enormity of the fuzzy black and white creatures as he regaled what it was like to be in their midst and feed them from his own hand.

I experienced the fear (then relief) as he told me about the time he and his buddies were out in the Atlantic, swimming and goofing around off the side of their boat, when a shark came up behind them, and they had to swim for their lives. Luckily, they all made it to safety and were able to have a good drunken laugh over out-swimming "Jaws."

I giggled until my stomach hurt when he'd recount the many stories of how he'd prank his brother and sister mercilessly throughout childhood, and how he once convinced his poor grandmother that he had made her a special chocolate cake that was actually made of mud. If he hadn't been her favorite, she swore that he'd have gotten the beating of his life, he joked.

I could listen to his stories for hours on end and wish I had the kind of daring experiences he had been through. Whether they were actually true tales or not, who knows? But listening to them was like experiencing an art form of words. Poetic and engaging—like his photography and his love notes.

Oh, *l'amour*. Enchanted.

***

I was charmed by his charitable heart—the one that had such a soft spot for kids. Over my too-short winter break, I accompanied him to that local hospital he volunteered at during one of his weekly visits to the sick children's ward, and I watched with such deep admiration while he read them a story.

But Blake didn't just read it; oh no, he reenacted the scenes to bring the story to life and had them laughing, giggling, and transported to a world anywhere but in the harsh reality of their terminal lives.

Some of the children came right up and sat on his lap or asked Mr. Blake what a certain part of the story meant. When the reading was done, he asked them questions and played a fun little game where he had them take turns making up a different ending. It was truly endearing to observe from the sidelines.

Then there was his Little League side business with his friends. It was so sweet to see Blake interact with those kids on my spring break; he was a natural with them, taking the time to coach each child individually to fortify their strengths and work on their weaknesses. He, along with his buddies, Dan and Eddie, taught them the importance of teamwork and served as true role models in the community. I loved watching him come alive with pride during a game, with me quickly becoming their biggest cheerleader.

Witnessing these moments of tenderness with children, I saw "amazing father" written all over him. And for the first time ever in my life, I felt the yearning pangs of motherhood, which caught me completely off-guard.

I never thought I would ever envision myself wanting a baby, but seeing Blake's tenderness with kids, I found myself wanting to be the mother of his.

***

I was charmed by the depths of his vulnerability.

We'd spend hours talking about our dreams, our past heartaches, our family dynamics, our career paths—anything you could think of. We never struggled for conversation, and yet, also found comfort in the sound of silence wrapped tightly in each other's puzzle-perfect arms.

There wasn't a subject that remained untouched by our intimate sharing.

I learned more about his love of photography, and how he had accidentally registered into an after-school class that introduced him to this unknown passion. I showed him my little bucket list journal of places I wanted to explore one day, and he promised to take me to as many on my list as he could.

We talked openly about our childhoods in the safety of each other's embrace, sharing emotional details that connected us on a deeper level. It was so easy to open up to Blake about all my insecurities, from my difficulties making friends and never having a boyfriend before to my parent's strict rules and my dad's seesawing alcoholism. He listened so intently and supportively that I wasn't ashamed to tell him about my heartaches and my dreams.

And when he confided in me about his earlier hardships, they were just so heartbreaking that all I wanted to do was rescue him from the pain and be his eternal band-aid.

I cringed when he revealed how his dad physically abused him—and not just the daily spankings with a relentless leather belt. We're talking hardcore cigarettes burning into the skin. One day, he cried in my arms as he admitted that his dad was once so incensed over a failing grade that he took Blake's hand and held it over the hot stovetop and singed his skin, telling him that this was what losers deserved.

He feebly disclosed how the constant abuse drove him to attempt suicide once, which was thankfully thwarted by his trusted sister who got him to the hospital in time without his parents ever knowing. If his dad had found out, it wouldn't have been a wake-up call to the abusive parent; no, it would've been an invitation for more punishment.

I hadn't met the man yet, but I wondered how I would ever be able to look into his father's eyes without seething anger for what he had done to an innocent child. I could understand why Blake thought the world was stacked against him.

In one of our many intense discussions, Blake was also brave enough to reveal how an older friend introduced him to heroin at a party, turning him into an addict instantly. He shamefully confessed how he would shoot up every day after that, rocketing more and more into darkness, until one night, he just decided to stop and completely cure himself. He threw away the needles, dumped the drugs, and never looked back.

The struggle for sobriety was unimaginable, but he couldn't go on hating himself anymore. He wanted more out of life than to be a useless druggie.

Besides, he had met me, and it had given him hope that he could have a better future, he revealed.

In fact, he said his heroin history was the real reason he avoided going on a date with me last summer; he thought I deserved better than a drug addict. Now that he had kicked his habit, he was so relieved that I was still willing to be with him—though he still feared that he wasn't worthy of me.

"Blake, don't be silly. Everyone deserves happiness, love, and second chances. I see the man you are on the inside, and that's all that matters to me," I assured him as he gently wept into my embraced shoulders.

It wasn't the right time for me to dive into the anxiety this little unveiling caused or question his problematic history further. I'd have to shelve my curiosities for another time; it was clear that Blake needed my support and unconditional understanding in that moment. How agonizing it must have been for him to live through that torturous time period. How unbelievably tough it must have been for him to come clean with me about something so dark and painful.

Who was I to judge the mile his shoes had walked?

"I don't know, Em. I sometimes feel like you are too good to be true. I'm so scared that one day I'm going to wreck everything and lose you."

"You won't," I soothed him, running my hands through his sticky, gel-stiffened hair and bringing his troubled head to my chest so he could hear my heart beat with compassion for him. "I don't care who you were or what you did in the past. I only care about who you are now. And who you are is someone I really like."

I did like Blake. Very much. His mere presence had a power over me I couldn't explain, and I wanted to explore this potential union with him further. I sought to unravel all the layers that made this man so kind, so charismatic, so gentle. His complexity was utterly appealing to my inquisitive mind. Though, inwardly, his addictive past didn't always sit well with me.

My words of reassurance that night betrayed my true fears.

One night, I finally found the courage to share how his drug addiction triggered my experience growing up my dad's drunken sickness. How we had to walk on eggshells during his outbursts and hangovers. The pressure on me to perform like an academic circus monkey to make up for his shortcomings. It apparently was up to me to restore the bright future of our family, to bring joy and pride into their dull lives—at the expense of my own dreams.

I couldn't go through that kind of oppression again, I told him. I wouldn't.

But Blake reassured me that his addiction was under control and that he would never be like my dad, and I felt safe to let myself trust his promise. He was clean and would never return to that way of life ever again. The fact that he was so vulnerable and honest was proof positive that he was nothing like my detached, unfeeling father, who would never vow to give up his precious bottle for anyone.

"Em, I will never be the kind of man your father is. I swear it," he earnestly pledged, looking gravely into my eyes with such conviction that he made my insecure heart feel a little safer to care about him and open up more.

"How can you be so sure? I've seen my dad and his battles, and it's not an easy path," I said in almost a whisper, hesitantly. I was afraid to upset him yet needed to confront this nagging worry of a childhood trauma resurfacing in my future.

So many times, I can remember hearing my dad's

pointless apologies. His meaningless oaths to get sober. His failed attempts to be the man our family needed. My scars would not let my mind rest until I was certain that I would not be repeating my mother's history.

I was stronger than that.

But I could not judge Blake based on the sins of my father. He was his own man, and I had to believe that he was different. He merited the benefit of my doubt.

"I'm no longer the same depressed, fucked up person I was a few months ago. You changed everything for me, Emily. You make me want to be a better person. I *choose* to be a better person," he declared.

"You already *are* an incredible person, Blake. Never forget that. You are worth so much more than your father ever made you believe. You have every right to be happy," I replied. "And you make *me* very happy," I added, reaching up for a light peck and gentle hug.

"You are the first person to ever make me this happy, too," he replied sincerely.

I heard all that I needed to hear. I felt safe and secure, confident in who we were as a couple and where our future was headed. We supported each other's dreams and swore to integrate them into our relationship. We wouldn't lose sight of the big picture. And we'd never have a reason to worry as long as we let honesty be our foundation.

"You came into my life at the perfect time," he hummed into my ear one night after a mild make-out session. "You know, it's crazy how we ended up together."

"Oh, really?" I asked, intrigued, settling into his strong arms on the couch. I loved how they perfectly curved around me as if they were divinely designed just to fit my body.

"Yeah. Truth is, my friend Leyla and I were becoming close right before you came back from college. She told me that she was interested in being more than friends," he divulged sheepishly, not sure if he was making the right decision in sharing this particular full disclosure.

"Oh," was all I could muster up as I instinctually stiffened my heart and my body.

Memories of past heartbreaks resurfaced—including Marcus—as repeatedly, I was told how I was so incredible that no one ever wanted to lose my friendship, so they didn't risk being with me romantically. I was so tired of being the friend and never the lover, and so scared that Blake wanted to join that crowd. He was probably bored of being with a chaste economics major, and who could blame him with the fascinating life he led? But I remained brave, bracing myself for the inevitable breakup as he continued.

"Honestly, I didn't know whether to date her or pursue you at the time. You two are a lot alike in your persistence, that's for sure," he jabbed in a failed attempt to lighten the mood. I'm sure he noticed the change in my body tension, though, and figured out quickly that humor wasn't the right approach in that moment. Clearing his throat, he continued.

"It's hard to think about her like that, even now, because she's always been special to me. I've known her for quite a few years, and she's always understood me in a way that others haven't."

Yup. There it was. The bombshell I had feared all along. That all too familiar pang of rejection in favor of someone better. I took a deep breath in, fighting back a wayward tear that wanted to escape, awaiting the final verdict. I was just so relieved to have my back to him at that moment, so he couldn't see the devastation that took over my face.

"That is, until you came along," he continued. "There's just something about you that I couldn't resist. You and whatever love potion you conjured up won me over," he assuredly confessed to my absolute shock, his words trailing off into a spellbinding, unexpected kiss that sent charged sensations throughout every part of my body.

Relief. Disbelief. Passionate acceptance.

Someone finally chose *me* as his number one. I pushed down that evil, little voice that tried to ruin this rejoiceful moment, hinting concern over the fact that there was another woman out there vying for his affection. That didn't matter. Blake wanted me, not her.

The cycle of rejection had been broken. My heart melted instantly, and I believed in what destiny promised me the day we met: we really were meant to be together.

***

The longer we were together, the more we would share. It continued to challenge us, but I feel like it only made us stronger. Like when I revealed some of my fledgling experiences with men, which just so happened to activate his dread of being cheated on again.

I couldn't fault him, though. His last girlfriend, Brittany, left some really deep scars on his heart when she hooked up with one of his friends. There were songs I couldn't listen to because they reminded him of her. He was slow to trust me, too, because I had been flirty with other men prior to meeting him, and he was worried that I would betray him like she did.

So, to soothe his own anxieties, Blake wanted to know every last detail about my past. He'd ask me about the men I'd made out with, and I begrudgingly disclosed the intimate details of my oral indiscretions, including an unsavory incident with Marcus and his friend that didn't bode too well with Blake.

Replaying all those scenes to him made me feel a bit ashamed, like my past semi-sexual encounters were beyond what he'd ever done or would do. It made me realize that in my personal connections, I was the total opposite of my professional persona, where I was strong and resilient. I had to face the truth that although a willing participant, the only way I could feel attractive to men was to offer a plea bargain—one that only gave out pleasure and never expected any in return. That was such a hard pill of awareness to swallow.

But being with Blake was teaching me personal confidence and reciprocation, and I didn't feel the need to sacrifice myself for his attention like I did for others. I tried to explain that to him, but I'm not sure he accepted this psychologically analyzed rationale for my behavior.

Usually, he listened to my heartfelt life confessions with empathy and understanding, but he struggled to accept this particular part of my past. I think it might have made him apprehensive about his own ability to perform when or if we took our relationship to that level. It was probably why he never went further than breast fondling or over-the-clothes-only suggestive explorations of our lower regions.

Well, could have been that, plus the fact that his grandmother had raised him to believe that sex was meant for marriage. I respected that because of his upbringing, he himself was not openly sexual, waiting to be intimate with the right woman—his wife.

I knew that was going to require a lot of patience on my carnally reluctant part. But I wouldn't need to worry about that if I couldn't repair the damage my past was doing to our present relationship.

Even though I had never had actual intercourse before, I began to feel like I was not virginal enough for Blake, like I had to repent for even seeing another penis before in my life. But I did it, pleading for forgiveness and penance, understanding how physical intimacy was revered by him.

"Blake, none of those men meant anything to me. I've never felt for anyone the way I feel about you. You have to believe that."

"I do believe that," he acknowledged, "but it still doesn't change the facts. Imagining you being with other guys like that just—it's just hard for me to wrap my head around, okay? How you can be so sexually cavalier with them. But then you swear you've changed and just want to be with me? I don't know, Em."

"But I *have* changed. Can't you understand that I

was so desperate for love and attention that I didn't realize what I was doing? All I wanted was to be liked by a guy, and yes, I see now how wrong I was to degrade myself for the tiniest token of affection. But I'm not that girl anymore, Blake. I don't *want* to be that girl anymore. I want to be the girl that you deserve."

"I need some time to think," was all he could mutter as he gestured to the door for me to leave. My heart almost shattered into a thousand pieces in that moment.

Days passed without a single word from Blake. I was convinced that he was going to walk away from our relationship because of this difference in our sexual standards and experiences. I thought I was going to lose him forever, and it pained me beyond any emotion I thought possible. I cried myself to sleep more than once over it, scared that my one chance at true love was destroyed. Perhaps I was doomed to be the old, retired executive spinster after all.

I was tainted; I was not the kind of woman his grandmother would approve of for her Catholic-bred grandson. I started to regret the woman I had allowed myself to become while waiting for the perfect man to enter my life, and now I was going to pay the ultimate price for it.

Was this truly going to be a dealbreaker? I obsessively fretted until I heard from Blake again.

A few days after confessing my sins, Blake finally called me to tell me that he forgave me and that my honesty made him realize that he could trust me. It no longer mattered what happened in the past; he didn't want that to ruin our future. The same words I said to him about his drug addiction resurfaced in his own unconditional acceptance of my intimate misgivings. We were equals once again; different baggage, but similar regrets.

"I appreciate you telling me the truth. I know how hard that must have been for you. I had to come to terms with it, but I realized that no one is perfect. You were willing to be honest with me, and I shouldn't give up on what we have over something in your past. But that's all over now, right?"

I swore with all my soul that I would never be promiscuous like that again; that I was committed to Blake and only Blake. And just as he'd need to reassure me that his addiction was a thing of the past, I'd have to keep promising him that I was not Brittany and that I would not hurt him like she did—ever.

He seemed to be satisfied with my declaration, and he resumed his charming pursuit of my heart.

With our deepest secrets out in the open and reconciled, it was time to take our relationship to the next level: meeting each other's family and friends.

4. INTRODUCTIONS

Blake's natural ability to charm didn't end with me. Oh, no—he was intent on fully mesmerizing every single member of my family, including my skeptical mother who had no qualms about voicing her opinion about whether an under-educated, wannabe traveling photographer was good enough for this ambitious daughter of hers. Thankfully, she agreed to curb her pre-judgment and halt her verdict until *after* she met him.

You can only imagine how nervous that made me to introduce Blake to my parents as I'd never brought home a boyfriend before, and their expectations were already of underwhelm. Still, we had been dating for a couple of months—long enough to know that we were serious about each other—and I couldn't avoid the inevitable meeting. Besides, deep down, I wanted their blessing.

I nervously paced back and forth, waiting for him to arrive. Mom was in the kitchen finishing up her homemade shrimp scampi, something I knew Blake would absolutely love. Dad was settled back into his worn-out brown recliner, remote in hand, trying to decide between football and a cooking show—thankfully, sober. My younger sister, Kerry, was nose-deep in a book, not the least bit interested in who she was about to meet.

After what felt like eons, the doorbell finally rang. I could feel the excitement rise like lava as I realized this was really happening—Blake was about to enter my whole world.

But to my chagrin, it was only Jess. Apparently, that disappointment was written all over my face.

"Nice to see you, too," my best friend of twelve years snarked as she pushed through the door with a platter of her freshly baked brownies. I had decided to get it all over with in one shot—both family and best friend around the dinner table with my new beau in one evening. Selfishly, I also thought that if things started to go south, Jess would be an amazing buffer. She was fully aware of my intentions when I coaxed her into joining us that evening.

"Where's lover boy?" she quipped as she plopped down on the couch next to Kerry. "I'm supposed to be the one fashionably late. Is he upstaging me already?"

"No one can upstage you, Jess," Kerry teased with a little sister's love. As if on cue, there came the next doorbell, and with my heart in my throat, I opened the door to welcome Blake into my family home.

With a respectful kiss on my cheek in greeting, I responded with a big yet nervous smile. He came prepared, I noted, with a beautiful bouquet of yellow roses, no doubt meant to soften up my mom with her favorite flowers. I introduced him to everyone, who were all very courteous and warmly welcoming, to my relief.

As we sat around the dinner table, the silence was powerfully awkward.

"This is one of my mom's best recipes," I gushed to break the ice, glancing over at Blake to encourage him to speak.

"It's really delicious, Mrs. Davidson. It's one of my favorites, actually," he responded.

"Thank you. Emily mentioned you'd enjoy it," my mother answered graciously. "So, tell us a little bit about your work. Emily says that you are a traveling photographer?"

Oh, shit. There it was. She was already going to start in with her interview about his questionable career choices instead of easing into it.

Really, Mom? No warm-up? I asked her with my darted eyes, which she blatantly ignored with a turn of her nose toward Blake to await his response.

"Yes, ma'am," he answered with a big grin, his passion for his work shining through his eyes and smile. He was not going to be fazed by any interrogation—I saw that now. I forgot how diplomatic he can be in front of a crowd; his power of persuasion was like no other. I took a few solid breaths and let him take the floor. I had nothing to worry about, I reassured myself.

"As a kid, I always loved taking pictures. Mostly of nature. Sunsets and sunrises, birds in the sky above the beach, blooming flowers. But as I got older, I became more interested in the exotic—the pictures that not everyone else captures.

"That's when I learned more about travel photography and where my passion really took hold. I get to take pictures of free-roaming pandas, or red-eyed tree frogs in the rainforest, or the layers of sunset behind an Egyptian pyramid. Publications will reach out to photographers to help capture images for their freelance writers, and it's quite the adventure."

"And you do this on the side? Is the convenience store just a temporary job then until the big break?" my dad interjected, to my utter embarrassment.

"Dad!" I grumbled through my clenched teeth, irritated that they insisted on grilling him instead of getting to know him outside of a professional capacity.

I understood their concerns that this man— who was two years older than me—did not have a college education or certified technical training of any sort. Just a few specialty classes under his belt wasn't acceptable in their futuristic eyes. I know they worried about how he would support me in the long run if we were to get married, but part of me resented their assumption that we both had to have our acts together in our early twenties for us to have a successful future.

It's not like he planned on being at that dead-end convenience store his whole life—but what if he did? Did that make him any less worthy of a human being and undeserving of my love?

How snobby and elitist of them to project their expectations of me onto this good-hearted person they just met. Why couldn't they ask him about his weekly hospital visits or Little League team? Or about his adorable German grandmother? I was seething inside.

"It's all right, Em. Your parents have a right to know about my life intentions," he said, giving a quick squeeze of my hand under the table to reassure me that he's "got this."

"For now, sir, I'm just starting out. Building my

portfolio and reputation. The more that different publications are exposed to my work, the more opportunities that come in. Just like with any career, we all have to start at the bottom and work our way up. I'm sure it was the same for you and Mrs. Davidson when you were younger," he said, discreetly alluding to their own non-collegiate career progression. I watched him in muted awe as he alchemized the line of questioning to his favor. Boy, did he hand it to them in the most respectful and polite way I've ever seen anyone dish my parents' pretentiousness back at them. He was truly remarkable.

"I happened to have gotten lucky to start off with the right opportunity that asked for repeated job assignments and referrals," he continued. "So, to answer your question, yes, sir, I do intend for this to become my full-time work. It's what I am passionate about."

"That's very admirable, son. Good for you. I mean that," countered my dad, impressed with Blake's ability to succinctly explain himself against a parental firing squad. Dad seemed content enough with the answer to move on, but the shots weren't quite over yet.

"I agree, I think it sounds wonderful," acquiesced my mom. "So, does it just start out as job assignments here and there and build into a full-time position? How does that work?"

"It's considered independent contracting. Typically, very few companies hire for permanency, though if I find a few happy clients, then there is stability in contracted services over freelancing. That's where I'd ultimately like to end up."

"Well, I don't see what the problem is," piped in my little sister, finally acknowledging Blake for the first time since he piqued her interest. "I'm absolutely fascinated by it. I actually want to be a photographer myself—but I'm more of a people person than nature. I like taking candids and capturing a person's unexpected moments."

"Is that so? Well, whenever you are ready, I'll just have to direct you to the right conventions and connections," he said, winking at Kerry before turning back to my parents. "That's part of my training, going to these conventions to stay up on the latest trends in the industry. Plus, we attend workshops that help us hone our craft."

"Yes, Blake goes to an annual show in Milan," I added with pride. "I'd love to go with him one day."

"Actually, there's an assignment coming up in London next month. With your permission, Mr. and Mrs. Davidson, I would love to be able to bring Emily with me. But only if you are okay with it," he quickly added, seeing my dad's jaw clench at the thought of his baby girl going away with a strange man they just met. Sensing his fatherly overreaction brewing, my mother surprisingly swooped in to the rescue. I guess Blake had won her over with his smooth answers after all.

"That's very sweet of you to ask permission, Blake, but Emily technically is an adult. I think she is old enough to make her own decisions. Don't you agree, Bob?"

"Yeah," my father grumbled, then succumbed to a small grin as he saw the excitement in my eyes. I had no idea that Blake was even going to London, let alone that he was going to ask my parents about it. Tonight had really gone better than I could have ever imagined.

Although my family was hesitant to accept a "menial" high school graduate as my beau initially, by the end of the evening, it was clear that they all ended up adoring him as much as I did.

He knew just the right things to say to make my mother warm up to him; I heard them laughing from the kitchen, where Blake was insisting on helping her do the dishes. My dad took him into his confidence as well later in the evening, down into his beloved man-cave of a basement, where he could show off his treasures to a son he never had. Kerry lit up at the amount of attention he paid to her, particularly since she discovered they shared a similar passion for photography.

I could tell from her face that Jess also gave her stamp of approval, which she was dying to share with me the second I kissed Blake goodbye for the night. The door barely closed before she dragged me by the arm into the seclusion of my bedroom.

"Jess, you hardly said a word all evening, and that's so unlike you. You're killing me! What did you think?"

"I think you got yourself a real lothario there. I was quiet because I was just watching him work the room and win your parents over. I can't believe he got Gloria and Bob to back down like that without them actually eating crow. He's good," she chuckled.

"And you?"

"Of course I liked him! He's hot and suave, and clearly, very much into you. He gets two big thumbs up from me," she nodded with a wink and gave me a big hug.

"I'm so relieved," I answered, finally breathing after the stressful night. I don't remember ever being so nervous about anything like that in my life. None of my academic or extracurricular activities presented such an emotional challenge, so this was all new for me. Having my parents' and Jess' approval of Blake meant the world to me, more than I even realized.

"So, I've been dying to ask," Jess interrupted my exhale with her propensity for gossip. "How is he in bed? I thought I would have gotten a phone call about your first time!" she chided.

"Um, we haven't slept together yet."

"What do you mean, not yet? It's been a few months now, and you've been waiting for this your whole life. I know you well enough to know you're not the one holding back. So—what's his problem?"

"Nothing. He just grew up with very strict morals and is honoring his grandmother's advice to wait for marriage." She looked at me skeptically, as if I had two heads.

"You're kidding me, right? Blake Denton does not have the virginal vibe about him. I mean, just look at him. He doesn't strike me as the religious type, either. You need to change his mind, sister."

"No, Jess. I respect his values. If he wants to wait, I'll wait with him."

"If you say so," she replied, a little too unsupportively, as if in disbelief we were really having this conservation. "But I bet you a million bucks that it won't be long until he sacrifices his sainthood to make a dishonest woman out of you. Just promise me

I'll be the first to know!"

I couldn't help but shake my head and laugh at her dramatic but reasonable best friend request. "Fine, I promise." Satisfied with my answer, she hugged me once again, and we walked out to the living room, where both of my parents were waiting to acknowledge that Blake was indeed "a very nice boy."

Yes, Blake had performed his magic that night, and I got the blessing I was wishing for. I oftentimes wondered if they liked him better than they liked me, to be honest.

He quickly became part of the family, always there with a listening ear and a humorous anecdote to lighten any sour mood. Kerry was totally enamored with him in a non-romantic way, eventually referring to him as her brother. My parents considered him the son they never had.

He became great at playing mediator whenever any of us argued—especially when my dad surrendered his sober streak and obnoxiously downed a few too many drinks. Boy, was I grateful to have someone so reliable and steady by my side when that happened. Blake would hold my hand and lovingly talk me through the betrayal and pain. How refreshing to finally have someone to talk to about these things instead of keeping them repressed.

And I was that calming force for him as well. He didn't have the best relationship with his parents, revealing that it felt like his grandmother was the one who really raised him with any kind of love. I listened to his stories without judgment and with endless compassion for a good man who battled such foundational traumas.

"You are so lucky to have such a wonderful family. No one cares about me in mine, except maybe my grandma. My parents think I am useless and treat me like a nobody. I have no one to talk to—well, I had no one, until I met you," he said with a meek smile and puppy-dog, watery eyes that met my sympathetic gaze. "Now I know I won't ever feel alone like that again."

Oh, how my heart hurt to hear him speak like that. I was so glad that I could provide the comfort and security he so desperately lacked. Even with all my family's issues, at least we still let love bind us together and acted like a family unit when it mattered. Blake didn't have any of that—his home situation was dysfunctional to the max, which made it even more nerve-wracking when it became my turn to meet *his* family.

***

I already had the predisposition to dislike his abusive father and cold-hearted mother. Although his siblings weren't too bad, according to Blake, Camille was supposedly all self-absorbed, and Joey was constantly in trouble and needing to be bailed out. Plus, I wasn't sure how warmly they were going to take to some new girl in his life after Brittany tore his heart out not too long ago.

Gratefully, his beloved Grandma Wilma was going to be there, and out of everyone, she was who I was most excited to meet.

Meeting the Dentons was almost exactly what I

had expected, to my dismay. His parents were both polite and hospitable, albeit aloof. His mom eyed me up and down, probably not unlike my own mother did to Blake, assessing this new person in her firstborn's life. The nerves shot up my spine as I wondered how I would ever get this woman to like me if she couldn't like her own son.

His father was even more non-committal, greeting me cordially, but then leaving me to the "womenfolk" while he returned to watch football in the other room. I was tremendously grateful for that as I'm not very good at hiding my distaste in people, and I couldn't help picturing a smaller version of Blake being beaten as I looked at the man.

Thank goodness my parents at least instilled in me how to be respectful and civil in uncomfortable scenarios, and I drew from that well to try to make the best impression I could with such a cool greeting.

I wasn't as smooth as Blake was in difficult situations, preferring to cower down into a corner and die of shyness instead of channel inner confidence and metaphorically kiss babies. His energy helped to alleviate the tension in the room with a few of his famous witty quips to elicit muffled chuckles, though there was no breaking through the polished ice that was his mother.

Mercifully, a sweet little songbird voice and presence swept into the entryway and changed the entire vibe.

"Oh, you must be Emily! You are even more beautiful than Blake described," exclaimed his endearing, short and stout German grandmother, with delicate wrinkles surrounding her sparkling green eyes and a big smile that was missing just a few teeth. I fell in love with her immediately as she grabbed me into a big bear hug as if she'd known me forever.

"It's nice to meet you all," I managed to reply, still anxious about what was in store for me that evening. "Thank you for having me over."

"Oh honey, no need to be so formal around us!" she insisted, even though the glaring eyes of Blake's mother indicated otherwise. I had the feeling that he was right about his mom not being the affectionate type—certainly not to the level his darling grandmother obviously was.

"Why don't you come inside and sit, Emily?" Ruth Denton invited, wanting to exert her role as mother and hostess. She certainly did not want to be bested by a bubbly grandparent. "Camille and Joey should be joining us shortly."

"I'm looking forward to meeting them. Spencer, too," I commented, remembering the poor little cat with the brain tumor.

"I'm sorry? Who's Spencer?" his mother asked abruptly, perplexed.

Oh my goodness, I hope I hadn't stuck my foot in my mouth. What if Spencer had passed since Blake told me about him over the summer?

"Your cat," I replied hesitantly, looking at Blake, who joined all of us in a state of confusion.

"What makes you think we have a cat? I never said we had a cat," Blake rebuked with a nervous chuckle.

"Sorry, I must have misunderstood," I embarrassingly replied, quickly changing the subject and moving toward the living room. I could have sworn Blake mentioned that cat before. Well, no use in dwelling on my mental clumsiness. I had to find a way to smooth over my silly faux pas so his mom didn't think I was a complete twit. I was an intelligent girl; surely, I could find something to say to redeem myself.

"You have a lovely home, Mrs. Denton. I adore the artwork, and I'm a big fan of antiques."

That comment saved the entire evening, pleasing his mother profoundly, and excitingly engaging her in a conversation about each of her favorite pieces. If that woman had any passion inside her body, it was solely for artifacts.

The rest of the evening went a lot smoother after that as I watched the antics between his sarcastic-tongued sister and goofball baby brother. I could tell they weren't the closest-knit family, but there was some warm camaraderie among Camille, Joey, and Blake at least. Probably due in part to Grandma Wilma's loving influence.

That woman animated the stiffness of the house, and I could tell she genuinely liked me. At the end of the night, she managed to pull me aside away from the others to reassure me that I was now considered part of her family.

"You are like an angel sent from Heaven for my dear *knuddelbär*," she began, misty-eyed, unknowingly exposing her German pet name for Blake, which I later learned meant 'cuddle bear.' "He hasn't had the easiest life, and he is quite the handful," she warned with a grandmother's love. Her big heart and generosity were obvious, and most certainly passed down the line to Blake. I could see that without any doubt. "But you are just the sunshine he needs in his life. I hope that you will always look inside to see his heart, even when he's not very good at showing it."

"He's good at showing it to me, Grandma Wilma. I promise to love and protect it," I swore.

She seemed relieved to hear that, knowing how sick she was and probably not much longer for this world. She counted on me to be the window that opened as her door closed one day on Blake's life. Realizing how much I was coming to care for Blake, I was certain after meeting the rest of his family that I was the only one who could carry on that loving legacy she started.

***

Meeting our inner circle of friends was much simpler than meeting our families. Since Blake and Jess already met at our family dinner, it was easy enough to gather my closest group together for a triple date—me and Blake, Jess and her latest boyfriend, Karl, and our other friend, Kayla, and her longtime beau, Steve.

We enjoyed a quiet night in at Jess' house where we feasted on the latest local 24-hour diner "delicacies" and played board games. I was delighted to see Blake get along so well with Karl and Steve— relieved, more like it. I was so nervous that he would have an issue with them like he had with Marcus after our conversation about my past. Then again, they are my friends' boyfriends and never put me in an uncomfortable sexual situation, so he had no need to be protective of me or jealous of them. Though he did seem to have an interesting opinion about Jess as we drove back to my house.

"I think your little friend was jealous that all of the attention was on you and not her tonight. I'm guessing she's used to being the highlight of the party?" he joked.

"Usually, she is," I laughed, acknowledging her tendency to steal the limelight. He was right; I typically am the one under the radar, so it might have just set off a little, baby green monster.

It would smooth over, though. Even if she made a few comments here and there questioning whether he was the man he seemed to be, I wouldn't let her resentment dissuade me from my heart. She was just going to have to get used to the fact that I finally had a boyfriend, and we were on equal dating ground for once.

Hanging out with Blake's friends was a lot less dramatic. They were so easygoing, and the girlfriends embraced me into their clique with sweetness. We ended up joining a bowling league with Dan and his fiancée, Karen, and Eddie and his new girlfriend, Melinda. Melinda and I especially hit it off right away, having so much in common as introverted bookworms.

It made us both laugh that meek mice such as ourselves could have boisterous, histrionic boyfriends.

I really liked that meeting Blake expanded my own circle of friends, who were starting to feel more like high school hangovers instead of futuristic supporters. Maybe we were just growing apart, but I began to prefer spending time with his friends instead, as I felt more at ease with everyone in the group and didn't have to run any envy interference, like I increasingly did with Jess.

Most of the time, we bowled, went to dinner, or to the movies. Nothing too crazy. One night, their mutual friend, Jack, was having a big party, and I was so excited to meet everyone else in his world. Blake couldn't wait to show me off, and I didn't feel all that edgy about it because I knew Melinda and Karen would be there, like a security blanket. I wouldn't need to hide in the corner with them around.

But not even they could prepare me for the unexpected meeting of Leyla.

As I heard her name called from across the room, I turned to find her eyeing me and Blake with a sad intensity. She was a pretty girl; shorter and slimmer than I was with a blonde pixie-cut and big, blue eyes. Eyes that felt heartbroken to me.

How close did she and Blake get before we started dating exclusively?

I couldn't dare ask, nor did I really want to know. A part of me liked to live in a bubble of denial when it came to the "other woman" who could've stolen Blake's heart from me. If I could've run off in that moment to spare myself the sudden insecurity, I would've bolted for the back door.

But knowing that he couldn't avoid the awkwardness, Blake took my hand firmly and moved us over to where Leyla stood to make a formal introduction. I couldn't help but see her mixed, raw emotion of anger and longing, and I felt the clamminess of his palms as he swallowed with nervousness before speaking.

I didn't know how to feel myself. I guess I

shouldn't have been surprised. He did warn me that they still ran in the same crowd, so I should've expected seeing her at a party like this. Yet, I could sense the history between them, and it made me uncomfortable. Jealous, even. For the first time since I met Blake, I was the one struggling with the pang of possessiveness.

Now I know why he scowled whenever he saw me talk to Marcus. That's exactly what my insides were doing, and I prayed that my body language or face didn't betray my attempt at civility. It wasn't her fault that Blake turned her down.

Mercifully, Leyla didn't stick around for long after the polite hellos, but she did part rather cryptically. "Nice to finally meet you, Emily. You seem like a smart girl. Don't let yourself be fooled by this one," she bit and walked away before I could question her further. Blake intercepted before I even asked what she meant by that.

"Em, she is still upset that I chose to be with you over her. It wasn't that long ago. I didn't mean to hurt her, but truth is, I did. I don't blame her for being angry."

"I guess you're right," I conceded, feeling sympathy for the girl who lost, remembering how many times I was that girl. I knew her pain, and I knew how wonderful Blake was. It made me even more grateful that he chose to be with me.

"I know I'm right. She can tell how much I care about you, and how you light up my life," he caressed with his words. "In fact, I almost forgot..." he trailed off to mischievously steal a blatant kiss, as if to cement our standing with everyone in the room.

He wasn't subtle about his public display of affection either, turning my cheeks all shades of crimson as a few rounds of hooting and hollering acknowledged his moves.

My Blake. Never one to back down from a performance.

After that, Leyla left the party, and we quickly moved on from that uncomfortable situation and into a playful banter of storytelling with the guys. One of them repeated the Jaws story, another mentioned how they moved a kid's car onto the soccer field right before a big game without getting caught, and another teased Blake about how troublesome he and Joey were, always causing problems for their "poor" parents.

I listened to a few impish stories before chiming in with one of my own.

"I remember Blake telling me we couldn't go on a date once because he had to help his dad repair a wall that Joey had punched his fist through," I giggled, feeling a little intoxicated and uninhibited from the beer we were served.

"Em, what are you talking about? I never said that," Blake denied after one of his buddies claimed that was out of character for Joey. If anyone, Blake was the one with the wall-punching temper, Jack mocked.

"Yes, you did, silly," I argued teasingly. "You told me you weren't free that weekend in August because you had to go to Home Depot for drywall and spackle. Remember?"

Irritated and a bit inebriated himself, he took to the defensive. I wasn't sure if it was the alcohol or the fact that I had embarrassed him in front of his friends that made him more callous than I had ever seen him.

"Are you sure you're not confusing me with *Marcus?*" he said bitterly, walking away and leaving me engulfed by his friends, who were not-so-subtly whispering and gossiping about our first little public tiff after such a magnanimous declaration of passion.

Utterly confused, I began to doubt where I had originally heard the story. Was he right—was it Marcus I was thinking of who told me that story? I could have sworn it was one of the reasons Blake couldn't go out to dinner one night. I wondered if I was losing my mind, but clearly, if it never happened, then I had to be the one mistaken.

I felt so ashamed about recalling a memory that happened with another man—especially one he hated—wrongfully thinking it was Blake. *How that must have hurt him to mix up a memory like that,* I berated myself. And in front of his friends, no less.

I ran after him and apologized for the error. I told him I'd be more careful and certain about my claims in the future before making statements like that.

But it was more than just the wrongful accusation—it was the thought that I had confused him with Marcus that was really cutting him to the core. He accepted my apology and we hugged it out, but I could tell from his body language and withdrawal that he wasn't really okay with it.

Ever since I told him about my past, he had been even more belligerent about my friendship with his work nemesis, and I could tell it irked him more than he let on. Even after that night out with his friends, he tried to let it go, but after a few too many confrontations between the two over me, he went into full-on protective mode one night after work.

"I need you to stay away from Marcus. I don't even know why you are still friends with him."

"He's been really good to me, Blake," I said in Marcus' defense, not prepared to go another round as referee between the two hotheads. "I've known him for years. He's like a brother to me."

"A brother wouldn't treat you like that," he fumed. "He's not the righteous guy you think he is, Em. I hate to tell you this, but he confronted me today and said some nasty things about you and your little escapade together. He's lucky I didn't kick the shit out of him."

"He wouldn't." No. Marcus wouldn't have dared to bring that up and humiliate me. Not even if provoked. Not the Marcus I knew.

"He would, and he did. He's not your friend, Em. I wish you could see that, but you're too damn nice to everyone."

"He never meant to hurt me, Blake. It was an innocent misunderstanding." Yet, as soon as the words came out of my mouth, I could feel Blake's anger rise as I championed a man that he believed had betrayed my honor.

"How could someone who claims to care about you put you in a situation like that? Can't you see? You were a joke to him and his friend, who just wanted a blow job. You were nothing more than a mouth with a purpose."

I was completely stunned by his bluntness—but he was indisputably right. How it pained me to realize the truth that Blake was speaking. Even though Marcus never intended to hurt me, his idiot idea to leave me alone in the car with his best friend, who had a crush on me, to simply talk and make out if we wanted to, was not an action a true friend would take. He put me in jeopardy—physically and emotionally.

How could Marcus pawn me off like that to his friend? How could I not see before how terribly he treated me as a woman—as a *sister*?

But once Blake shone a light on what my alleged good buddy was really about, I had to admit to myself that what Marcus did really wasn't something a genuine friend would do. I felt so used and embarrassed. How naïve I had been.

Blake could sense my shame and softened a bit.

"I'm sorry, Em. I didn't mean to be so harsh. I just care about you so much that I hate to see you taken advantage of. It makes me so mad to think about how carelessly he's tossed your feelings aside—first with dismissing a kiss between you as meaningless, and then putting you in a compromising position with his friend. You are too trusting, baby. I just don't want to see you hurt anymore."

He pulled me into his arms and kissed me on the forehead, holding me as I sobbed in acknowledgment of a friendship gone wrong. I had trusted Marcus. I had confided in him, believed in him—loved him even. He was my biggest supporter, or so I thought. But I had been blinded by my old infatuation with him and couldn't see him for the traitorous man he really was.

This revelation was so painful, it made me feel empty inside to face the facts that I had been blind to. Luckily, I had Blake by my side to get me through this. He was my protector, stepping in as my knight in shining armor to shield me from the injustices of my world with his love.

I knew what I had to do. It was time to confront Marcus.

"I can't believe you are letting this asshole twist what happened," Marcus spewed in anger. "I made a stupid mistake in high school, and I've regretted it ever since. Do we really have to end our friendship over this?"

"I'm sorry, Marcus, I really am. But how can I believe you truly care about me when you think so little of me?"

"I think the world of you, don't you know that?" he countered, becoming visibly upset in the alleyway outside of the convenience store where we took our mutual afternoon work break. "I love you like family. We've known each other for years—but instead, you listen to this jerkoff, who you've dated for only a few months?"

"You're the jerkoff, Marcus. I wish you could support my relationship with Blake, but since day one, you've been against him. Why can't you just be happy for me?"

"Because I'm worried about you. He's not good enough for you, and the way he is manipulating you proves that."

"He warned me you'd say that," I half-laughed at his predictability, thanks to Blake's tutelage on the male mind. "*You* are the manipulator, Marcus. I'm sorry that I was too 'sister-like' to be anything other than your friend, but it doesn't give you the right to make me feel bad about someone who actually *does* care about me enough to want to be my boyfriend.

He never tossed my heart aside like some piece of trash and then served it up to his buddy as a sloppy second. That was *you.* "

"Wow. He really has done a number on you," he said with genuine surprise. "If you truly believe that, I feel sorry for you, Emily. Go ahead. Go be with your perfect boyfriend. Don't say I never warned you."

And with those words, my friendship with Marcus ended. Only a few weeks later, he left the convenience store to get a new job, far away from my life forever. It saddened me at first, but I knew I had to let go of users like him in my life. Blake had helped me see that "friends" like Marcus were just out to take advantage of me in one way or another, and he swore an oath to protect me from them from now on.

And I was going to protect him from the cheating Brittany's, pushy Leyla's, and all the other women of the world as well. Our history was no longer going to be our future.

5. LOVE

Deeper and deeper, I fell in love with this man over the course of the next year.

We wanted to know every little thing there was to discover about each other. Like how my favorite color had always been green—the sparkling, shade-of-his-eyes kind of green. His was red, which explained why those ruby-soaked lips finally sunk him into submission, and how every time I wanted something from him, a little red dress was all it took to turn the tides in my favor.

He was amused by my weird collection of seahorse figurines, and I uncovered his obsession with hoarding Batman paraphernalia like the closet superhero geek he was—though it suited him quite well as he could be a bit dark and brooding sometimes. It was an interesting contrast to his typical class-clown personality.

Our two seemingly opposite personalities and lifestyles attracted and balanced each other out perfectly.

He brought out the more playful parts of my ambitious persona, turning me on to the luxury of international escapes and exclusive parties. It was like I was a groupie being led into the world of her now-famous rock star lover, completely starstruck and posing for pretend paparazzi. His fantastical realm was much more exhilarating than my economics degree-led future promised, and I was sucked into a modest limelight without warning.

I remember the very first time I accompanied him on one of his assignments as a budding professional: that photo shoot in London for an exposé on Buckingham Palace.

Holy shit. I'm going to London with my dreamy boyfriend, was all I could verbalize in my head as I packed for the summer trip of a lifetime.

My very first overseas excursion was even better than I had ever envisioned. We had the opportunity to explore everything that the beautiful city had to offer before he had to report to work, and we made the most of it. A humorous drive with a trivia-happy cabby named George took us into the heart of the city, dropping us off at the infamous Big Ben, where we embarked on a self-guided walking tour of the hottest London spots.

Energized by the notion of being in another land, I continued to gawk and gaze my way past the Houses of Parliament, St. Margaret's Church, the Jewel Tower, and more before landing at Westminster Abbey. Quite a landmark to behold, the decades of British history and architecture astounded me as I breathed in the beauty and wondered what it would be like to get married there.

I pictured myself in a stunningly simple, white satin dress, walking slowly toward the lovelorn man standing at the end of the altar: my handsome, irresistible Blake.

Known for his iconic ripped jeans, 90's-style

flannel shirt, and work boot ensembles, seeing him dressed up in business casual as a professional photographer made him subtly sexier—inviting me to daydream about how enticing he would look in a groom's tuxedo.

I shook the image from my mind, reminding myself that we'd only technically been together for about six months and to slow it down. We hadn't even made love yet, and most of our six months were spent apart while I continued college studies and my internship in Virginia. Yet, I couldn't resist thinking of the future whenever we were together.

"Hey, where'd you go just now?" he asked, breaking me from my reverie.

"Oh, nowhere," I replied, flustered. "Just in awe of everything, that's all." I could feel the rosiness rise in my cheeks as I told my little fib to cover up my mental wedding fantasy.

"This church is amazing. Could you imagine getting married in a place like this?" Wait—how on Earth was he able to read my mind, and so mystically think the same way? It's like we really were soulmates who shared the same energy. I felt relieved that I wasn't the only one imagining our future nuptials.

"It would be incredible," I responded with a blushing smile. "Like a dream come true."

"You never know, Princess," he suggested as he affectionately moved a flyaway lock behind my ear and leaned in for a respectful, church-approved kiss—though I had anything but reverent thoughts arise in my responsive body.

Walking hand in hand down the city streets toward Trafalgar Square, I could feel my love growing for this amazing man, who gifted me with such an enriching experience. Our hands fit perfectly together, I noticed, as I felt the smoothness and warmth of his manly strength wrap around my delicately polished fingers.

He gave my hand a tight squeeze and looked at me and smiled, pleased that I was so enraptured by our adventure together—an adventure he painstakingly designed to spoil my every whim. Just like he always did. On our first date. On that photo shoot. And now on this trip.

If this was what life with Blake would be like, I was ready to sign up right then and there to be his Buckingham Palace Princess forever.

It was indescribable to tour the palace itself; though, to my laughable chagrin and Blake's obvious amusement, the queen wasn't there to greet us. But her absence enabled us to walk through several of the gloriously decorated State Rooms, up the Grand Staircase, and even catch a glimpse of the Throne Room! I felt like I was transported into living the fascinating life I had always imagined as a child.

As if the trip wasn't already so perfect, Blake arranged for us to have afternoon tea in the Buckingham Palace gardens. He somehow always "had a guy" with the connections to make the impossible possible, though I never got a chance to meet these wish granters. But that didn't matter. It was all so hypnotic; I was free to explore a real castle in awe, while he was granted permission to document every last majestic detail with his sophisticated lens.

I didn't know which of the two I loved more: the romantic palace setting or watching Blake passionately take photographs. The way he'd move ever so gently to the right and measure the light coming into the room; how he'd take several pictures at once and cutely frown in disgust at some duds; or how he'd gleefully show me his most favorite shots with pride. I was quickly engulfed into this extraordinary world, knowing this was only the beginning. Our beginning.

***

Being with Blake was unavoidably intoxicating. As my first real boyfriend, I didn't want to go too far too fast, but man was it difficult to slow down those brakes as time went on—especially when alone with him in London. If it weren't for his grandmother's morals assuaging my conflicted mind that I didn't have to give my virginity away just yet, I'd spontaneously strip him down naked and have my way with him after imbibing a few too many beers at a local pub before returning to our joint hotel room with a plush, king-sized bed.

The passionate kissing and heavy petting started as it normally did, but there was something different about the way Blake grabbed a hold of me that night. He laid me down on the bed, urgently consuming me with an animal-like desire that my body feverishly responded to.

"I want you, Emily Grace. All of you," he pleaded breathlessly, to my absolute shock. Could he really be giving us the green light?

"I want you, too, Blake," I assured him in between lustful tongue entwining and the electric power of our mutual fondling.

"Are you sure?"

"Yes. Yes, I want you with every ounce of my being."

"Tell me what you want, baby. I want to hear you say it," he lovingly demanded, unable to stop kissing and caressing me.

"I want you to make love to me," I finally said, breaking months-long tension that kept us from the most sacred of intimate acts. He stopped for a moment, and I thought I might have misread him and asked for too much, but then I saw him look long and lovingly into my eyes. His smile made time stop as he moved off of me to slow us down and savor every second of our impending union.

Fear, excitement, anxiety, lust—all kinds of wayward emotions moved through me. Was this really going to happen? I had fantasized about this moment for so long that it never crossed my mind how intense I'd feel when it finally came.

I was so self-consciously nervous as I allowed him to undress me as no man ever did before, but Blake put me at such ease. He kissed me tenderly on the lips and then let his sweet nibbles trail to my ears and neck. I couldn't help but release soft moans of pleasure as his very touch sent shivers through every part of my body, which only heightened his own arousal.

Our hands wandered over each other's bodily terrain as we explored, touched, and tasted. Although I had orally pleasured other men before, this fully immersive experience was on a completely different level than those meaningless hookups in some random guy's car or those restrained nights on Blake's couch.

It was sensual and caring and slow. Blake caressed my breasts with his tongue while tugging ever so gently at my nipples with his teeth to trigger lightning bolt sensations throughout my body. He then took his time to ready my inexperienced womanhood with his pulsating fingers, each thrust heightening senses I didn't even know I had.

It was comforting that he seemed to know exactly what to do and was gentle and respectful as I gave myself to him completely. He asked me once again if I was sure before he slipped on a condom, parted my legs, and urged himself inside me with a plunge that brought tears to my eyes.

Both pain and pleasure devoured me at once, and I was grateful for the slight inebriation that dulled some of the aching's of a newly-penetrated vagina. I'd worry about the inevitable soreness in the morning; in that moment, all I wanted was to feel the depth of our union as Blake melodiously moved within me until his final release.

I finally experienced the heaven so many of my friends told me about. It was more exquisite than I ever imagined, to be bonded with another human being on that level. Maybe next time, I would even achieve my own orgasm.

Waking up in his arms the next morning only reinforced the surety of my feelings as he leaned over to kiss me "good morning" and told me he loved me for the first time.

"You are the most beautiful woman I have ever seen," he whispered, wrapping his strong, toned arms around my naked body and kissing my neck gently from behind. "Even with that freshman-fifteen booty of yours going on," he teased with a light slap as I tried to discreetly rise from bed without him seeing the fullness of my body in the light.

"Oh, stop," I whispered shyly, uncomfortable with his ease of expression and even more insecure about my not-so-perfect body. Had I gained more weight than I realized over the last few months?

But then he turned me around so that I couldn't avoid seeing the sincerity in his eyes as he professed his feelings, and I dismissed his comment as simply lighthearted.

"I'm serious. The moment I saw you, my entire world stopped. Emily, you are the woman of my dreams. I love you, Princess."

"I—I love you, too," I naturally responded, tears of joy springing to my eyes and heart, exploding into an awakened kiss of unconditional devotion.

Finally hearing the words I yearned to hear my whole life from a man, we soberly and intensely made love for hours. The outer worlds of London, home, and the entire universe no longer mattered.

Until I opened my big mouth about wanting to share our most intimate experience with my best friend.

"Jess is going to lose her shit with jealousy when she finds out my very first time happened in London," I snickered in glee as I started to get dressed for the day. We were headed out to explore a few more sights before catching a plane back home that evening, though I would have much preferred spending those hours in that glorious bed instead.

When Blake didn't respond, I turned to find him still in bed, stiffened and sitting up defensively.

It didn't take me long to realize that my lack of experience as a girlfriend and amateur social skills once again were about to ruin a perfectly splendid morning.

"That is private between us. It's none of her damn business," he said rather angrily. I was taken aback, not expecting him to react so strongly to innocent girl-talk. Surely men know that we disclose certain milestones with our chosen sisters, right?

"But we always talk about stuff like that with each other. We've been there through every minute of each other's lives since we were eight years old. I can understand not disclosing our most personal details, Blake, but how can I not share with her one of the biggest moments of my life?"

"Because it's not about sharing with her—it's about comparing. Have you noticed how she always has to have the latest fashions? How she has to be the one with the first boyfriend or have the best this or that? Is she really your friend, Em, or does she use your failures to make herself look and feel better?"

"I know she seems to throw her money and boys in my face, but she's not really like that. She'd be happy for me," I swore up and down in her defense, though I couldn't help noticing Jess' patterns through Blake's eyes.

"You keep telling yourself that. But then ask yourself how many times she wanted to talk about her new boots when you were about to cry about your grandmother being sick. How many times she knew you were lonely, yet she talked endlessly about her latest boyfriend—or ditched you for him. She's not a real friend, Em. You're out of high school now. Time to grow up and see her for who she really is. She doesn't deserve to hear about our private moment and dirty it to her satisfaction. Making love to you is special to me. Don't turn it into girl gossip."

I was upset with myself for tarnishing one of the most wonderfully intimate memories we'd ever have in our lives, but I was even more upset about the blind revelation about my best friend. Blake gave me a lot to reflect on during a long, 7-hour plane ride home—like how many times Jess let me down. How materialistic she really was. How she flaunted her popularity in my face. How she wasn't truly there for me emotionally and that everything had to be a competition between us—one in which she always had to be the winner.

So, by the time I landed and Jess called, wanting me to fill her in on all the juicy details of my "expected" virginity loss in London, I almost verbatim repeated his words in disgust. I was not going to give her any more emotional ammunition against me for her own internal, conceited validation. I was not going to engage in this game of who had it better or worse. I was not going to be her chess piece pawn any longer. I so much as told her that, and she agreed that perhaps our friendship had finally run its course. Our childhood was officially over.

And I was okay with that. Blake was all the best friend I'd ever need, and I was committed to loving him for the rest of my life.

***

After London, our relationship took a bit of a

turn, which I guess is only natural once you cross the line from chaste curiosity to unabashed lovers. In some ways, intimacy brought us together, and in other ways, it brought new challenges. Though it wasn't the smoothest of romances anymore, or the most erotic, it swept me away, nonetheless.

I suppose I foolishly embraced one too many fairytales as a child, not realizing just how much compromise went into a relationship on the way to happily ever after. I was navigating a whole new world that led me to different emotions, perspectives, and considerations than I ever imagined.

Like about sex itself, for instance. I was so intrigued by this sensual box of discovery that we opened up that I'd hunger for more—more often, more exploration, more interesting—but it seemed like Blake was very much reserved in this area. I underestimated the impact his morals had on his overall beliefs and ideas about what making love should be. Maybe he regretted not abstaining until marriage.

I learned quickly that he was uncomfortable performing oral sex on me and that he was equally dismayed by the thought of touching himself—and forget about experimenting. Intimacy was very black and white with him, and that was something I needed to accept early on in our relationship. I struggled with that a little, but out of respect, I decided that my fantasies were not all that important. Not when I found a man as wonderful as Blake to love me for the rest of my life.

Thankfully, our love was built on more than just sex.

Adventure became one of the foundations of our relationship instead. We'd go on his growing number of photography job assignments to places I had always wanted to visit, just like he promised. We journeyed to New York City frequently, as well as ventured to Niagara Falls, the Grand Canyon, Hawaii, and France—each trip even more incredible than the last. I was quickly beginning to check off my global exploration bucket list sooner than I had ever anticipated.

The excitement of his blossoming career, trekking around the world, and seeing him in the middle of his passion were all so fascinating. He was my drug that I couldn't get enough of. I was undeniably addicted to Blake Denton.

The people we'd meet and the parties we'd attend were first class. He'd go to trendy photography conventions with a circle of like-minded friends, and they'd gather in amazing places to learn new techniques and sample the latest equipment and technology. Sometimes, I was able to tag along and found myself enthralled by the art of photography and its surprisingly cliquey scene.

Although it became increasingly difficult to alter my school and ever-demanding internship schedule to accompany him all the time, I couldn't turn down the opportunity to join him in Milan for one of his big annual conventions. I can't even explain the feeling I had as he proudly showed me off to his colleagues and took me behind the scenes as if I were part of the event itself.

"This is my Emily," he beamed as he introduced me to the convention coordinator.

"Ah, the elusive Emily. We've heard so much about you. It's a pleasure to finally meet the woman who makes this man so besotted."

Besotted? Wow. That's a word you don't hear every day. To hear someone who barely knew us share his perception of Blake's feelings for me was humbling. I felt so important; so included—so loved. I was his, and he wasn't afraid to make it known to the world.

Everyone knew who I was and went out of their way to make me feel so special. It was a wonderfully different dynamic to be the center of attention instead of the mouse in the corner, and I found myself liking the spotlight—a lot.

Blake was so protective of me in these large crowds of strangers, never allowing me to be alone with anyone. On the rare occasions I couldn't be with him, he made sure that I was in the company of another friend's guest who he trusted to watch over me.

"It's not that I don't trust *you*, Em," he insisted. "You don't know these people or this city like I do. I don't want to see anyone take advantage of you."

"How is that possible, Blake?" I asked, rolling my eyes at this overly masculine display of showmanship. "I'm pretty sure I can handle myself. I manage to survive unprotected at college. Surely, I can handle a photography convention."

"Now's not the time to argue with me. You'll stay with Evelyn, and that's the end of it. I will come get you when I am finished here."

It wasn't worth the fight for my independence, so I indulged his demand. At least I knew I could count on him to have my back and be the man I needed as

I entered this new, fast-paced world of his with my innate naiveté. He made me feel so safe and protected that I couldn't fault him for wanting to look out for me. It was just another way for him to show me his love.

When I was able to be at the convention live with him, I was enraptured by his ability to work a room. I'd watch him make his way from colleague to colleague, knowing just the right things to say to each person to make them smile. He also had an intelligent mind and quick wit, which those in his sphere found fascinating.

He'd lure people in to look at his latest photographs with that signature storytelling that made even the simplest picture of a blade of grass that much more interesting. In fact, he'd be one of the best sellers of the postcard-sized prints that attendees were allowed to exhibit during the conventions. His booth was always a hotspot.

And though his pictures were quite breathtaking, I do believe it was his innate salesmanship and charisma that drew in his captive audience, who paid a little more than they needed to for the added benefit of the Blake experience. My, how beguiling that man was.

In between adventures, we'd continue our deep conversations, yearning to learn even more about each other. Every day, it was as if a new layer of our lives was unraveled.

He grew to appreciate my love of Broadway musicals, and I learned to endure his love for bowling—I was starting to get really good at it, too!

I championed his love of photography, and he

encouraged me to keep my secret fashion design portfolio growing. In fact, at times he seemed to be the only person who cared about this creative part of me that I usually had to hide in favor of a respectable career and reputation.

"Em, these are incredible. Did you really design these?"

"I did. I used to sew clothes for my dolls and loved to dress them up. It's been my dream since I was a little girl to be a fashion designer."

"That's such a pity, Em," he said, shaking his head in disbelief like he was disappointed in me. "I still don't get why you are majoring in economics and interning at an investment firm instead. It's so—uninspiring." I couldn't help but nervously laugh at his direct honesty and observation. He had a point, but I had long given up hope on silly little girl wishes.

"Perhaps—but one day it will pay the bills pretty well! Beckingers is setting me up for a lot of great opportunities to advance my career. You know that. It's secure and stable. Fashion design won't exactly provide that for me." I almost shuddered as I repeated the words I heard so many times from expectant adults.

"I guess," he relented. "Secure and stable definitely suit you, so it makes sense why you'd like it. But I think you should keep designing. You're really good at it, and it's kind of nice to see this more fun side to you. You're way too serious all the time."

"Hmm, well someone in this relationship needs to be. Not everyone can just go off and live their exciting dreams like you can," I teased with mock jealousy.

"Hey, I'm not all fun and games, you know. I'm

very serious about loving *you*," he emphasized as he grabbed me into his arms for a spin before throwing me onto his bed for a very serious and passionate lovemaking session.

***

We continued to be there for each other during the challenging times, like when poor, sweet Grandma Wilma passed from a heart attack the winter of our first anniversary. Oh, how devastated Blake was to lose that woman; she was his entire world. I was by his side the entire time, and I witnessed the poignancy of love that existed within his own family. Perhaps I had been wrong about their level of dysfunction.

I expressed my deepest condolences to Mrs. Denton, who clearly was torn up over the loss of her mother, as different as they were. But in trying to empathize with her grief, good old Emily once again added insult to injury with my misunderstood family facts.

"I'm so sorry for your loss," I began.

"Thank you, Emily," his mother murmured, trying to keep her composure.

"I know it's been a difficult year for your family. First your niece, Monica, and now sweet Grandma Wilma. I didn't know her for long, but she was like another grandmother to me, and I loved her very much. If there is anything I can do for you, please let me know," I said with the deepest, sincerest attempt at consolation I could muster.

"My niece Monica? Emily, I don't have a niece by that name, nor has anyone else died in my family this year. Just my mother. If you'll excuse me," she said, rattled and annoyed.

Blake caught the tail end of the conversation and quickly moved me away from disturbing his mother further, chiding me for once again confusing him with someone else.

"This is not the time or place for your memory loss games, Emily. Why do you keep doing this to me? Today of all days?"

"I'm so sorry, Blake. I didn't mean to upset anyone. I—I was just trying to express my sympathies." But my plea fell on deaf ears. Clearly, I was not the source of comfort he needed in that moment. "Maybe I should go before I say something else stupid. I'll see you later at the house?"

"That might be best," he replied coldly, but I understood his detachment. He was so distraught, and I was only making things worse. I knew him well enough to know when he needed space to cool off, and the last thing I wanted to do was start an argument at the wake.

But as I drove home, I couldn't help but replay the memory of him canceling on me because of his cousin's death. I was absolutely bewildered—how was it possible that I kept getting these stories all wrong? Blake had been my only boyfriend, and I didn't have all that many male friends, so who could I be confusing him with this time?

Maybe he did say it, but just didn't remember it, I supposed. It could have been one of those embarrassing situations where he was feeling unworthy of being with me because of his drug habits, and just made up an excuse on the fly to let me down easy. Surely that kind of lie was understandable, wasn't it?

Yet, on the other hand, I shouldn't be made to seem like I was crazy for making stories up! I *knew* what I heard. Didn't I?

The whole inconsistency of "I said, he didn't say" started to irritate me a little, but then I remembered where I just came from. Grandma Wilma's wake. She entrusted her precious *knuddelbär* to my care when she passed. As I envisioned her portrait aside a closed coffin, her words reverberated in my head.

"I hope that you will always look inside to see his heart, even when he's not very good at showing it."

I would honor her expectation to be that door that kept Blake's heart open.

I knew that meant patience, understanding, and sensitivity. It meant being selfless and doing whatever it took to make the man I loved happy. It meant thinking twice before saying something hurtful and humbly asking for forgiveness when I was wrong.

I wasn't going to be my parents in an endless cycle of blame. I was going to take responsibility for my mistakes and forgive Blake's—the grownup way of being in a partnership.

"Blake, I didn't mean to add unnecessary stress or heartache to you or your mom today. I don't know what I was thinking when I brought up the death of some random person neither of you knew. Can you ever forgive me?"

"I love you, Emily, and so, I'll forgive you for embarrassing me—yet again. I don't know anyone else who would put up with being confused with other men all the time, you know."

"I know, and I am so sorry. I sincerely thought we had that conversation, but obviously, I was wrong. It won't happen again."

"I hope not. You were really out of line today."

"You're right. It was really insensitive of me to not think before I spoke. I was trying to be supportive, but I guess I'm just not very good at it."

"Agreed. But you know what hurts the most about all of this? That you turned to me with this look of doubt, as if you thought *I* was the one who lied to you about some dead cousin. Why would I do that? I've trusted you with my deepest secrets. I asked you to be by my side as I buried my Grandma Wilma today. Does that sound like someone who wants to lie to you? I'm grieving, Emily. I don't deserve your mental insecurities right now. Or ever."

"No, you don't," I admitted with shame. "And I know you wouldn't lie to me, Blake. I just thought— well, it doesn't matter what I thought. Like you said before, I need to stop overanalyzing everything. I keep letting my brain get in the way, and I'm sorry. Do you really forgive me?"

"Of course, baby. Just promise me you'll stop making up these stories, and we'll be fine," he assured me.

"I promise," I said as I stood there and took his lecture to heart.

"Good girl. Now, I know the perfect way you can make it up to me," he hinted—to my relief. I hadn't screwed things up between us, so I was more than willing to please him in any way he desired, to alleviate his grief over his beloved grandmother and his hurt heart over my thoughtlessness. As long as it meant we were okay, I would say or do anything to make things right between us.

Thankfully, Blake was open to accepting my apology this time. Since he had just lost his grandmother, he swore he didn't want to lose me, too; he loved me way too much to let some silly misunderstanding come between us. We were stronger than that and could get through anything.

Blake and I truly had an incredible bond. We laughed, we played, we laid still in the moonlight. We rarely fought, but when we did, making up was always spectacular. He taught me the art of compromise and how to be less selfish.

He showered me with the most thoughtful gifts and gestures, and we wrote love letters whenever we were apart. He'd tell me repeatedly how much he loved me and how devastated he would be if I ever left him. I never realized I could be so deeply loved by another human being.

"No one will ever love you the way I do," he declared, and he meant it.

We became close in every way that mattered and had the makings of the perfect love story.

6. DOUBT

Life with Blake promised a never-ending dance of adventure, fun, and laughter. And yet, even with all the magic that surrounded our magnetically predestined union, it sometimes—surprisingly—felt like something was off.

Either that or the looming certainty of a lifetime of devotion scared me senseless.

As much as I adored Blake and looked forward to these incredible escapades, or dreamed about our future together, I began to feel claustrophobic. Our roles had subtly reversed—shifting from me being the one in hot pursuit, fantasizing about wedding plans in my head, to him taking the lead in making our relationship the utmost center of his life, especially after Grandma Wilma passed.

"What time are you getting off work? I feel like I haven't seen you in days. Your boss spends more time with you than I do."

I couldn't help but put in overtime to secure my place in the new company I was working for off-semester in hopes that it would turn into a full-time position after graduation. I had officially turned down the offer to work for Beckingers, resolving to return to New Jersey permanently to focus on making something of my degree there. And admittedly, the new job afforded me some breathing room from both my family and Blake, who were always on my case about something.

"I can't wait until we can wake up in each other's arms like this for the rest of our lives."

I did love those rare mornings we were able to wake up together, but the enormity and permanence of that statement rattled me a little, drawing attention to the fact that it meant I would never be independent again. It made me shudder, to be honest.

"I hope our little girl has your cute nose and big brown eyes. How many kids do you think we'll have?"

Kids weren't on my short-term radar, but the thought of having Blake's children was certainly endearing. I secretly hoped we'd have a long courtship before a marital commitment so I could blow off motherhood for a few years; needless to say, I was meticulous about birth control.

At first, it was a fantasy come true that I was someone's whole universe and that I had found the love of my life. But slowly, the attention and expectations became overpowering, and I wanted so badly to take a step back; grasp a single moment to catch my breath while traveling on this runaway love train.

As we approached our first anniversary, shortly after the funeral, I had started to feel overwhelmed by all of our togetherness and just needed to get away to sort out some of my new emotions. I decided I was going to visit my older cousin, Julie, in Weston, Connecticut, for a few days before our private celebration and before returning to Virginia for my junior spring semester. She always had great advice, so if anyone could help me figure things out, it was Julie.

Blake seemed supportive at first when I told him I wanted to visit her. He said he'd miss me, but then hugged me tight and let me be to pack and enjoy my trip.

That was, until a few hours before I was set to leave, and he showed up on my doorstep in tears.

"I needed to see you. I had a nightmare last night that someone stabbed you, and all I could think about was how I couldn't lose you like I just lost Grandma. I needed to make sure you were okay—I needed to see you with my own two eyes. I couldn't take it if anything happened to you. Please don't stay away too long," he begged with grief-filled anguish.

It was a lot of baggage to have dumped on me right before a 4-hour drive. I tried to be empathetic to his mental scare, but he violated my desperate need for some space, and it was the first time I was ever truly angry with him, even if it was irrational of me to feel that way.

He could have easily just called me, but I guess it wouldn't have been as impactful without the visual of his tears. I still remember the bitterness that crept up inside me that I had to push down so as not to make him even sadder.

"As you can see, I'm fine," I replied tartly before softening. "It's only for a few days. I'll be back before you know it."

"Every day you are away feels like an eternity. I'm just so scared I'm going to lose you."

"Honey, you are not going to lose me. I'll call you when I get there, okay?"

"Yeah. But I'd feel much better if you called me every day so I knew you were okay."

"Fine," I agreed with a forced smile and terse hug goodbye.

I never asked him for much. All I wanted was a few days with my cousin, and now I was being made to feel guilty about leaving him so soon after his grandmother's death. It was more than I could bear in that moment, but seeing the messy man standing in front of me, I knew I had to be the bigger person and be strong for him.

I didn't know why I always had to be the one to repress *my* emotions; deny that *I* had the right to matter more sometimes.

Yet, instead of voicing my objections, I promised Blake that I wouldn't be gone for long and that I'd stay in touch every day—which actually defeated the whole purpose of my Connecticut breather. Still, I was determined to go and hopefully find some kind of clarity before I destroyed what we had with my romantic inexperience. I had become way too cloudy in my brain, and I didn't like where my resentment was heading.

I enjoyed some much-needed bonding time with Julie, whose own experience with men and my family helped me see both sides of the relationship story.

"From what you're telling me, Em, it's hard to say what's really going on without meeting Blake myself. I mean, on one hand, you could absolutely be experiencing a fear of commitment. Look at the role models you have. It's not exactly like Aunt Gloria and Uncle Bob have the most loving marriage, so I can see how you'd be afraid that you'd end up in the same kind of relationship and want to shut down and run away from love completely."

"I do worry about that, Jules," I admitted. "Especially because of Blake's own history with addiction. I trust him completely, but is that even a guarantee that he will be sober forever?"

"Yeah, see, that's the other thing, kiddo," she said lovingly. "I don't want to pass judgment, because like I said, I don't know Blake personally, but I think you're valid in your concerns. Addiction is not something to take lightly."

"I know. But he has never been on drugs around me—ever."

"As far as you know," she suggested, much wiser than I was about these things. "Listen, Em, it sounds to me like you really need to come from your heart on this one. Only you know if he is the right person for you or not. No one is perfect, and you need to figure out what lines cannot be crossed and which ones can be compromised. It's a give and take. Trust, but look out for red flags. They'll never steer you wrong."

"You're right, but I don't know if I could spot a red flag if it hit me in the face," I joked.

"We usually don't until it's too late," she laughed back with the knowledge of being through it before with her most recent ex-boyfriend. What a dick that guy was—I was certain that Blake was nothing like him at least.

"I guess I just need to figure out where my heart begins and where my head fits in. You know me, I'm probably overthinking everything like I always do," I bemoaned.

"Probably," she agreed. "But as you overthink, the

question you honestly need to ask yourself is this: are you in love with Blake or the *idea* of Blake?"

With the dropping of her wisdom bomb—exposing the question to end all questions—she left me in solitude to reflect on her words.

It was a seed of doubt that would haunt me over and over. A chilling nerve was struck. It was exactly what I had been avoiding asking myself, but her verbalization of it made it so raw, so real—so possible.

Could it be that I was so wrapped up in the storybook of love that I was resistant to reality?

Unfortunately, before I was able to truly sit with that query, Blake's weepy breakdowns led me to cut my visit short. The entire trip was overshadowed by his now recurring nightmare of my death, which he reminded me of in his daily phone calls, and I felt like I needed to get back to him for his own peace of mind. *Once again, putting his needs first,* I thought as I reluctantly packed up my car to head home.

Even though Julie lovingly advised against it and urged me once again to think of what my heart really wanted, I couldn't let him fester in his fearful worry.

What kind of person would I be if I didn't care about how distressed he was? He literally just lost his grandmother—his original lifeline. I couldn't be so selfish as to put myself first right now. To put girl time with Julie ahead of soothing his brokenhearted sorrows. Above all else, I did care deeply for him. He was in pain, and it would be callous of me to disregard his oversensitivity. Wouldn't it?

"I missed you so much. I hate when we are apart like that," he cried as he hugged me close to him. This was so unlike Blake; we'd been apart for several weeks at a time whenever I left for college, and he's never been so weepy or attached before.

I tried to be understanding through my growing irritation, which was becoming increasingly difficult to control. He was visibly tormented, and I didn't want to add to his anguish, but didn't my feelings matter to him—even a little? He made no acknowledgment whatsoever that I had come back early just for him.

I sighed deeply. I resigned myself to accepting that this was just how things were going to be. When Blake was more needy, I'd simply have to take a backseat. It wasn't any different than how it was with my own family whenever Dad's drunkenness would tear through us; I was the rock for everyone else, and so I'd stuff it all down to listen and comfort them.

Though with Blake, I was determined to still try to somehow communicate my own needs, hoping they didn't fall on deaf ears.

"I know. Me too. I just wanted to enjoy catching up with Julie, you know? And have a little bit of space to think. I'm not used to being someone's girlfriend, and I guess I'm learning what it's like to not be alone. I sometimes wish I could have a little time to myself, that's all."

"You make it sound like I need to be with you night and day," he accused, standing back offendedly with his arms crossed over his chest. "All I was saying was that I missed you. Is that so terrible?"

"No, of course not, babe. I'm sorry, that's not what I meant. It just came out wrong."

Well, that backfired. So much for honesty being the best policy.

What could I say to make it better? How could I

express myself without making him feel worse? I felt like I needed to come up with a good excuse as to why I was trying to distance myself from him to avoid a fight. I didn't want a fight. I wanted everything to be perfect again.

Please, God, help me smooth this over. I don't have the strength to defend myself in a verbal war today. I just want us to be all right. I'll think through my confusion later; right now, all I desire is peace. *Please help me find the words to make this right,* I prayed.

"Maybe I'm just working too much. Or maybe I'm reacting to my parents. It's hard for me to live back under their roof with all their rules when I'm used to being on my own at school. I'm feeling a little overwhelmed, and I didn't mean to take it out on you."

"It's okay. I know your parents can be strict, and you absolutely work too much. Honestly, I'm starting to feel neglected. We should take a trip somewhere and spend some time by ourselves away from it all. How does that sound?"

"Okay," I managed with a weak smile before he seduced me into a few rounds of lovemaking and spring break vacation planning. He wasn't getting the hint that he was part of my engulfment, but who's fault was that? I shut down and didn't want to pursue the issue. I chose peace, and I'd have to deal with the immediate consequences of that choice.

Perhaps when he was less emotional, we could try the conversation again. I had to, for my own sake. I needed him to understand that having personal freedom was important to me; I missed my solitude.

Part of me didn't know how to get that solitude

without causing a breakup, though. That's not what I wanted either. I only wanted a little bit of "me" time.

Could I hit pause without ruining this seemingly great thing we have?

I didn't know if I could, but everything inside of me had been crying out, as if maybe he loved me a little too much; wanted to see me a little too much. I couldn't tell if it was merely my fears or one of those Julie-warned, early red flags that said "run for the hills" that had me examining whether this relationship really was everything I fantasized it to be.

My cousin's question kept replaying in the back of my head. *Am I in love with a person or an idea?* The answer kept struggling to bare itself, but I denied its persistence. Now was not the time.

Only time could reveal what my inner voice was desperately trying to tell me.

***

So, until I took that time to listen to my own heart and needs, I pushed down any sense of confinement and challenged myself to let Blake more and more into my heart and my life.

I am just having cold feet, I'd tell myself, even though we weren't engaged or anything. Though marriage did come up quite frequently—enough to unnerve me into the epiphany that this wasn't part of my 5-year master plan.

Marriage and kids weren't supposed to be in the cards for me right now. I was so caught up in the romance of falling in love that I was neglecting the dreams I had independent of a relationship. So, whenever he would talk so intensely futuristic, I'd want to run and hide from the conflict that plagued my mind.

Did I forget about my career goals? Am I losing myself to this tumultuous ecstasy of unexpected love?

I'd reflect on this, over and over, as I pondered what a future with Blake would mean.

It meant wonderful, worldly adventures. We would never be bored with a mundane life, that's for sure. It meant endless conversations, sharing our innermost secrets, and building a trust that would last a lifetime. We were a reciprocal source of support and could count on each other for comfort, for laughter, for understanding.

He generously doted on me with fascinating dinners, experiences, and gifts, which although a little extravagant for my taste sometimes, showed me how profound his love for me was. Like when he imported a beautiful red satin fabric from Paris and encouraged me to take a class so I could use it to make my own designer dress for myself, which I did and wore on a very romantic dinner date.

And oh, his poetic side sometimes just knocked me off my feet. For our second Valentine's Day, he surprised me with a very strange arrangement of a 4-flower bouquet of pink, red, yellow, and white roses. I looked at him quizzically until he prompted me to read the handwritten note that accompanied it:

Pink is for the growing affection I feel for you every day.
Red is for the passion that you stir within me.
Yellow is for the sunshine you bring into my life.
White is for the purity of my love, forevermore.

How could I not adore this man with every fiber of my being?

Even though I was originally hesitant, we imagined what it would be like to have a few kids—both boys and girls—and talked about who they would look like, what activities they might enjoy, who they might want to grow up to be. We fantasized about owning a home in the suburbs a little further away from our families so that we could begin our own life together. Sometimes, we even looked through catalogs to inspire our future interior design, or choose china patterns for our registry, or find the perfect nursery theme for our firstborn.

It was so dreamy that it made all those professional goals of mine seem so cold and empty. What good was a life of an executive if I didn't have a wonderful family to share it with? *I could have it all,* I reminded myself once again. The fairytale family, the successful career, the picturesque home. My 5-year master plan didn't have to be abandoned, I finally grasped. It only needed to be embellished with the majesty of love's newest blueprints.

I resolved then to not run away from what Blake and I could be.

***

We had the promise of a beautiful future, of that I was certain; but, as with every well-laid plan, it would not be without its thorns.

Especially as the "honeymoon" phase faded further to unearth revelations of our mutual imperfections. We both surely had our quirks. Growing pains were a normal part of the relationship cycle, and we had entered the stage where pet peeves came into play. Our irritation with each other was completely natural and understandable, I told myself.

I, of course, was a little too serious for Blake's taste and an obsessive clean freak. I became annoyed too quickly when someone talked during a movie, and I was indecisive whenever we went out to eat. I worked a little too hard and a little too often, my ambition sometimes overpowering my affection. I could also absolutely acknowledge that I was a nagging pain in the ass at times and worried too much about money and what my mother thought of my decisions.

But Blake? Well, some of the stories he told me didn't match up to a comment his mother or a friend would make, and I wondered if sometimes he became too caught up in his own elaborations that he didn't remember what was actual and what was fiction. Then I'd find odd, un-Blake-like items in his new apartment, which were typically attributed to his troublemaking little brother.

Like when I discovered a rather large bag of pot in his linen closet while getting out a towel for a shower. He explained how Joey had stopped by and hid it in there away from their mother without Blake's knowledge or consent. Totally plausible, but I was uncomfortable with the thought of drugs being so accessible in a former addict's home, even as mellow as marijuana was compared to his hardcore heroin. It made me really edgy, but Blake immediately put my mind at ease by flushing it all down the toilet, out of his reach.

A few days later at a family dinner, I casually

informed Joey that I would keep his secret this time—if he promised to never ask Blake to hide his illegal drugs for him again. Joey looked at me with sincere confusion because he never even tried pot. I was infuriated by the lie and didn't want to press the issue, but I couldn't let the presence of these drugs remain unaddressed. I had to confront Blake.

"We promised to always tell each other the truth, Blake," I pleaded.

"Okay, you're right. It wasn't Joey's pot," he finally admitted after some coaxing that I would listen without judgment. "I was trying to avoid telling you this, but it was actually your dad's. I'm sorry. I didn't want to upset you, knowing how mad you would be. I was stuck in a hard situation and didn't know what to do. He wanted me to keep it from your mom, and I didn't want to let him down. Please don't be mad at me or tell your dad. He's the only man who's ever treated me like a son, and I don't want to ruin that. Please, Em."

I seethed with anger that my father would put Blake in such a position, but Dad didn't know about Blake's past, and he was right; confronting him would only start a World War, and I already knew that my mother was at a breaking point with him. Divorce was on the horizon, and I didn't want to be the one to tip the scales. For her sake, I let it go, but warned Blake if my dad ever approached him again, he needed to be firm and tell him to find another scapegoat.

Then there was the super strange experience of finding porn magazines under his bed one day when I was cleaning out his disorderly apartment. Porn magazines—from a man sworn against masturbation and illicit sexual fantasies. I paled at the sight of them. Blake was never all that into sex, but was it because I was terrible in bed? That thought hadn't crossed my mind until I held a stack full of busty blonde boobs in my hand.

"Oh, baby, those aren't mine," he assured me as I wiped some threatening tears away. "They really are Joey's this time. He brought them over here thinking I would want them, but I told him you are all the turn-on I need. You know I think this stuff is gross. I guess he just didn't take them with him when he left the other day."

That one I could believe, knowing Joey and his womanizing tendencies. I instantly blew out a sigh of relief and let him prove how much he desired me. He put every effort into his sensual touches, to the point where I almost orgasmed for the first time. We'd never been successful before, probably because of my inability to surrender.

I read somewhere that some women have psychological blocks to orgasms, and Blake agreed that it must be the case with me because he tried his hardest to please me. At least I had the proof of knowing I satisfied *him*.

Witnessing the intensity of his attraction for me that afternoon, I knew those couldn't be his magazines. But still—he needed to stop covering for everyone! Finding these random things rattled my insecurities way too much. I didn't like how it felt to interrogate Blake, as if I didn't trust him. I trusted him more than anyone else in the entire world. He was my rock. My protector. My everything.

Even if he was a little on the flighty and forgetful

side. It was part of his charm.

Which brings me to his financial management. As an economics major, it completely baffled me how someone with such promising income could be so irresponsible with his money, going on spending sprees before paying his bills. He made girls look like grinches when it came to retail therapy.

Sometimes, I'd find his overdue electric bill open on his desk with a shut-off warning and think it peculiar, that with all his money, he had any issue paying his most basic expenses.

He also had to pay everything in cash, he said, because he wasn't able to get credit cards. Since he and his uncle shared the same first and last name, his credit would be mistaken for his debt-ridden uncle's, and he had been unable to establish good credit for himself. I'm sure that must have been incredibly frustrating to deal with all the time.

But then some of his bills weren't even *his* bills. Why was Camille's cell phone statement on his desk?

"She didn't want Mom to know she got another cell phone, so I let her use my address for the new account. Ruth can be a pain about that shit, and Camille didn't want to sit through another round of her third-degree lecture on irresponsibility," he explained to my satisfaction.

Okay, so maybe Blake wasn't the most responsible when it came to money and had some issues in this area. He tended to be a little too generous when it came to helping others, myself included. He bailed me out a time or two when my savings had been depleted, and I needed some new clothes for work or an emergency car repair. And not everyone has a budget-conscious mind like an investment planner in training, so I was willing and able to help him sort out his finances as we built our future together.

It was the least I could do to pay him back for all the support he had given me.

Odd thing was, as I began to help him, I started noticing more incongruencies and patterns that didn't add up. If the phone bill was Camille's, then why was it for Blake's phone number? On the defaulted electric bill, why was his uncle's middle initial used and not Blake's? A run of his credit report revealed a whole slew of approved credit cards that were not only maxed out but defaulted—*with* his appropriate middle initial.

What in the hell was going on?

Of course, he'd have a clever answer for everything. It was the vendor's fault for the mix-up, and those *really* were Uncle Blake's credit cards. And the phone bill? Well, it started out as Camille's, but when she defaulted on paying it, he took the phone line over and got her a different number. On and on piled the weird excuses.

And I'd just accept them, because, well, they fit Blake's claim of never-ending bad luck.

Sometimes, my investigative probing became a little too much for Blake, and he'd retaliate with some mild-mannered threats that if he wasn't making me happy, then I should leave him. He quickly discovered that the idea of Leyla was a weakness of mine, so that came in pretty handy for Blake's toolbox of warnings. Whenever I would aggravate him, he'd casually remind me of his power to choose.

"Leyla is still interested, you know. She won't leave

me alone—she's a lot like you in trying to chase me down. Don't make me regret my decision to be with you instead of her."

Other women became the dangling carrots that made me step back and realize that if I pushed him too far, I would lose him forever.

It wasn't just Leyla, either. Brittany left countless remnants of scars on his vulnerable heart. So sometimes, his fears would cloud his judgment, and we'd get into some volatile tiffs during a miscommunication.

Like when we were supposed to go to an important work event of mine together. He ended up getting sick with a mild rash that evening, and I went to the fundraiser anyway—and then kept plans the following night to go out for a friend's pre-planned birthday celebration. Since I was so busy, I didn't get to see him that weekend. That didn't go over too well with my ailing love, who thought my extravagant outings would lead to my eventual cheating.

"Two nights in a row? Wow, it must really be important for you to be out living it up with everyone. I just had a severe allergic reaction, and you're out partying? If you were sick and had to go to the emergency room, I would have been by your side instead of going out with my friends drinking. But maybe that's just me. Hope you enjoyed yourself."

"Blake, I tried to call you to check in on you, but you wouldn't return my calls. You know how important being at that fundraiser was for my job. I *had* to go. And I couldn't exactly cancel on Linda—we've had this planned for weeks since I was actually going to be home. It was just a minor skin inflammation—even the doctor said you were okay."

"Just a minor skin inflammation? You have no idea what this did to me—to have my face look like it was hit by a shovel and not know what to do about it. You really let me down, Em. The doctor said it was a reaction to all the stress going on in my life with my asshole landlord evicting me out of nowhere and not having any new job assignments come up. I was really scared, and it hurt that you chose to go out with friends instead of being there for me. I thought I could count on you."

"Honey, you can count on me. I'm so sorry. I didn't realize it was that severe. I wish you would have told me. I would have changed my plans if you said you were going to the emergency room. How was I supposed to know?"

"You're my girlfriend, Em. I shouldn't have to tell you to be there for me. You should just know when I need you. But don't worry about it. I ran into Leyla, who happened to be the nurse on call at the hospital, and she talked me through it," he said right before he hung up to leave me to my guilt and fear that I had fucked up royally.

Sometimes, I really did wonder if the magic had died and if I was dragging this out longer than I needed to. But no two people are exactly alike, and no relationship is ever perfect. These were just quirks of Blake's or mutual misunderstandings that I came to accept and push to the side like they were no big deal. If I gave them any fuel, I'd be risking a downward spiral that we couldn't recover from.

Besides, it's not like we didn't still have amazing moments together. He surprised me one night while

I was back at college, showing up at my dorm with a bouquet of spring flowers and an invitation to a hot air balloon ride that evening. He had sweetly worked it all out in advance with my roommate, who was more than happy to give us our space for the weekend.

We needed this jolt of romance back in our relationship. As we soared high above the skies, witnessing the grandness of the world below, I felt at home in Blake's arms.

"It blows my mind to think of how small we really are in this vast universe," I reflected.

"And yet, the universe conspired to bring the two of us together, despite the odds," he thoughtfully pointed out as he squeezed me tighter and placed a delicate kiss on the side of my neck, sending chills through me.

"We really are lucky, aren't we?"

"Yes, we are. At least, I know I am," he hinted. "It's nice to hear that I matter to you."

"Of course you matter to me, baby. I love you."

"Good. Because there isn't anyone else in this world I'd want to spend the rest of my life with. No one will ever love you like I do," he reminded me once again. "Never forget that, my Emily Grace."

How could I ever forget? I knew his love for me ran deep, and I could feel it in his welcoming embrace. His words carried me through the rest of the gloriously peaceful ride and back down to Earth, where he tenderly made love to me the rest of the weekend. When things were good between us like this, life was spectacular.

***

But it never lasted for long, it seemed. There continued to be more highs and lows between us, never any consistency. Romance boosted us, then arguments fragmented us. Over and over. Whenever something didn't feel right, I was tempted to just pull the plug and break up with him. I couldn't handle all this up-and-down drama when I was trying to keep my grades up and get my career path settled.

But I never had the courage to end it. I always talked myself out of it—or got talked out of it. It's like Blake sensed the impending doom and stopped me before I had the chance.

Every single time.

"I'm not good enough for you. You are so smart and successful, and I barely graduated high school. I can't believe someone like you could love a loser like me. I don't deserve you."

Signal the need to boost his ego and convince him that I am no better than he is and that he absolutely does deserve me—tossing my own oversensitive needs to the side. He was already feeling down; I couldn't bear to add to his burden. A few more days wouldn't hurt...

"I'm so grateful to have found you. Last night, I was thinking about Grandma and how much I missed her, and I really needed a hit. It was so bad, baby. I was itching hard to score some drugs. But then I thought of you. You've given me the strength to stay sober, Em. I can't wait to marry you. I love you so much."

Now, how could I let myself be the reason someone so fragile falls back into a drug addiction? I wouldn't be able to live with myself knowing I had single-handedly destroyed Blake's sobriety or will to live. Maybe when he is feeling a little stronger...

"I scored us two tickets to *Les Mis* in Chicago for Memorial Day weekend. I know you've always wanted to visit the 'Windy City,' so I figured we could take a few days to sightsee and catch a show."

Exploiting my weakness—Broadway *and* a trip to one of my bucket list destinations? He was so sweet and big-hearted with his gestures, and we always did have a good time whenever we stepped away from our hometown. Perhaps things weren't all that bad...

Yes, whenever I would feel unsure, Blake would do or say something to make me second-guess myself, and I would mistrust my reasons for wanting to end things between us.

What was I running away from? I would scold myself. I thought I had already worked this out in my head that the good outweighed the challenges. Not to mention, if I left him, would I ever find anyone who loved me as much as Blake did?

Way too often I let that false sense of security win out over what was most likely my intuition.

I began to ignore Julie's wise wisdom to probe whether I was in love with Blake or in love with the *idea* of love. I realized that I no longer wanted to know the answer; I was in too deep and unable to turn away from this Cinderella story and my reckless hopes for a happily ever after.

And so, I carried on with our relationship full steam ahead—smothering affection, shortcomings, and all.

But then there was a turning point during school when our relationship temporarily became that of nightly calls and weekly love letters, and it seemed to suit me just fine. After all, he was still a drug to me, and I needed regular doses of his humor, encouragement, and attention.

Yet while I was away, I was afforded some much-needed breathing room to really reflect on all that I was feeling—which continued to be a plethora of mixed emotions. Some days, I wondered if there was something or someone else out there for me, and then the next day I'd be designing my wedding dress and dreaming up flower arrangements. I never strayed, but an increase in attention from some new men around me on campus stirred up even more confusion. It took my doubts to a whole new level.

Was I missing out on life experiences because I had already found "the one?"

No, I needed to stay true, I reminded myself. I deflected the advances of other men and stayed faithful to my word and to the love of my life. I could choose to experiment and explore my curiosity, but I'd be giving up the assurance of a forever kind of love with a man who undoubtedly loved me to his core.

Case in point: Blake would send me pictures of himself snuggling with my favorite blanket I left behind at home; my mom would tell me stories about how he visited her every night so he could feel closer to me; and every week, a new, sappy love letter, accompanied by an occasional mixtape that professed his undying devotion, arrived in my mailbox.

He had no doubts—so, why did *I?*

I had every intention of picking up where we left off when I returned home after two long months away, right before our planned Memorial Day weekend trip to Chicago. I wasn't ready to face my real feelings just yet, so I decided to keep it status quo. I convinced myself that I was happy enough and nothing had to change; I was in it for the long haul.

But when we saw each other, *he* was not convinced. Blake saw my eyes shift with uncertainty and felt the physical wall I had slowly started to build with each creeping reservation. When he confronted me about it, I tried to lie and spare his feelings, but he begged me for the truth. Fearfully, I allowed myself to speak it—at the risk of destroying the best thing that ever happened in my life.

"I can tell something is wrong, Em. What is it?"

"It's nothing, Blake. I'm just tired." I did just finish driving in ten hours of traffic, and I really wasn't in the mood for a dramatic confrontation. I prayed that he would let it be, but he didn't.

"No, there's something more to it than that. I can feel it. You're pulling away from me, and I want to know why."

"Can we please talk about this tomorrow? I honestly just want to go to bed. It's been a long day."

"Fine. But just tell me this one thing: do you love me?"

Please God, please don't make me have this conversation tonight. I beg of You, let me get some rest tonight and then I promise I will have the deepest, most open and honest conversation with Blake in the morning...

"Of course I love you, Blake."

"But are you *in* love with me?"

Fuck, he went there. Time paused, and the small, purple bedroom began to spin. The nausea came over me in waves like a tsunami that engulfed an entire coastal town. *How in the hell do I reply to that?* It was different when Julie asked; I could avoid her and refuse to answer. But I couldn't ignore the question when it was posed by Blake himself.

I could try to lie, but his eyes were honed in on mine, and he'd see right through me. He already knew the answer but needed to hear me say the words. I wanted to puke all over my lily-white bedspread and disheveled open luggage, but I held back the months of silent bile.

I had no choice but to meekly respond with what was genuinely in my heart. I barely whispered it as I hung my head down and away from his tortured eyes. I couldn't bear to see what my truth would do to him.

"I don't know."

With those three words, I watched a man's heart shatter into a million pieces and a future destroyed.

Fuck. What had I done?

"Well, I know how I feel about you," he finally said after a minute of silent agony. "I love you and have no doubts that I want to spend the rest of my life with you. You know where to find me when you figure it all out in that messed up head of yours."

And with that, Blake stormed out of my parents' house, and it was over.

7. BETRAYAL

Well, maybe it was over between us as a couple, but it wasn't the end of us going back and forth about what happened as Blake sought further clarity—namely how I could so easily give up on our great love. After several conversations and tons of profuse crying, Blake swore he understood why I was confused and promised he would be content if I just wanted to be friends for now, as long as I remained in his life. He even wrote me a beautiful poem professing his surrender.

> *"There was a chocolate-eyed girl my heart once knew*
> *She had a dazzling smile that lit up the room.*
> *We spoke through our heartbreaks, and laughed at the incredible*
> *Without her, life will most definitely lose its spark, it's inevitable.*
>
> *As I let out a lovelorn groan and a sigh*
> *I kissed her gently on her forehead between her eyes.*
> *I held her for a moment, and released her like a dove*
> *Forever knowing her as my one true love."*

My heart instantly puddled at the thought of him loving me so much that he would be willing to let me walk away—in the hope that I would come back, of course. I knew those were just selfless words and that he truly didn't want to let me go; he was willing to wait for me to remember where my heart belonged. I was relieved because I didn't want to move on just yet, either.

I didn't know why I couldn't just make a clean break and not look back.

After a few days of seesaw emotions, in between pleading with me to tell him what to do to win my love back, he'd interject some real soul twisters that made me question why I couldn't just give him my whole heart.

"You know the moment we met, it was destiny. Are you telling me fate had this all wrong? That all the signs pointing to our union were wrong? That would be like saying there was no God—that this miracle He created to bring us together was a lie and not real."

"I bared my soul to you. Men don't get vulnerable with women the way I got vulnerable with you. I guess I was right all along—you deserve someone better than a loser like me."

"Are you sure you really want me to walk out of your life? I may not be around when you get back from whatever it is you think you need to discover about us. The grass is not greener on the other side. I'm not saying this to be mean, but you'll never find someone who loves you the way I do."

"I slept in your bed when you were away at college. I waited for you to come home. I wrote poems and love letters to you. How could you not love a man who recites such words of love to you off the cuff?"

It was too much to absorb. The guilt plagued me day in, day out as I reflected on his words.

I did think God had divinely brought us together.

We did have an intense vulnerability that not many couples I knew shared. I didn't think the grass would be greener, but I had no point of reference to compare us to. I did absolutely adore the sweet, sensitive, romantic man that he was, who wasn't afraid to show his devotion in so many poetic ways.

I wondered time and again how I could doubt my love for him. I didn't know why I couldn't just force myself to feel what I was supposed to feel. Endless nights, I would berate myself for being so messed up in the head that I'd choose to destroy a beautiful relationship instead of fight for it.

To exacerbate the situation, everyone seemed to be on Blake's side of the breakup. Even my family was mad at me by this point. He had become so close to them that I started to feel like an outsider in my own unit. My parents interrogated me about breaking Blake's heart and letting him walk out of their home in such a distraught state. Kerry chided me for turning my back on a wonderful man and potentially ruining her own relationship with her infallible big brother.

I would hear lists of reasons why I was wrong about letting Blake go.

"He's so wonderful to you, sweetie, and it's clear that he loves you very much. I'd give anything for your father to be the kind of man Blake is. Why are you running away from the love of your life?"

"Poor kid. I'm going to miss him coming over here and hanging out in the basement with me. It's too bad you couldn't work things out. He's a good man."

"Ever since you met him, you've been a way cooler sister. Now you'll probably go back to being the self-righteous bitch you always were. He made you a nicer person to be around."

If that was my own family's reaction, I don't know why I thought his friends would remain neutral. After all, they were Blake's friends first, and when push comes to shove, they knew where their loyalties lied. So, I hung my head low as I left the bowling alley for the last time after they made it clear I was no longer welcome on the team. I deserved to lose them as my own friends.

I told myself over and over again that I deserved everything I got for wounding him so deeply by telling him that I wasn't sure if I was *in love* with him. That verbal self-punishment helped to appease the enormous sense of remorse that overpowered me.

But Blake was still not ready to give up on me. We continued to remain "just friends" and hang out over school breaks, and our overall relationship seemed to be on the mend. He'd spend more time with his buddies, and I'd see Kayla and Linda. Our time together was much more easygoing now that I had unburdened myself with the truth. The fun that was behind our friendship blossomed once again.

He even gave me a beautiful blown glass seahorse figurine for my birthday to prove how much he still cared about and doted on me. He was so patiently lavish with his gifts, with his time, with his kindness.

But the hurt I caused was undeniable. I saw it when he wished me a happy birthday; when he'd come over to see my family; when we'd platonically sit close together on the couch watching a movie.

To make matters worse, our uncontrollable, innate attraction overcame us one steamy night. One thing led to another, and we had sex. Since it had been so long, there was an electric power to it.

Our connection was indisputable. The passion was as real as our very first night together. The way he kissed me, touched me, moved inside me, was all so familiar and safe and comfortable. I couldn't deny that even with doubts, I was drawn to him like no other.

"Would any other man ever be able to make you feel like this?" he asked as I glistened in his arms in the aftermath of our intense connection. "I don't think you realize how strong my love for you is. I would protect you and love you to the moon and back, Emily. If only you'd say you'd be mine again."

I couldn't respond with words. I felt guilty for not being able to mouth all that he longed to hear, so I kissed him hungrily and invoked another round to escape from dealing with a confrontation of commitment. He simply and tenderly repeated what he had said so many times before:

"No one will ever love you the way I do."

Could he be right? Was I just being stupid and insecure about our inevitable forever after?

Although I considered getting back together with Blake after that night, I was still not ready to make that life-altering decision. He graciously endured my uncertainty, and we continued to have occasional sex as if we were a couple, but without the label. It was complicated, but we both were seemingly getting what we wanted. He got me, and I had the freedom to navigate my feelings. No strings attached.

So, if I happened to kiss a guy when I went back to school for my final fall semester, I was technically not doing anything wrong, right? Surely it was okay for me to test the theory that no man could ever make me feel the way Blake did...

Yeah, not my best hour. Engaging in a hookup with an old college crush was one of the worst decisions I had ever made. It was bound to come back and bite me in the ass.

Michael—sensual, attentive, seductive Michael, who was equally charming and made my stomach twirl with butterflies—was simply irresistible. While on this official dating break, I succumbed to a single fiery kiss that left me wondering if there *really was* more to life than being with Blake.

"You are so damn sexy, Emily," Michael crooned as he pressed his rock-hard body against me and let his mouth take over mine. He unapologetically possessed me, stirring up fantasies that I pushed down because Blake wasn't interested in sexual diversity. The power with which he threw me up against the dorm door shot images of naughty whips and chains through my innocent head.

Where did *that* come from?

All I could do was moan in response as he trailed his tongue toward my ears and took a playful nip. He began sucking on my neck to mark me as his erotic victim, and I couldn't get enough. His hands started to move up my shirt to unclasp my bra, and I froze as he whispered, "I want to fuck you so hard right now."

I knew what Michael was offering, and I craved it. I wanted to know what it was like to be fucked and not made love to for once. I wanted to know the rawness of pure lust; to give in to my secret fantasy to be with at least one other sexual partner before settling down with a single man for the whole of my life. I yearned to be with someone who might lick me into an insatiable orgasm. *Just once.*

But I couldn't go through with it. I freaked out instead of surrendering to my hungry desire. No man but Blake had ever seen or touched my naked body, and his emotional hold over me was so strong that I felt like I was being unfaithful to him. I pulled away from Michael apologetically.

"I'm sorry. I'm not ready for this. I—I have to go," I whimpered, adjusting my shirt, grabbing my purse, and running toward the door.

"Emily, I'm sorry if I made you feel uncomfortable. Shit, I didn't mean to push too far," he said in regret as he blew out a frustrated breath of hot air and ran his hands over his head. I softened guiltily, knowing that he didn't do anything wrong.

"Oh, Michael, it's not you. You didn't do anything I didn't want you to do," I assured him. "I just—I thought I was ready to be with another man, but I guess my head is still a mess thinking about Blake. I know that's probably the last thing you want to hear."

But Michael was unbelievably understanding. "Nah, it's cool. I was just worried that I was crossing a line. Although I did mean it when I said I wanted to fuck you," he nervously laughed, "I respect you too much to pressure you into anything. We good?"

"We're good," I smiled. "Thanks for understanding."

"Yup. See ya around, Davidson," he said, escorting me to the door like a gentleman, even though I must have bruised his masculinity quite a bit.

Although I didn't sleep with Michael, I felt this enormous sense of shame as if I had betrayed Blake, nonetheless. My mind replayed that kiss over and over all night long as I laid restless in my lonely bed.

At the end of the day, I was no better than Brittany was. A technicality doesn't change the fact that this was a cheating of the heart.

And for what? Pushing aside the strong passion of Michael's touch and the pleasure of his kiss, I ultimately thought about Blake and how it really didn't feel the same. He was right about that. Another man could not measure up to the comfort and connection I had with him.

Let the self-punishment and contempt commence once again.

I was mortified that I could bring myself to even let another man touch me in any romantic way. It would crush him—not to mention infuriate him—since Blake had met Michael when he visited campus once, and they had shared an instant dislike for each other. This had a Marcus-style explosion written all over it.

No way was I poking *that* hornet's nest. I've seen how his jealousy played out before, and I knew better than to repeat history.

I ended up forcing my attraction to Michael off to the side out of respect. Afraid of what Blake would do if he ever found out, I swept the mistake under the rug and never told him about it. I couldn't bear to hurt him like that again, especially after the way Brittany deceived him—and how I devastated him with my uncertainty.

Since Michael seemed cool with the fact that we couldn't be anything more than friends, I was able to put the whole scenario behind me and move forward. We agreed not to utter a single word about it, as if it had never even happened.

No harm, no foul—right? On I went with my studies and internship, withdrawing from many social events to protect myself and Blake from any more of my physical fuckups.

It worked for a while, anyway.

Until one day when Michael innocuously asked me to go to a basketball game with him. His buddy had canceled at the last minute, and he didn't want the ticket to go to waste, and he knew I enjoyed an occasional game. He promised he was asking just as friends, so I accepted his invitation and went.

We had an amazing time and kept to our agreement. We didn't even kiss or hold hands. One hundred percent platonic, and it was a much-needed break for this overworked academia nut, who was still trying to earn a 4.0 in between dealing with all my love drama.

But somehow, word got back to Blake that not only did I go to this game, but that I had sex with Michael afterward. To this day, I don't know who could have been so cruel as to start that story, but the rumor created a shitstorm of epic proportions.

As expected, it was as if I stabbed Blake in the center of his loyal heart. Like breaking up with him wasn't painful enough... let's add some salt of betrayal into the wound. There wasn't much I could say to ease his anguish, but I was determined to try.

"When were you going to tell me that you hooked up with some other guy?"

"It wasn't like that, Blake. We just went to a basketball game—as *friends*. I swear."

"If it was so innocent and nothing happened, then why didn't you just tell me you went to the game with your *friend,* Michael? Why did you hide it from me?"

"Because I knew you would react like this—all jealous for no reason. Plus, I know you hate the guy, so if I told you I went with Michael, you would have gone nuts and thought the worst of me. I was trying to avoid this right here—this unnecessary confrontation."

"So, you just decided to lie like it was no big deal."

"I didn't lie, Blake. I didn't think it was a big enough deal to start a fight over. I don't have to tell you what goes on in my life every second of the day," I defended.

"It was a lie of omission, *Princess.* And as long as we're sleeping together, I do have a right to know about you going on dates with other men—especially assholes like Michael."

"I get it, you're right. I should have told you. But how many times do I have to tell you it wasn't a date?"

"I don't buy it, Emily. Any of it. You have no problem having sex with me, yet you still don't want to get back together. Is it because of him? Is Michael the reason you want your damn freedom? So, you can fuck around with whoever you want but still have me to come back to?"

"No! It's not like that at all. Yes, I was attracted to him. Yes, we kissed *once*—but not at the basketball game. We really did go as just friends. I swear to you—nothing happened. We *never* slept together. After kissing him that one time, I knew it was wrong, and I told him I wouldn't cross that line again because of how I felt about you."

"And what is it you feel about me? I'd love to know myself."

"I don't know," I frustratingly confessed. "At times, I want to be with you wholeheartedly, but I'm still confused. I thought we'd have this break, but we went right back to hanging out and having sex as if nothing changed. You keep talking about marriage, even now, and it frightens me.

"I don't know if I am ready to say I'm in this forever with you. I haven't even graduated yet. You make me feel like I have to say yes to a proposal before I can even say yes to just being a girlfriend. I feel this enormous pressure and I just—I can't do it right now, Blake. I have school to worry about. I need more time."

"Don't flatter yourself into thinking I'd want to marry you after this. I don't know if I can ever trust you again. Take all the time you need. I might not be here waiting for you, though."

Out the door he walked once again, this time with my crushed heart in his hand.

I didn't blame him. I did violate his trust. On a break or not, he did deserve to know if I kissed another man while I still willingly warmed his bed. And I deserved any retribution he wanted to dish out for all the pain and suffering I had caused him because of my foolish, inexperienced doubts and lies of omission. I broke us, and I had to learn to live with the consequences of my selfish actions.

I lost the Blake that I had come to know forever, and I would chastise myself for violating his trust for a very long time to come.

***

Blake eventually came to forgive me, though I'm not sure he ever believed that I was telling him the truth about Michael. The next few months went on as friends, and I continued to abstain from getting mixed up with any other men. Until I knew what it really was that I wanted, we both agreed that it would be best if we didn't have sex either.

I even told him that he should move on and not wait for me any longer. I knew there were other women showing their interest in him—Leyla at the forefront, as he continued to remind me. It was unfair for me to string him along, and I was letting him go find the happiness he deserved.

Blake wouldn't accept it, though. He said he would hold on as long as it took until I was ready to make that commitment.

He was slow to trust me again, understandably. I thought we were headed in the right direction, reestablishing a solid foundation of friendship, until one night we were alone in his apartment. Things took a surprising turn and became mighty steamy. We weren't supposed to have sex until I was ready to commit, but he couldn't keep his hands off of my body—and my body didn't want him to.

His fingers found their way down my pants and into me, pulsating hard and quickly bringing me to an almost orgasm that I sensed was finally going to happen—but then he stopped before my release. I moaned into his mouth, relieved when I realized he had only paused to remove my panties so I could be fully exposed to his touch.

"Does this feel good, baby?"

"Oh, yes, Blake. Don't stop."

"Do you want to feel me inside you?"

"Yes. Deep inside me." He allowed his fingers to resume their position of pleasure, heightening all of my senses almost to peak once more.

"Did Michael make you feel this good, baby?" I froze at the mention of another man's name, but he kept on pulsing while talking. "Answer me, Emily. Would you rather it be Michael that was making you moan right now?"

"No," I responded, tears of remorse starting to pool in my eyes. "Only you."

"Say it again," he ordered as he swiftly positioned me under him, holding off on penetration until I obeyed his demanding eyes.

"I only want you," I cried in a whisper, trying to bring him closer so that his touch would eliminate the distance between us. I wanted to feel him inside me again. I needed him, his touch, his closeness. But instead, he got up off the couch and zipped up his pants.

"Remember that the next time you want to be with another man. I may not be so forgiving next time."

And out the door he went, leaving me half-naked, confused, and ashamed that I could ever want to be with anyone else. I was stunned that he could be so cruel as to bring me to the brink of ecstasy and then just drop me like that and walk away—yet that was exactly what I was doing to his very soul with my game of confusion.

His message was loud and clear: choose him, or he was leaving forever.

The clock was ticking.

I needed to stop fucking around with his heart

and make a decision. I know what he did that night seemed utterly vicious, but my selfish obsession with keeping him in my life, while I figured out if he was good enough to be my future, was a million times harsher. I was the worst kind of scumbag, toying with him like that. My parents, my sister, my friends—all of them constantly shared their opinion of my callous treatment of sweet, loyal, steadfast Blake Denton.

After that night, he turned the charm back on. His pursuit mirrored that of my initial one. He was so determined to convince me that I was only postponing destiny—and that the sooner I realized he was the only one who could love me with his entire being, imperfections and all, the sooner we could start our beautiful life together.

Love letters, gifts, and kind gestures continued to court me back to him. An invitation to an upcoming job assignment in New England over spring break, where we could drive through the blossoming colors of rebirthed trees and hike through the mountains during a spring sunrise, was hard to resist.

A rose gold bracelet in the shape of an infinity symbol with the inscription, *Forever My Princess*, melted my heart. One night after a long day at work, he was waiting at my parents' house with scented oils to give me a non-sexual massage to ease my tension, though it backfired as I had to fight my seemingly unrequited arousal.

Blake went from being cautious and distant to pulling out all the stops to win me over. It was starting to work, but I would be lying if I said I was confident about my future with Blake.

I didn't know why I still hesitated when the man

of my dreams was practically begging me to come to my senses and tear down the wall around my heart. If only there was a way I could be unequivocally certain...

Then came the nightmare bomb that rocked my world.

***

Blake was diagnosed with polycystic kidney disease, and the doctors didn't know how long he would live with this condition since it was uncommonly advanced for his age. They proactively registered him on a kidney transplant list, and the praying and research began. All the doubts that had tortured me were instantly surrendered the moment Blake's mortality stared us in the face.

"I'm so scared, Em. I don't want to die."

"You're not going to die, baby. We're going to find a cure, and you'll live a long, healthy life. I'm going to be here to help you get through this. I promise."

Never in my life had I been so scared to lose someone. With God's intervention, all the sins of our past (*my* past) were washed away and forgiven. All that mattered was saving his life, and when I say I spent days—weeks even—on finding alternative supplements, treatments, and cures to slow his progression or ease his symptoms, it wasn't an exaggeration.

I sent him letters and music of encouragement to not give up and reassured him that I would be there by his side through this entire ordeal. And I meant that.

BEAT ME WITH YOUR WORDS

"And when the night is cold and dark
You can see, you can see light
'Cause no one can take away your right
To fight and to never surrender"
-Never Surrender, Corey Hart

I once abandoned him in his time of need, choosing work and a girlfriend's birthday instead of caring for him when he was sick. He was so upset that I wasn't there for him when he needed me most.

This time, he would not be alone, and I would find a way to save him, even if the doctors couldn't. Even if we couldn't find a match right away. I would be the light that would give him the hope to live.

The thought of living a life without Blake hit me hard. I finally saw it clearly: he was my present and my future, and I wasn't going to waste any more time wondering if this was right or not.

The rest of my life took a backseat, and I dedicated all my free time to saving Blake from this tragedy. I even helped him confide in his parents about his diagnosis, though he was extremely resistant to do so. He begged me not to tell anyone because he didn't want their pity, but I insisted that the people he loved deserved to know that his life could be cut short— besides, what if they could be the match that saved his life? This wasn't a secret I was willing to keep for him, and begrudgingly, he allowed me to stand by his side as he shared his pain with his family.

It was to be as expected, with lots of questions Blake didn't know how to answer, but thankfully, I was there to fill in the blanks from the hours of research I'd conducted.

"I don't know how I would get through this without you, Em. Thank you for being here for me," he said as I embraced him close to my chest after all was said and done.

"I'm not going anywhere, sweetheart. We'll fight this together."

"When you say it, it makes me believe I might have a chance at beating this. You give me hope."

"And I'll keep giving you hope until the doctor says you're healed, or you get a new kidney. I'm not giving up on you, Blake Denton."

"And I'll never give up on you either, Emily Grace Davidson. You have changed my life in so many ways. If these are to be my last days, I wouldn't want to be anywhere else than here in your arms."

I literally remember the moment when I decided that he was the one for the rest of my life. We permanently reunited during that special photography trip we took to New England, shortly after breaking the news of his kidney disease to his parents and then to mine. It was romantic and full of love and fireworks of our own making. It was as if I had already said yes to the impending proposal. Our time together was pure bliss as I pledged myself to him once and for all.

I couldn't help but let my doubtful heart give way to the love I felt for Blake in that moment. I don't know if I had ever before, or ever since, made love to him in such a way that bound our souls together in a sacred union. It wasn't just our bodies that slowly and sensually joined, but it was as if our two souls merged into one, and however long the good Lord let Blake live on this Earth, I would never take another moment for granted; I was going to show that man how deeply he was loved every second I could.

"I'm sorry I put you through so much crap, Blake. I love you and never want to live without you again. I'm yours, now and forever." I kissed him tenderly with all the love I had in my soul. I had given myself to him fully, and he accepted it willingly. He took a deep breath, smiled, and kissed me affectionately on my forehead.

"I've waited a long time to hear you say those words," he began while stroking his hands through my wavy locks. "You know, I have to be honest with you—this getaway was almost like a last chance for us. If you weren't ready to get back together this weekend, I was going to walk away for good. I couldn't wait anymore—with the little time I might have left to live, I was so close to letting you go so I could find the love I needed. I'm so glad you finally returned to me."

Blake's ominous assertion hit me hard with immense fear. I was on a secret time limit, and the hourglass almost ran out.

Thank goodness I had come to my senses, I thought instantly. I could have lost him forever. How sincerely grateful I was to be given this final chance and that I hadn't ruined things after all. How lucky I was for his forgiveness, understanding, and loyalty.

His near surrender gave me serious food for thought, though. It was more than discovering just a silent ultimatum. There was an underlying threat that he could, and would, walk away from me. How self-absorbed I was to think that he would pine away for me indefinitely. How humbling to realize that he wouldn't.

I couldn't help but wonder if there was a possibility that he could change *his* mind about *me* one day.

Feeling vulnerable about my epiphany, I shared my worry over him retaliating against me. Would he turn around and hurt me the same way I hurt him if given the chance?

"Baby, that could never happen. Do you honestly think I would stand by all these months, fight to win your love back, just to dump you? I love you more than my own life. Please don't ever doubt that," he pleaded.

I believed him, yet the fear always remained lodged in the depths of my subconscious throughout the entire course of our relationship. As was the constant internal reminder that I had almost lost the love of my life because of my confused heart and betrayal. How lucky I was that he took me back.

8. PROMISES

It was only a few months after our reunion and right after my graduation when Blake whisked me away to Hawaii for an exotic vacation.

It began with a lovely little dinner on a Maui beachfront. The sun was setting over the pristine, blue Pacific, and the streaming descent of reds, oranges, and yellows melded with the ocean horizon. We indulged in piña coladas and dined on the most tender barbecue ribs as we listened to the live music of an acoustic local.

I had never felt so in love as I did that night, gazing into those sparkling, emerald eyes and feeling his dazzling smile burst to try to hide his modesty over my attention. We held hands in between courses and whispered countless "I love yous" as the singer crooned words that were undoubtedly meant for us.

We had come so far in just a short amount of time. I no longer had doubts and was completely, fully, undeniably in love with Blake. Our existential romantic crisis known as my love phobia melted away into the unspoken distance. We rarely talked about the past anymore, choosing to focus on the future.

Except for tonight.

As dessert neared, Blake became apprehensive, his legs shaking nervously under the table, and his eyes shifting in and out of focus. I thought maybe it was the free-flowing alcohol, but then he became uncharacteristically quiet and serious.

"Em, we need to talk. Something's been bothering me for a while, and I just need to know..."

"Know what?" I fearfully urged when he paused. My heart was in my throat, and immediately my thoughts ran their wayward marathon. Chills coursed through my veins as I anticipated the moment my world would come crashing down and I'd receive the payback I knew I deserved. My gut sank. I knew this was all too good to be true.

I prepared for my life to be shattered by his "I changed my mind" confession.

"I know this is way in the distant past, but I can't help but wonder how I measure up against other guys you have been with."

Well, that took me completely off-guard. I heaved a sigh of relief that it wasn't an automatic breakup. *Really, Emily, sometimes you can be so mentally dramatic.*

Though, that didn't stop my mind from wandering in a new direction. What had I done to him? Instead of my heart breaking for myself, it broke for him and how I still made him feel like he wasn't good enough.

"Oh, Blake. No one has ever compared to you." He flushed, smiling a little, but there was something more. I could tell.

"That's not it. I mean—um—well—the other guys you were with. Like Michael. Marcus. His friend. Did you find them hotter than me?"

I was flabbergasted at what he was asking. It was completely random and out of the blue—and very unlike my confident Blake.

My mouth went dry. I didn't understand, in this beautiful setting, on this gorgeous night—one of the most romantic dates we had ever been on—why was this at the forefront of his mind? Where was this coming from?

"Blake, why would you ask me such a thing?"

"Because I need to clear the air once and for all. Be honest, Em," he urged, not backing down. "Were you more attracted to any of them than you were to me?"

It was evident he wasn't going to stop until I genuinely responded, as absurd as this conversation was. I needed to tread lightly; my whole future could be decided based on how I answered.

"The moment I met you, Blake, I had never felt as instantly attracted to a man as I had to you. But it was on this deep level, more than physical attraction. You know that. It was soulful, emotional, mental—absolutely everything at once."

"But?" He sensed my attempt at a roundabout coverup.

"But, I will admit that I also felt a powerful spark with Marcus' friend, Evan, if you insist on knowing. Not the one he left me in the car with. The other friend of his that I told you about." His jaw tightened a little, and I could sense the jealousy rise.

"I remember that story quite well," he responded bitterly as he envisioned me going down on yet another one of Marcus' friends. I don't know what he expected from me. If I lied, he'd be pissed. If I told the truth, he'd be hurt. I couldn't fathom his purpose for having this dumbass discussion that made us both feel terrible. And yet, he probed further. "Do you think he was better looking than me?"

"Oh my God, Blake. Really?" He nodded his head, and his eyes dared me to continue. Uncomfortable to the max, I obliged. "Yes, he was hot. All right? But so are you. Why does this all even matter?"

"It matters to me. A lot. Was he bigger than me?"

"Excuse me?"

"His dick. Was it bigger than mine?"

"You have got to be fucking kidding me." Apparently, the other diners wondered the same thing as they looked over in our direction at my heightened irritation.

"Lower your voice, please, and just answer the question. I have to know. Please, Emily."

"Fine," I hushed bitterly, leaning in so that eavesdroppers would have to struggle to hear anything further. The sooner I gave him what he wanted, the sooner we could drop the whole subject.

"He could have been, but I don't remember. I didn't bring my ruler with me that night," I spewed calmly yet sarcastically from gritted teeth, unable to control the anger over his incessant line of questioning. "Might I point out that he never used it *in* me, nor has anyone else. You are the only man I have ever made love to, the only man that I have ever loved, and the only man I want to be with for the rest of my life. Anything else?"

I was fuming. If he wanted to break up with me, then he needed to just say so instead of playing these mind games. I wasn't going to be made ashamed anymore of life decisions that happened years ago. I thought we were past that, yet here we were, digging it all up again.

I pushed my plate aside; I lost my appetite and wanted to be anywhere but here with this psychopath investigator. I almost stood up and walked out, but Blake gently grabbed me by the arm and nudged me to sit back down with a beseeching expression.

"I'm sorry, Emily. I shouldn't have brought this up. But thank you for being honest with me. Believe it or not, I feel more secure now in our love. I didn't mean to test you like that. Can you forgive me?"

My jets cooled a little to see the rationale behind his cross-examination. I had put him through hell quite a few times before, and he needed validation that I was committed to him and that I didn't regret choosing someone else; that I *didn't want* to choose someone else. I softened as his tormented inquiry transformed into a gentle, loving smile and a caress of my hands across the table once again. His eyes pleaded with me to understand.

"Of course, I can. But please—promise me that we can put this all behind us now? I love you, Blake, and only you. Please believe that, once and for all."

"That's all I needed to hear," he whispered as he got up, walked around the table, and bent down to give me a sweet kiss on the forehead. "Thank you."

The subject fortunately changed to something more lighthearted, and before I knew it, our intensity had shifted back to that of tender love. My previously disturbed emotions had faded into the night as we walked hand in hand down the chilled beach toward our luxury hotel. We stopped for a moment to let our bare feet sink into the cool sand and stare out into the receding horizon.

"You are more beautiful than the sunset, Emily

Grace," he murmured melodiously, continuing to butter me up. "I am the luckiest man in the entire world to call you mine. You and me forever, right?"

"Right," I replied instinctively. "Forever."

After that super awkward dinner interview and moonlit walk on the beach, Blake led me back to our room where he surprised me by getting down on one knee and straightforwardly asked me to marry him. As I was half-naked on my way to the shower, I was completely caught unprepared by the gesture.

I obviously couldn't have predicted it at the time, but that peculiar dinner conversation was intended to be his segue into a marriage proposal. In his mind, Blake needed to be certain that his future wife had no more doubts and would say yes to him.

It wasn't exactly the romantic proposal I had fantasized about my whole life, but I was touched by his nervousness. He was so adorable and helpless down on the floor, the ring box opened to expose a delicate princess cut diamond ring. His eyes were so sincere and full of love, and I knew when this moment came what my answer would be.

I let him slip the ring on my finger, kissed him with enthusiasm, and readied to make love to my husband-to-be—that is, until he casually mentioned his original idea didn't pan out the way he planned it.

"I was going to propose at sunset along the beach tonight and ask you if you would be eternally mine, but the live musician canceled at the last minute. I figured here would be as good a place as any, though. I'm so glad you said yes," he hummed as he began to take the remainder of my clothing off and move me toward the plush bed.

Even his sensual touches couldn't shake the thoughts running rampant in my mind. I knew I shouldn't have been upset about how the man I loved asked me to be his forever. But hearing about what he had planned—how poetic, how magical, how lovingly intentional this once-in-a-lifetime question would be asked—disappointed me. Depressed me, even.

Even if the musician canceled, couldn't he have still gone ahead with the beach part? Or said those amorous words? We were *right there*. We had that perfect moment.

Why did he even bother telling me all this, I wondered. *What was the point?* I frustratingly asked myself before giving in to the lustful aggression of my new fiancé.

I admit, my head was too out of sorts to feel the connection I should have felt with Blake. It was as if I let him have my body while my detached soul ruminated in disenchantment. I could feel him touching me, hear him moaning, and yet, the usual sensations that inspired me to devour him in return were absent. I hoped he hadn't noticed, which was doubtful, as he came quickly and turned over almost immediately to fall asleep.

Wide awake and restless, I decided to finally make my way to the shower. I let the hot, sweltering water run over my hair, face, and body as I stood there in silence recounting everything that had just happened.

This whole night had been strange. Not at all very Cinderella-like. I would have never dreamed up a dissection of my past crushes as a prelude to what should have been the most magical question of my entire life. To go from a shameful penis contest discussion to a lackluster engagement was not what I had envisioned from my prince charming.

Perhaps my expectations were way too high, but I wished for fancy outfits, candles, rose petals, champagne, poetic words like he spoke so many times before—*the works*. Or at least, something thoughtful and special, like his beach idea. That would have been wonderful as well.

There were so many ways he could have asked me, I pouted to myself as I dried off and got dressed in a pretty red negligee that would go to waste now that Blake was in a deep slumber; now that I didn't exactly feel inclined to make love again as long as these childish thoughts stormed my self-absorbed brain.

I was being ungrateful, I told myself. What's important is that we decided tonight to cherish each other for the rest of our lives, for better or for worse. The fantasy disillusioned, I just had to accept that our very basic pledge was at least forged in one of the most beautiful places in the world.

Just like the rest of our relationship, his tactics were a little unorthodox, yet I could understand why he felt anxious, given my propensity to waver in my devotion. And odd proposal or not, I vowed to love this man until his very last breath.

***

Which ended up being postponed quite a bit, thanks to some medical investigation on my part.

After a second opinion, it seemed as though Blake didn't have polycystic kidney disease after all—only minor kidney stones. He was destined for a long and healthy life, the new doctor assured us. How ecstatic we were that our prayers were answered!

No longer did the impending doom of his mortality weigh against our life plans. We were free once again to visualize our own home, the children we would have, us growing old together without any fear of time restrictions.

We were truly blessed.

Never once did I question the authenticity of his original story like some family and friends did. When I told them about the miraculous news, quite a few shared their unsolicited concerns.

"Are you sure he was even sick to begin with? His diagnosis was pretty serious. Not sure how a medical professional could get something like that so wrong. Did you ever see the test results?" Kayla quizzed.

"Don't you think it is a little convenient how he was sick when you were broken up, but now he'll live a long, happy life after you got engaged? Something doesn't make sense, Em," my intuitive mom probed.

"I'm so glad he is okay, but how is this possible? He was on a kidney transplant list, and now he's cured? Sounds like he used one of his famous stories to tug at your heart and lure you back if you ask me. Oh, Emily, I'd be careful with that one," Julie warned.

I hushed them all quickly—how *dare* they make me doubt my soon-to-be husband. What they were implying was almost unforgivable to me. Blake would never lie to me about something like that— about *dying!* He even told his parents about it, albeit reluctantly, which made it *real*.

The love of my life could never manipulate me into reuniting with him under the false pretense of death. That deception would be unthinkable. Who on Earth would do that to another human being?

Like Blake said, the skeptics were just jealous of our happiness.

Not allowing supposed loved ones to address the matter further, those nay-sayers silenced their opinions and embraced our engagement. Nothing and no one was going to tear us apart ever again—now that we'd finally found our way back to each other for the rest of our lives.

In fact, we almost immediately began with the numerous plans that needed to be made for the wedding—in between my long hours at my fancy new job, as Blake liked to call it.

The location, the flowers, the music, the centerpieces, the invitations—on and on the decisions went. Blake would chime in with some of his opinions but seeing as though I was fully engrossed in the details, he surrendered the reigns to let me design our most perfect day.

It also gave me the chance to get to know his mother and sister better, now that they were officially going to be family. I could sense his mother warming up a bit to me, allowing herself to get excited about being part of the festivities. She dazzled as she tried on different dresses as the mother of the groom.

"Oh, Mrs. Denton, this one is absolutely stunning. I love this shade of violet on you," I gushed. "You look radiant!"

"Thank you, Emily. You know, I was thinking," she said as she turned for one last look at herself in the mirror before circling back toward me. "Now that you will be my daughter-in-law, I think we can do away with the Mrs. Denton thing. Call me Ruth, darling."

"Well, I was actually wondering if I could call you Mom," I shyly proposed, to her surprise. I could see baby pools make their way into her hazel eyes but stop short of falling. I had touched this seemingly untouchable woman.

"I would love that," she managed to reply. I looked over to Camille, who simply winked at me in her emerald green, A-line bridesmaid dress, giving me the sign that I made my future mother-in-law's day.

The lunch that followed was full of laugher and warmth, and it was a wonder I had never seen the possibilities before. His mother had an underlying kindness that was hidden beneath a hardened exterior. I was thrilled that she felt comfortable enough to break down some of her walls and let me in. I even heard new stories of what my mischief-making love was really like as a little boy.

Speaking of the devil, Blake showed up to surprise me at the end of our girls' day with a huge bouquet of bright pink lilies.

"I hope it wasn't too painful spending the day with Ruth and Cam," he teased, as if the flowers were my reward for enduring a traumatic experience with his family.

"Not at all," I replied happily. "Mom, as I call her now, was quite lovely, and Camille helped me pick out some gorgeous shoes to complement the girls' dresses. I quite enjoyed the alone time with them."

"*Mom?*" he asked in bewilderment. "You never cease to amaze me with your magic, Emily Grace. Has someone finally won over old, callous Ruth Denton?"

I had indeed. Involving her in some of the

planning was one of the best things I could have ever done to open the door to a wonderful new relationship between us.

And just like I had to involve his side of the family, mine made no qualms about their participation, either. My mother had countless suggestions about the decorations, the diversity of music, and even the originality of the favors. I was grateful for her wisdom, but I was beginning to feel a little overshadowed. Thankfully, Blake kept me in check.

"Remember, this is about you and me, not your mother," he'd subtly remind. "Don't let her control our wedding like she tries to control everything else."

"I won't," I promised. I did need her input on some things, but I was firm with everyone who lent an opinion that I would have the final say.

While my mother was busy looking into décor and entertainment details, Kerry and Kayla accompanied me to select floral arrangements as maid of honor and bridesmaid, respectively. I felt a pang of regret as we sorted through different options, wishing that Jess were here with me like we had always talked about since we were kids. I never imagined planning one of the most important days of my life without her by my side, but in the end, I had to remind myself that it was for the best that she was not there to try to selfishly upstage me. Kayla was a much less dramatic and more supportive friend than Jess could ever be.

"Hey Em, what do you think about these for the centerpieces? The tall vases won't block your guests from talking to each other around the table, and I just love the whimsical nature of the cascade. Very you and Blake-like," she suggested perceptively.

"Oh, I love them. Good call, Kay."

"This is so exciting. Thanks for letting me be a part of this. It's giving me so many great ideas for my own wedding."

"Wait! You're engaged, and you didn't tell us?" reprimanded Kerry. "Details, girl!"

"Oh, no! I didn't mean it like that. I mean, I think he's going to propose soon. At least, I hope he does."

"He will," I replied excitedly. "He'd be crazy not to! And then we can do this all over again for your most magical day."

"I can't wait! But for now," she redirected, "we need to focus on yours and finalize our bouquets!"

With so many lovely assortments to choose from, I ultimately settled on the elegance of burgundy-colored roses sprayed with luminescent gold sparkles against a sea of robust green leaves. The flower girl would have matching petals, and the décor would intertwine the best of both colors. Breathing a sigh of relief that I could check something else off my list, we were almost done with our errands for the day.

Next up: dress shopping!

Mom joined in at this point to help us scour the local boutiques, and it felt like I tried on every dress imaginable, until we found the perfect one. When I looked at my reflection, I almost lost my own breath. It was more emotional than I ever imagined. I couldn't believe that I was standing there, in an exquisite white gown, my family and friends crying with joy around me. This would be what I would walk down the aisle in to wed the love of my life. It was almost exactly how I had envisioned it that day in Westminster Abbey.

Everything was falling into place for the most

wonderful day of my entire existence. I couldn't wait to be Mrs. Blake Denton.

**

Naturally, there were some hiccups along the way to our promise of forever. Even with the threat of death downgraded to treatable stones, the path to the altar still had a few ups and downs.

I guess it was inevitable that we would leave our second honeymoon phase and re-enter grownup land, but I had high hopes that we'd get through our actual honeymoon first. But then we wouldn't have a taste of what the real world was like, now would we? And what didn't hurt us, made us stronger as a couple. If we could get through a few minor hurdles before the "I do's," I was certain we'd master this marriage thing.

So, I learned to adapt to a few of his idiosyncrasies along the way.

Like his really poor accounting skills and continued money mishaps. Quite a few of Blake's paychecks never came in—either because his clients couldn't pay or because the checks were lost in the mail or bounced. It was frustrating how Blake never tried to rectify the situation or hold any bosses accountable to their agreements, but it's not like I had access to fight for him. It wasn't my fight anyway, I resigned.

Thankfully, I had started a great job near our New Jersey-based apartment which afforded us the ability to not only pay for our wedding but to start our life off together on stronger financial ground.

That helped to ease a lot of the tension that started to form between us. Who knew money could be such a relationship tester?

I remember one particularly large paycheck of Blake's that went missing—not too long before our wedding, and an important income source we needed toward the venue down payment. I cried my eyes out over the boss' deception, only angering Blake more.

"What do you want me to do about it? I can't force someone to pay me, Em. It doesn't work like that in this business. They all talk, and if I go against one, I might as well give it all up."

And so, I worked overtime to make up for the loss. It became a habit of mine—recuperating the income that either never came in or was otherwise allocated for some unplanned scheme.

Right before the wedding, as I was unpacking our boxes and settling us into our new place, I came across something that almost changed our course forever.

I found the paystub of the alleged never-paid check that I was told he was never going to get.

Truth flashed before my eyes. The enormity of the lie was soul-crushing, and in that very moment, I questioned if I was ready to commit to a life of this kind of delusion and ongoing financial fabrications.

Has this happened before? What other money has he been hiding from me? Was it really his uncle with the credit issues, or had it been him all along?

I spent the entire evening alone in that new apartment, seriously weighing my future. I cried for a good two hours, going over all the curious questions I mentally asked myself in the past but always pushed down or blew off as no big deal. I couldn't ignore what was right in front of me now. I was devastated that my fairytale was no longer this sparkly, beautiful story.

How could I possibly marry this man now?

But then another question rose up to taunt me: how could I not? Wasn't it too late to turn back, after all these plans were made, after we invested so much time in our relationship, after I finally made a commitment vow? I couldn't put Blake, or myself, through another round of confusion. We would be destroyed; there would be no coming back from that level of devastation ever again. I was certain of that.

Scared to lose the only love I ever had, I stuffed down my feelings and ignored these blatant warnings. Oh, I was going to confront him all right, but not with the intention of breaking up with him. No—with the intention of hearing his beautifully spun lie of gold so that I could go on with my plans to marry him, as if this was not a legitimate game-changer. I needed to be convinced this time, otherwise my happily ever after was going to implode.

And what a beautifully masterful gold weave it was that he told.

"I needed the money to pay for an emerald and diamond love pendant I bought you for the wedding. It was supposed to be a secret," he scolded. "I wanted to give you something special to show you how much I love you, and well, since you manage all of our money, I didn't know how else to pay for it without tipping you off. I'm sorry I lied, but it's only because I wanted to be able to surprise you with a gift from my heart."

He lied so he could buy something so elegant for me? No one had ever given me something so expensive or full of meaning before, and my walls came tumbling back down. I forgave him. Quickly—and repeatedly.

I mean, he was right—how else could he use his own money to purchase something so generously expressive when I was watching our funds like a hawk?

His little white lie wasn't worth calling off the wedding, I decided.

Nor were the increasing arguments over practically everything. We were having some major communication breakdowns, probably from the stress of the wedding planning and my parents trying to control the details—including where we would live. It put a damper on our sex life, which was becoming less frequent amidst the angst.

I thought that once Blake was cleared of his dangerous kidney condition, we could resume lovemaking as normal, but between our money arguments and his slowing photography assignments, he wasn't always in the right state of mind to connect on that level.

It was okay, though, I kept telling myself. Once we got married and started our honeymoon, that would change everything, and we'd be back to normal. We just needed to get through the planning hurdle.

My anxiety was starting to get the better of me, and one night I pushed Blake too far. I found myself worrying—yet again—that I'd make him so miserable that he'd leave me one day or do something to deeply hurt me for all the pain I had caused. The last time I dared to voice my fear of his retaliation, his ominous words never left me.

"If you keep saying it, you just might make it come true."

And with that, I shut up and let our life unfold as it was meant to.

***

Our wedding day was the most beautiful day of my life. The sun couldn't have shone any brighter while delicate winds kept the temperature down during an unusually warm October. The autumn leaves had just started turning their vibrant, earthy shades of yellow, orange, and red, setting the natural backdrop for some truly magnificent pictures.

As I stepped into my long satin dress and watched Kerry enthusiastically zip me up and move some loose curls from my back, I sucked in my breath and couldn't believe this was really happening. This was the day I would marry my soulmate and pledge an eternity to him in front of family, friends, and God.

"I'm so glad you came to your senses," Kerry squealed. "You are perfect for each other and will have the most incredible life. Just don't screw it up again," she advised with a sisterly giggle.

"God and your grandmother are shining down on you through that glorious sunshine," my mother mused, knowing how much I wished my Nana could have been alive to witness this blessed day. "I'm so happy for you, baby girl. I wish the two of you only the best that life can bring."

I took a deep breath in, never remembering a moment in my life when I'd felt happier. I was saying

"I do" to the man of my dreams—my best friend. Life promised a long, adventurous future filled with love and companionship. Nothing but joy coursed through my veins; there wasn't a hint of apprehension as I excitedly got ready for the big day.

We opted out of a church wedding for a great package deal that included an antique gazebo outside for the ceremony. Rows of white chairs with dark, shamrock-green ribbons seated supportive loved ones alongside the aisle, which was delicately covered by a flowing, white fabric decorated with loose, burgundy rose petals.

My sweet little cousin, Krista, was our flower girl, who tossed out even more flower petals as she walked beside Blake's cousin's shy little boy, 2-year-old Georgie. The kids walked nervously through the crowd toward Kerry, Kayla, and Camille, who were already standing up at the altar alongside Joey as best man and his groomsmen, Dan and Eddie. What a perfect crew we chose to stand up for us.

As my tearful, rarely emotional dad took my elbow into his to lead me down to my future husband, all those pre-wedding concerns faded away when I locked eyes on my handsome groom. There he was, standing tall as I always pictured him, in a black tuxedo with a dark green cummerbund and bowtie that matched his eyes (done so, of course, at the bride's beseeching request).

His eyes lit up as large as my smile when we saw each other for the first time.

"You take my breath away," he whispered as he restrained from leaning in for a premature peck.

Magic was in the air and blessings were all

around as we exchanged our wedding vows and serendipitously kissed each other as man and wife for the first time.

The reception was even more enchanting, full of food, dancing, and friendship. We were high on life, and our playful side showed as I tossed the bouquet not-so-secretly toward his sister—which was shortly followed by him taking my garter off with his teeth and then "accidentally" dropping cake down the front of my dress so he could lick it off of my cleavage. You can imagine how red I became as I thought about a room full of people witnessing his intimate retrieval of cake. But I loved every second of it.

When it came time for us to ceremoniously slow dance to Savage Garden's *Truly Madly Deeply,* I felt so much love within Blake's embrace.

"I can't believe this day has finally come," he murmured in my ears as he held me close, and I could feel our hearts beating together.

"I know. It's such a dream come true. I love you with all my heart, Mr. Denton. I can't wait to spend the rest of my life proving how much."

"I love you, too, Mrs. Denton. Together forever."

9. ADJUSTMENT

As I hoped, the honeymoon did help to spice things up in the tranquil world of the Bahamas, but not in the way I expected. I had packed several new pieces of lingerie that I was anxious to model for my new husband, but Blake seemed more interested in the shore excursions than bedroom activities.

"Come on, Em. We can do that later. How many times do we get to go parasailing and snorkeling in our life?"

His dismissal of my sexual advances was frustrating, but he did have a valid point. We had our whole life to make love whenever we wanted now that we lived in our own place and didn't have to sneak around like teenagers. We had to embrace the moment and enjoy the pristine beaches that waited for us outside, I relented.

Our honeymoon was amazing in that respect. The sparkling, crystal-blue waters were so clean and clear to swim in that we spent hours playing in the water. I had never gone snorkeling before, so Blake got a kick out of my mini-hyperventilation attack over not knowing how I would breathe once I stuck my head into the ocean deep.

But with him by my side, I was able to calm my nerves and finally submit to the waters beneath me and fall in love with the intense colors and textures of extraordinary sea life. Never could I have imagined the rainbow that burst in front of me, reminding me that there was so much out there I had yet to discover. This is exactly how I imagined a life with Blake would be: non-stop exploration of all the wonders the world had to offer. I felt free, peaceful, loved—if this was somehow just a trickster's dream, I didn't ever want to wake up.

It was so liberating to fly high above the ocean and see the shrinking, glorious planet below as we parachuted up and around the Atlantic. I closed my eyes and floated weightlessly against the salted air, not caring that I was far from the security of the ground. The only security I needed was Blake's hand in mine as we embraced this magical moment. The lack of gravity released me from all my past troubles, and I never wanted to come back down to reality.

The next morning, we continued having a blast in the translucent water, this time on jet skis. How lighthearted we allowed ourselves to be as we raced each other to an imaginary finish line. I almost fell over with hilarity as Blake curved too fast in his attempt to beat me and toppled over the side of his ski.

After a split second of worry, I knew he was fine, and I couldn't control my snickering as I glided into first place. He threatened to pay me back for being such a sore winner—and he did. After we dismounted our skis, he firmly scooped me up, carried my resisting body deeper into the ocean, and amusedly tossed me into its luxurious, cold vastness.

I didn't realize how much I missed this fun kind

of banter with Blake. But the stress of his health scare and the wedding planning was now over, so we were free to be our childlike selves once again—missing not a single second to take advantage of more tropical activities, like a bike ride along the beach and a banana boat excursion. There was so much to see and do, it's no wonder we were absolutely exhausted from the adrenaline rush of all we experienced every single day.

At night, we would indulge in the most incredible barbecues and fancy dinners, with mixed drinks and wonderful music. It saddened me for a moment that Blake didn't like to dance anymore like I did, as I could feel my body sway in the chair and want to get lost in the music. It made me feel alive to move my hips and seductively surrender to the sounds.

But just his presence, knowing this was the beginning of a wonderful future together, was all I needed. Dancing was not all that important anyway in the grand scheme of things.

The week flew by way too fast, but when we got back home to our brand-new rented apartment, we were both so excited to settle into married life. It was fun to figure out where we wanted to put all our new housewares and gifts, what color curtains and couches to buy, and when to have a housewarming party. It was all coming together for us finally, and life became easier.

"This is so amazing. Everything I imagined our life would be like, Princess."

"Me too. I couldn't be happier. I love you so much, baby."

"And you'll love me forever," he smirked as he

turned over to shut the light off to go to sleep after a quick peck good night.

We were blissfully happy together. Of course, we had our normal struggles, like most married couples do. I tended to work more than I should have, and Blake's assignments were few and far between, so he had more free time on his hands. We still ran into some bill snafus, especially when I wanted to keep us out of debt, and Blake wanted to keep planning these extravagant vacations.

Blake typically won out because, well—who doesn't love to be talked into an exotic adventure? He knew how much I couldn't resist an enticing travel idea.

One of our favorite trips had to be to the Grand Canyon, where we took a helicopter ride over its wondrous massiveness. Breathtaking couldn't even describe the views; the colors of sediment formed earthly sunsets, and its depth left you wondering what mysterious, lost civilization might be hiding at its bottom. Blake always loved when I let my mind travel to the illusions of what could be.

That amazing weekend jaunt included a huge in-room hot tub that we misjudged—boy, did we have a good laugh about how I poured in too many bubbles and flooded the room. I was bummed when we ended up calling for housekeeping instead of having the romantic champagne bath indulgence we had originally planned, but it made for a classic story to tell our kids one day. We were writing so many exciting chapters to add to our marriage book.

He later took an assignment in the heart of Texas, so we moseyed on down to a local dude ranch, where we rode horses, ate s'mores by the campfire, and enjoyed home-cooked hospitality until we couldn't fit in our pants. Blake had a much better way with the horses than I did, and I was grateful for that when my own steed sensed my fear and tried to take off.

Thankfully, Blake and the ranch hand were able to curb the runaway and bring me back to safety. I swore I'd never go horseback riding again, but Blake amusingly warned that he wouldn't let me give up on a future equestrian rematch. That evening, I felt the sore effects of that bumpy ride, but I easily relaxed into loving paradise as we stole away to a quiet corner of the ranch to be alone.

I remember the full moonlit night so clearly and how we laid in a pile of hay in each other's arms and gazed up at the glittering stars.

"It's like a painting," I observed in awe. "How incredibly beautiful the sky is when we stop and look up."

"It's how I feel when I look in your eyes," he responded. "I forget sometimes to stop and remember how beautiful you are, and how lucky I am." Delightful chills ran down my whole body, warmed up again by his words. "I love you with every ounce of my being."

"I love you, too. I wouldn't want to spend my life with anyone else in this entire world."

"Good. Because you are stuck with me forever, Emily Grace, like it or not."

"Oh, I like it very much," I replied, kissing him into the late hours of the stargazing night.

We never ran out of interesting new things to try or places to see—skiing in Colorado, horse races in Saratoga, and camping down shore. He was even able to persuade me to go whitewater rafting in the Poconos—something I was absolutely fearful of trying but survived!

Blake always pushed my limits like that; he refused to let my anxieties and seriousness get the better of me on our adventures. He reminded me how he was always there by my side and would protect me from harm. Feeling safe, I'd entrust him with my life, and he would always be right: the journey was always worth the risk, even if our own journey together was laced with challenges at times.

Like when we went to Las Vegas, where we ended up spending most of our time gambling at the slots instead of taking in a show or indulging in some sin city debauchery like I wanted to. Not a favorite vacation of mine. I had to hold my breath as Blake blew a few hundred on some unlucky Triple Diamond dollar machines—money that we didn't exactly have available to spend so foolishly when we were trying to save for our future home and family.

"Relax, Em. We came here to have fun. Lighten up."

"I'm trying to, but you're starting to go over our limit. If we are ever going to be able to buy a house, we need to watch our spending a little bit."

"I'm not asking your permission," he argued back, dismissing my repetitive pleas, the ones I could hear myself autopilot out of my mouth on a regular basis. "I'll be over there at the Monopoly station when you get your chubby knickers out of a twist. Do us both a favor and order a drink, will you?"

He wasn't always this condescending—just when I pushed his money buttons. When I wasn't doing that, we had the most extraordinary time. Occasionally, I would get some time off work to join him on an assignment, and we did love our annual trip to Milan for his convention. He even let Kerry go on a few of his conferences with him to help with her own budding career. He had fully inspired her to become a photographer herself, venturing into the modeling world instead of his preferred landscapes.

Blake and I also loved to eat out a lot as neither of us was very gifted in the kitchen. And we never tired of our weekly bowling nights, occasional Broadway plays, baseball games, and concerts. Every weekend was a different sensational escapade.

We certainly had our share of good times, which seemed a little alarming to my overly worrisome mother, who felt the need on several occasions to point it out.

"Emily, you go on an awful lot of trips. Are you sure you can afford all this?"

"I know what I'm doing, Mom. I'm an economics major, remember? If we couldn't afford it, I wouldn't go," I reminded her authoritatively. Who was she to question my adult decisions with my husband?

"I know. I just mean that you've talked about getting a house and having kids at some point, but I don't see how you could possibly be saving for that with all these elaborate vacations. And with Blake not working consistently? Honey, I'm just concerned about you."

"I appreciate that, really, I do. But we love our time away with each other. Blake's a gypsy like that, always on the go. He's never been one to stay in one figurative spot for too long. You know that."

"That I do," she miffed, trying to make her point. "I know you are your own woman now, Em, and I don't mean to butt in. Just remember that marriage is much more than just having fun," she advised.

But it wasn't just fun to us, I thought to myself. We also were there for each other through the tougher moments in life, and that's what made our relationship so strong and lasting.

Somehow, someway, we were able to lift each other's spirits to keep going during the rocky times, knowing we were in this fight together. Blake did a better job at comforting than I did, though. Where I always fumbled with the wrong comment at the wrong time, like at his grandmother's wake, he conversely always knew the right thing to do or say whenever my heart was heavy.

When my great-aunt, Carolyn, died, he knew part of my world had collapsed. She was one of the few people who never judged me and had once wisely advised me not to heed everyone else's opinion and to follow my heart instead of what was expected of me. Oh, how sometimes I wish I had listened to her. Part of me missed my design dabbling and still yearned to be something more than a corporate math magician. She made that impossible dream seem so... realistic. Like I could still change my mind and choose a new path. Up until her very last breath, she believed in me.

Now, her guidance was gone, and it left a huge gap in my support system.

Blake being Blake, he poignantly surprised me with an enlarged picture of me and her from when I was a little girl. It meant more to me than any excursion or expensive gift he had ever given me; it was something I would treasure forever.

He embraced me as I expelled all the pain and grief of losing such an important person in my life. I felt his empathy, as he could relate to the deep feeling of loss after Grandma Wilma had passed, and he was steadfast in his comfort. It was moments like these where his kindness shined, and I was reminded of the depths of compassion the man I loved held.

He was also there by my side when my parents finally decided to get divorced. Now that Kerry and I were all grown up and out of the house, my mom declared she had enough of his drinking.

So did I. I had reached my own personal breaking point when my dad became visibly sloshed at a baseball game, not even trying to hide it from me. Fed up, I uncharacteristically blew up at him in public, not caring that the crowd around me was suddenly more interested in my family brawl than a lackluster game.

"What the fuck, Dad? Aren't you even going to try to stay sober?"

"It's just a beer, Emily. Relax yourself, kiddo. Have one with me," he slurred, laughing as if he wasn't doing anything wrong, and I was overreacting.

"Are you out of your mind? *Have one with you?* I can't even believe you would do this to me right now. I wanted a nice day with my dad and my husband at a baseball game to spend quality time together, and that wasn't enough? Is our company so terrible that you need to have a drink to get through it?"

"Don't start with me. I'm going through a rough time—or have you forgotten I'm in the middle of a divorce?"

"No, I haven't forgotten. Thanks for reminding me why, though," I said bitterly as I began to turn away.

"You're just like your mother," he spat. "A pain in the ass, little bitch. You should mind your own fucking business and worry about your good-for-nothing husband here instead. I don't need this shit from you, you stuck-up smartass. I'm out of here."

I stopped short with shock. Countless times I had heard him speak so viciously to my mother, but never once did he ever bring the cruelty to Kerry or me—and to bring Blake into the mix? That was completely out of left field, especially since he and his "son" spent endless hours together male bonding in the basement.

But there it was. No one was spared from his disease. His attack on us crossed a line I wasn't sure I could ever recover from. Although it fueled a lifetime of my anger and abandonment issues, Blake reassured my broken heart that estranging myself from him was best in the long run.

"He's sick, baby. He will always choose the bottle over you. You can't live like this."

"He's my dad, Blake. I can't turn my back on him, even when he's an asshole."

"And yet he has already turned his on yours. How many times are you going to go through this cycle of hoping he gets better, only for him to hurt you again? Sometimes we have to let the people we love go, Em. It's not easy, but sometimes, it's necessary for peace of mind."

He was right. I loved my father, but that didn't mean he needed to be in my life. I was an adult now, and I could choose to release the toxicity from my life and stand up for myself. Painfully, my father was all too happy to walk away from all of us after the papers were signed anyway, making the decision easier for me to lose contact with him.

Blake was that rock that I needed to help guide me through life's poisons. My dad wasn't the only disappointment he had to console me through, though. Work was taking advantage of me, but I thought my dedication would pay off in the end. I truly thought I was securing our future by throwing myself into my new career.

I loved my job with every ounce of my being. After one miserable year employed with a belligerent city investment company, I found my groove in the accounting department of a little family company only a few towns away from my childhood home. Parks and Associates.

I loved the feeling of family togetherness; they treated me like one of their own. I enjoyed getting to use all of my skills in the ultimate entry-level position. Plus, I had access to training that let me dabble in areas outside of my selected career path. My choices were unlimited, and I felt the stirrings of my inquisitive mind quench with new wisdom. It reminded me of how much I loved being a student, and I absorbed as much information as time permitted.

Time management seminars gave me great tips for juggling it all. Marketing classes reignited my design passion, and I found myself becoming more creative off-hours. I learned ways to streamline the company's financial processes and became quickly known for my efficient, team player attitude. It felt amazing to belong to such a wonderful organization.

"Your work is excellent, Emily," my direct manager, Mindy, would say. "It's so refreshing to have someone like you on the team. So enthusiastic, helpful, with a thirst for knowledge. It's like you fit in perfectly here."

"Thanks. I feel like I am learning so much from you—from the owners, too. Everyone is so amazingly supportive, like I really am part of the family. I am truly grateful to be working here."

"I expect nothing but great things from you," she stated. "Just don't become so great that you push me out the door!" she joked, though I wondered if there was a hint of truth behind her jest. Blake pointed out that she was probably used to being the one everyone relied on, and I shouldn't blame her for having to adjust to someone new receiving a bit of the praise now. Gosh, Mindy felt a little too eerily reminiscent of Jess in that respect, I realized.

That didn't matter, though. I knew she was too ingrained in the company's culture to be passed over even if I wanted to try! And I didn't. I was too focused on sponging up the experience to give a second thought to silly corporate power struggles.

I couldn't help but smile to myself when I thought of my professional future and how it was shaping up according to plan. So much growth and opportunity awaited me at Parks, and when you love what you do and feel inspired by the people you work for, it was effortless for me to want to dedicate my life to the job.

I admit, I might have been a little too dedicated, though. In the beginning, it was because I wanted to impress all my different bosses. With Blake going on lots of new travel assignments, it didn't matter that I was spending extra time on my career and building my reputation—not to mention my salary. If he wasn't going to be home anyway, then why not nurture this part of my life?

But once his career opportunities began to dwindle a little, his support for my job unfortunately plummeted with it. My late nights became more noticeable and intolerable.

I didn't fault him initially; I did become somewhat obsessed with my professional life, and I couldn't stop it just because he was home more often now. Living with a workaholic wife, he was always in competition for my time and attention. He was tired of hearing nothing but stories about my co-workers and boring projects.

He even once accused me of being in love with my department head boss, Alex, to the point where he thought I was having an affair. The reality was, I just loved being at work much more than I liked being with him at home.

That hit me hard when I made that emotional connection. I realized work was giving me the praise, affirmation, and value I never received from my father. Honestly, I wasn't getting as much from my husband anymore, either, when I stopped to think about it. And although there was no particular person I accredited the time infidelity to, I was indeed having an affair with my career. And Blake knew it.

Something else outside of our relationship was showing me how valuable I really was, and that raised the insecurity flags within him that one day, I would finally see that I was better than him and leave once and for all. It didn't matter how much I assured him that this would never happen, his jealousy over my commitment to my career reigned on.

It ended up being a moot point, anyway. It didn't take long for the company to show its true colors and disregard my loyalty to them. I was passed over for a promotion, and the extra income we expected—and *needed*—to carry our increasing expenses fell through.

I was inconsolable. I didn't understand why they chose another colleague over me, and I guess Blake was just waiting for me to come to my senses about this "perfect company." He saw what I couldn't all along, just like he always did. I was beginning to think my talent for assessment wasn't as sharp as I thought it was.

"It's not your fault, Em. You're just not as special as you think you are. You're just a number to them," he wisely pointed out.

I never thought he said it to hurt me. I thought he was showing mercy by opening my eyes to the way the world really worked. He didn't want me to live in a gullible bubble because, as he said, it would keep breaking my heart. I had a habit of believing the best in so many people who hurt me over and over— Marcus, Jess, my dad, now work. It's no wonder he was so overprotective of me.

"I thought they valued me. It just hurts because I gave them so much," I cried. "How could they do this to me?"

"You care about them too much—and you make it personal. They don't care about you the same way. It's just business, baby. They're going to take as much as you are willing to give as long as you keep giving it," he said, trying to soothe my tears with his worldly wisdom. "Maybe it's a sign that you should be home more often with me. Concentrating on us."

"You're right. You've always been right about them. It is time that I work less and pay more attention to my husband," I declared. And in a rare spontaneous moment, we connected and made love to cement my renewed pledge to become a better wife.

I kept my promise to be there more for Blake. More than just carrying the household, making his favorite dinners, and letting him have guys' nights out. Like that time he was in a terrible car accident and could have lost his life because some asshole veered into his lane and pushed him toward a tree. Or when he officially realized his dream of being a famous photographer might not come true, and he had to figure out a Plan B.

I knew we had to stick together, for better or for worse. God was going to hold us to those vows, as Blake always reminded me.

***

Life had its inevitable ebbs and flows, that was for sure.

We didn't always see eye to eye, and I was surprised when some of our mutual master plans took a backstep after we were settled into marriage: such as starting a family.

We talked incessantly about having kids during our courtship, and even though he was adamant about them pre-marriage, he seemed less enthusiastic about the idea now that it was a real-world possibility.

"I'm not ready yet. I want to enjoy being married. Once we have kids, we won't be able to take these vacations or go out as much. Let's just take a few years to have fun first. And then we can have the family we always dreamed of, okay?"

Putting my unexpected maternal needs aside, I did have to concede to him. Kids would change our whole dynamic, and until he settled into a career—whatever it ended up being—we really didn't have the financial security anyway to invest in such a life-changing decision.

We did spend some time in marital bliss before I approached the subject again. Yet he was still hesitant, even after I obliged his request to go on a cruise, travel to Alaska, and visit L.A. before he'd be open to parental talks. His conditional checklist was complete—so why was he still resisting the idea?

"Blake, I'm starting to think you don't ever want children."

"No, baby, it's not that. I'm just worried it will change everything."

"Of course it will change everything. But it will change everything for the better. Can't you just imagine holding a little version of yourself—of us—in your arms?"

"I can. I do think about it all the time. But I don't know if we're ready."

"I don't know if anyone is truly ready, honey. So, how about this? What if we just start trying? If it happens, it happens. And if it doesn't, then we're meant to wait."

"You and your 'leave it to fate'," he laughed

playfully. "Okay, Princess. We'll do it your way. But don't say I didn't warn you if it doesn't turn out to be the life you imagined it would be.

I didn't care what he advised—I threw my arms around him with such excitement that I ended up dragging him to bed and throwing caution to the fertility wind.

That would be one of the few times I could get him there after that conversation.

Turns out, the prospect of having children made him even less prone to have sex—until it dwindled down to only a few times a year.

***

"You know that's not normal, right?" Kayla stated critically, practically appalled at my admission over my waning sex life. I thought she was going to spit out her vanilla chai latte when I told her the last time Blake and I made love was on my birthday a few months earlier.

"Well, it's not exactly like I have experience in this area," I defended, reminding her that Blake was the only man I had ever been with, unlike her, who had quite a few lovers before she fell in love with Steve. "What am I supposed to do about it? Beg him?"

"Uh, yeah. Well, maybe not beg, but you have a right to have your needs met. Buy some new lingerie. Set up a sexy night. Maybe if you take the initiative a few times, he'll catch on' and you can spark that ol' flame again."

"I've tried that. I think he's afraid if we make love, I'll get pregnant. He's not ready for kids."

"Then it sounds like you might have bigger issues than sex. It's called birth control—and last I checked, it was just as effective as abstinence. Double up if he's so paranoid about it," she suggested, not realizing I already tried that route, too. "Wasn't he the one who pushed for kids before you even got married, anyway?"

"Yup. I don't know what made him change his mind, but he's terrified of being a father."

"Well, terrified of being a father or not, it shouldn't be an excuse to not have sex with your wife on a somewhat regular basis, Em. Some of the fire can burn out the longer you are married, but for me, unless you are a disabled corpse, that wouldn't stop me from getting my orgasm on," she laughed.

If only she knew that I'd still never had one.

While sleeping practically alone that night, barely touched once again, my mind began to wonder about what Kayla said and why we had become so intimately detached. She was right that sex was known to lessen when you were married, but that's usually as you grew older and experienced physical limitations. Not a few years in. Or so I thought.

Maybe it was me. Maybe it was my constant nagging about his finances or about how his few and far between job assignments weren't bringing in enough money. Maybe I was a little too married to my job still. Maybe I had added a few extra pounds that made seeing me naked a little less desirable. Or maybe he really was just so afraid to be a dad that he didn't want to take the chance, and that's all there was to it. Whatever the reason, it was disheartening, to say the least.

As I lay there unable to fall asleep, my thoughts strayed to another dimension of questions. Like Pandora's box of pondering, randomly exposing thoughts I had previously buried out of conscious reach.

The mind wanderings led me to remember some of his past inconsistencies, where I found myself tallying up a few of his more interesting fibs over the years. Especially when it came to his family, who I had grown closer to and found to be much more loving than I was led to believe.

Out of nowhere, I had the notion that maybe, just maybe, some of his childhood stories were slight fabrications. I was surprised by what entered my mind: why would I ever think something like that? The thought of a possibly fake past haunted me, but I had to know. My brain refused to let me fall asleep until my midnight meditations were answered.

There was one sure way to find out.

I looked over at my handsome husband. As Blake slumbered soundly under his goose-down comforter, the full moon shone in through our window and highlighted his peaceful, sweet soul. His snoring indicated that he would not be awakened easily by the additional lighting of the nightstand lamp. I carefully turned it on, scared of what I would find; *knowing* what I would find.

I gently moved his arm out from underneath the covers. He stirred gently but remained asleep. I turned his bare wrists toward me and took a long look at his muscled limbs. To my horror and disenchantment, I not-so-surprisingly observed that there were no scars. Not on his alleged cigarette and stove-burnt hands. Not on his suicidal wrists. And most certainly, no indication of old track needles all over his arms. I don't know why I believed his story that he could really just "stop" heroin at will without some kind of official rehab program.

Oh, Emily, I mentally condemned myself for being so gullible sometimes.

The only scar he had was under his chin from a childhood friend accidentally knocking him off his bike and into a metal fence—and that was actually a true tale, one that Joey loved to jab him about every occasion he could.

I should have been angry at the deception, but all I felt was sadness and pity. Maybe for myself as much as for Blake. I believed all of those childhood violations. All of those addiction claims. Every last desperate and melancholy detail. I thought this man had survived such tragedy and yet still lived with such kindness and gentleness toward others and expressed such love for me. I couldn't even imagine why he would feel the need to make this all up, as if he needed to win me over. He had my heart from the moment we met.

Knowing how painful these claimed memories were for him, I didn't say a word the next morning. I didn't want to belabor how things didn't add up. Truth be told, I needed to believe the duplicity anyway; believe that he suffered at the hands of an abuser and at the mercy of a needle. If I didn't, that meant there was a major flaw in our foundation, and I couldn't accept that. I loved this man, and so I began doing what he so often did to me—I lied to myself.

Maybe the scars weren't deep enough to be permanent. Maybe they were just faded, and I couldn't see them well enough with a small nightlight. Maybe the stories were true, but not the severity. Who was I to question the authenticity of his trauma?

Or the validity of his friendship woes?

The tension between him, Eddie, and Dan was beginning to build. For years, they continued to run their Little League venture together, and those teams and games brought us tremendous joy every spring.

However, the collaboration was not without its drama, at least on the business end of things. Who would organize the schedules, communicate with parents, pay the bills? All of it seemed to fall onto Eddie, who took the lead in managing the operational details. Blake and Dan were left as more of the creatives in coaching the kids and strategizing the plays.

Well, over time, money became an issue, and Eddie was accused of stealing from the Little League. Blake made a strong case for how Eddie was responsible for quite a large amount of missing funds, seeing as he was the one who managed the banking and had the access.

No one could prove otherwise. We all naturally took Blake's word for it. Eddie tried to deny it, but of course, a liar and a thief would deny his crime. So, we ignored his pleas of innocence—though from what I knew of Eddie, he always seemed like an upstanding guy, and his actions were hard for me to digest. It didn't sit right with me, and I wasn't sure if it was because I questioned his guilt or questioned my own ability to accurately assess his character, raising internal inquiries of my off-balanced judgments once again.

Could this man of seemingly high moral standards really be involved in such a horrendous scheme? Was it really that cut and dry? I wished I could have talked to Melinda to hear her side of the story, but she wasn't exactly the easiest person to get a hold of after it all went down. My calls went right to voicemail, and I took that as validation of a guilty admission.

Plus, by that point, Blake's rationale was way too convincing for any of us to give Eddie the benefit of the doubt, and I figured that Melinda would be his staunch defender anyway. We all simply decided that Eddie was a malicious, reprehensible human being for stealing from little kids and backstabbing his friends like that. And so, we turned against him, and the poor Little League team collapsed, as did their tight-knit group of friends.

It was like the ultimate domino effect. Eddie's betrayal caused the Little League breakdown, which trickled into the bowling team. That disassembled quickly, but no one really minded because once the couples in our group got married and others started having kids, it was expected that we would not be in each other's lives as often. We were all too busy by then, though Blake did see Dan on a weekly basis for guy time, so I was glad he held on to at least one good friend in the aftermath.

Time with my own friends was beginning to become less of a priority as well—considering Blake wasn't a big fan of the few confidants I had left. Any time I wanted to go out with Kayla to a casual lounge that offered dancing, Blake would put up a fight and remind me of how infantile I was being.

"I don't want you going to that place again," he

essentially demanded.

"What's the big deal? I rarely see Kayla anymore, and we just want to hang out for a little while. Why can't I spend one evening out with a girlfriend of mine? You go out with Dan all the time."

"I never said you couldn't go out with Kayla, but I don't like how she acts like you're still single. It's not appropriate for you to go out drinking and grinding up on guys, Mrs. Denton. Unless, of course, you've changed your mind about me again and are on the hunt for another Michael to experiment with?"

"Are you ever going to let that go? That was years ago, Blake, and I have no intention of finding another Michael," I irritatingly fought back, even though at times like these, the thought was tempting to lose myself in some hot Latin lover and release my pent-up sexual energy. Oh, how I could use a thorough penis penetration in that moment—to feel loved, to feel like a woman, to feel the power of almost ecstasy. I so desperately wanted to be desired again.

I couldn't help but recall that long-ago moment with Michael and wish that I had chosen differently; chosen the experience of a single, hard fuck that I always thought I wanted to experience. Way too often, I'd have these odd sexual longings overcome me, and I'd have to tame myself down to reality. I repeatedly convinced myself it probably wasn't all as satisfying as I fantasized it would be, and it certainly wasn't worth betraying my marriage vows. So, I found other ways to ease the erotic tension that built inside me on a regular basis.

Dancing helped me expel some of the physical frustration I felt without touching another soul, but

JENNY DEE

I couldn't exactly say that to my husband without triggering his insecurities as a man who was cheated on before and betrayed by me once already.

I brought my attention back to the moment and to Blake, shaking off my wayward trance. He was just so aggravating sometimes!

"In case you've forgotten, Kayla and Steve are engaged now. We're going *dancing*, not clubbing, for crying out loud! And for your information, the crowd that goes to *Elliot's* isn't exactly looking for booty calls. If you would just come with us one time, you'd see how respectful the place is."

"Do whatever you want. One day you'll grow up and realize life's not all about partying. And you think you're ready to be a mother?"

That one hit me in the chest. I couldn't deny he had a point, given that I was nearing my thirties. Perhaps I was still carrying on too much like a college kid and less like an adult. Whatever. I just didn't want to fight and ruin my mood any further. We ended up compromising, with me altering the evening to meet up with Kayla at a low-key, business-like martini bar instead. Suppressed once again, I pretended all was well when she tried to probe about the change in plans.

"I'm telling you, Kay, it's nothing. I got my period, and my cramps are killing me. I just wasn't up to dancing," I lied, pulling one of the old standby excuses women use to hide the real reason they didn't or couldn't want to do something.

"Seems to happen a lot lately," she muttered, silently acknowledging that deep down, she knew it had nothing to do with my cycle and everything to do with Blake's opposition to how we chose to spend our time together.

Eventually, our girls' nights faded away as we became more absorbed with our respective men, just like with Blake's friends. I grew up as requested and gave up on drinking, dancing, and gossiping.

But that's what inevitably happens, right? Friendships fade, and it becomes all about you and your immediate unit. It's an unspoken truth of adulthood.

What no one told me about that truth was that it would leave me so utterly alone, that once I was left with only an inattentive spouse, I was primed for depressive detachment from the entire world.

10. WITHDRAWAL

Although the beginning was full of extravagant fun and endless excitement, married life was not what I had pictured in my storybook version of it.

It was downright grueling at times.

The fights over money. Arguing over his increasing trips away or failed job attempts. Jealousy over my career success. The decreasing frequency of sex. Family disputes. His lack of assistance around the house, leaving most of the responsibility to fall to me.

Little by little, I could feel his love withdrawing and the resentment building. And everything began and ended with money arguments.

What started way back with that little mishap right before our wedding—the hidden paycheck that had my head spinning—set the stage for a lifetime of misunderstandings. He never meant to hide that money. He was so earnest about wanting to surprise me with that pendant that I couldn't begrudge his loving spontaneity. That time.

Or the time after that, or the time after that. It happened again and again.

It kept on happening, and I kept on overlooking it. I was finally sensing a bit of a pattern, and I berated myself for not seeing—no, acknowledging—it sooner.

Like when his one-time freelance boss was losing

money on printed publications as the trends turned more digital, and he couldn't afford to pay Blake in full for his recent work. At least, that was what I was told, until I found the paystub weeks later. That certainly felt like déjà vu.

When delicately probed about the alternative "truth," Blake had the most reasonable response.

"Oh, I just forgot to tell you that Tommy figured things out and was able to pay me after all. It's all good. I used the money to get the new tires I needed on my car last week."

He'd go on alleged lucrative work assignments and come home complaining how he'd never get paid; that all these different clients kept jilting him. When I asked why he didn't get a lawyer to go after them or insist on payment, he'd beg me to understand that doing so would be further career suicide, and he couldn't risk losing his livelihood because of one or two jerks who stiffed him.

Unfortunately, those weren't isolated incidents. It became more the norm than uncommon, and it worsened over time.

He'd finally get an amazing, genuine payment from a client, and I'd put it into savings for him—for us, along with my now wonderfully abundant paycheck contributions—so we could save toward our future home and children.

But, little by little, the funds started to deplete. He needed to lay out travel money, claiming we'd be reimbursed with his next pay (that rarely happened). Dan was in a bind, and he had to help him out. Blake made annual contributions to the children's hospital he volunteered at.

What could I say? It was *his* money, too, and I had no right to control it.

It didn't end there, though. New bills came in with his uncle's middle initial to Blake's address while previous defaulting accounts and collections were ignored. Never his fault, and since we were estranged from his uncle, I couldn't even speak up on Blake's behalf to stop the madness. Well, I couldn't stop *any* of the madness.

Money handling was just the one thing we couldn't agree on; it was our source of perpetual conflict.

It didn't help matters that he was on shaky ground with his unstable career choice, one that I irreparably damaged, thanks to Kayla and Steve's inopportune nuptials. Their special day happened to conflict with one of his rare photography opportunities. I knew it was unfair of me to put him in this position, but I had insisted that he attend the wedding since she was the closest person I had to a best friend now.

"Blake, I'm her matron of honor. How would it look if my own husband wasn't there to support my dearest friends? You always tell me I work too much and am never around, but that's how my weekends feel to me now. You're never here anymore. I just want to spend time with you and celebrate our friends' happiness together. Can't you give up just one little job for me? Just this one time? Please," I pleaded with all the persuasion I could muster.

"Fine, I won't go to Richmond this weekend because you're making such a big deal about this. It would have been really good for my career, though, Em. This better be a damn good wedding. I hope I don't live to regret this."

I felt guilty for making him choose what he considered ultimately to be a lame event over a wonderful new job assignment. I knew how important it was for him to keep building a name in a struggling industry, and there I was, making him decide between his wife and his passion.

Worse, we didn't even end up having that great of a time as I was busy helping the bride, and my neglect of Blake put him in an even fouler mood.

"I don't know why you wanted me there, Emily, if you were just going to ignore me," he muttered before giving me the silent treatment for the rest of our car ride home.

I felt even more remorseful when I found out the true impact of his not accepting the job: I eventually cost him his entire career.

Canceling that Richmond assignment made him appear unreliable in the industry. As a result, he was never granted another opportunity by that particular prestigious publication ever again, and that blossomed into him earning a bad reputation among his peers. Couple that with an increasingly digital world that he wasn't trained for, and his entire professional future was in jeopardy.

Had I known at the time that he ran the risk of losing everything, I would have never shamed him into accompanying me that weekend. Undeniably, I was the one to blame for his misfortune.

Blake tried to regain his status by attending even more shows and conventions, traveling more than normal, hoping to make that right connection. He was afforded a few minor in-country opportunities here and there, more like "favors" for an industry friend, but nothing substantial. He'd leave for countless weekends for long, overnight training sessions and workshops, feverously learning the ropes he'd need to survive in a modern photography world, but it didn't change the facts: Blake's career was practically ruined because he made the wrong choice between work and a wedding.

All it took was one faux pas and very few were interested in booking him anymore.

We could no longer rely on his sparse assignments to pay the bills, and it was taking a toll on our already strained finances. Making our matters worse was his need to front money for travel expenses for these conferences, training, and spare jobs in hopes of keeping that professional fire burning somehow. That's how it worked: expenses first, reimbursement later. Ideally, anyway. We didn't always see a return.

It was a burden to support at times, but he was desperate to reignite his photography aspirations, and I didn't want to hold him back. After all, it was my fault that he was headed toward ruin, so I wanted to be extra supportive of his endeavors going forward. I needed to repair the damage I caused. He begged me not to be the reason his dreams died for good, and so, I would just figure out a creative way to make it all work for him. I *had* to.

But it was a catch-22 situation. Supporting his ongoing getaways escalated into even more exorbitant money issues than usual. And back around we came to the arguments about how to handle our finances. Like a hamster spinning aimlessly around its wheel.

***

You see, I was always at fault for his fiscal indiscretions because I obsessively controlled the money.

I couldn't help controlling our finances, though. He wanted to enjoy our life together with dinners, trips, and sensational evenings out, while I held on too tightly to make sure we had a roof over our head.

"You know, this is my money, too," he'd argue. "I have a right to use it sometimes."

"I know, but every time you dip in without consulting me, you leave me in a hole I have to dig us out of. All I am asking is that you check in with me first."

"Do you know how humiliating it is to go out with the guys or business associates and tell them I can't do this or that because I didn't get enough 'allowance' this week? Jeez, Em, I look like a chump to everyone. I can't live like this."

"And I can't live with constantly fixing your mistakes. If you'd just talk to me instead of going behind my back, or if you'd care enough to help manage our bills and find a better solution, we could work through this instead of always fighting about it."

"Right. It's always my fault. I guess that's what you get for marrying a loser."

I'd then walk away, unable to debate the issue any longer, yet also ashamed that I made him look so pathetic to his friends and professional colleagues. What they must think of me, and the pity they had on Blake for having such a hard-ass bitch for a wife. It was no wonder I didn't really get to come around his friends or conventions anymore.

I lost my ability to have fun and became "Mrs.

Responsibility," and who wants to be around *that*?

Besides, it didn't matter what I said, anyway. Blake was going to do what Blake wanted to do, and he was right; he was an adult and not a child. I had to stop acting like his mother.

But it was still a struggle whenever he'd unexpectedly take out money from our savings account or try to get an extra credit card in my name (since I was the one with the good credit) to have some spending money. I knew his heart was in the right place, wanting to alleviate our burden and bring some joy back to our union, but he failed to see how he was only making things worse.

And I admit, some of the gifts he bought me, though on the extravagant side, were so incredibly beautiful and thoughtful. How could I be mad when all he wanted to do was express his love?

His desire to buy things for me out of love would become one of his most famous excuses for why money disappeared out of our accounts for years to come. He was trying to be thoughtful while I was being domineering. He wanted to bring fun back into our lives while I focused on saving our financial skin month after month. Eventually, the constant bickering made him stop wanting to rob Peter to buy Emily nice things, and so the thoughtful gestures dwindled down.

But that didn't stop him from his spending sprees. His irresponsible behavior didn't go unnoticed by my mother, either, who I tried to keep out of my personal business—but sometimes I just needed someone to vent to.

"It's just so frustrating that I always have to figure

out how to make ends meet. I feel like we will never get out of this hole. If only I hadn't ruined his big break by making him go to that wedding with me, things might be different."

"Emily, you didn't ruin Blake's career by making him go to Kayla's wedding," she said, practically rolling her eyes. "Why would you think such a thing?"

"Because it's true. If I hadn't guilted him into missing that Richmond assignment, he would have never lost so many future opportunities."

"That's utter nonsense. Is that what he's telling you?" I nodded earnestly. "Listen, you know I love that boy with all my heart, but sometimes I wonder about him and his little games."

"This isn't a game, Mom. It's his career."

"His career? Let me tell you something, Emily Grace. You have been supporting this *career* for years now, and what has come of it? Nothing. How many conventions has he attended? How many weekends has he left you for these trainings that never pan out? How many second jobs have *you* picked up along the way to bail yourself out of *his* messes? I'm sorry, love. I've tried to hold my tongue and let you make your own mistakes, but I can't stand by and watch his constant laziness while you support it all."

"Mom, please. It's not like that. He's so close to getting a new break. I have to support him and his dreams. He's my husband," I cried.

"Yeah, well, your husband needs to learn how to become a responsible adult and stop spending money like he's an aristocrat," she sneered. "Even when he's trying to do something nice for you, it always ends up costing you—your bonus, your time at another job, your mental health. Baby girl, time to take a good, hard look at the problem and stop living in denial. He is careless with money, and you need to work that out before it escalates beyond your control," she warned as lovingly as possible.

I refused to admit it to her face, but she was absolutely right. Blake loved spending money way too much. It was almost humorous when I stopped and connected how all those expensive presents I'd receive once we were married would not be paid in full—or would be paid with *my* extra source of money. Especially when his income began to dwindle and mine rose. As much as he bitched about my working so hard, he didn't seem to mind the salary I brought in—and what it could buy.

A surprise vacation to Aruba for our anniversary. We'd need to use a bonus check of mine to pay off the balance before we could go. Tickets to a Broadway show we never ended up attending were purchased on my credit card; one in which he was not an account owner on. Before long, this pattern switched from thoughtful gifts for me to expensive gifts that I didn't even want.

Like the GPS system he got me for my birthday that I didn't need, because I didn't drive anywhere, but he couldn't return it, for whatever reason, and so it became his. Ironically, he had just mentioned a month earlier how he really wanted a navigation system, and I had said we didn't have it in our budget at the time.

So, anything of extravagance he wanted to buy that he knew I would object to, he presented to me as a gift so he could ultimately have it; bought and paid for once again with my credit card.

The use of my personal credit became a favorite pastime of his. I couldn't stop it either—not legally. I actually looked into it in a moment of sheer frustration once. Turns out, once you are married, you are considered one person, so he technically never stole a dime from me. It can't be considered identity theft, even though he used my personal information to secure financial gains without my permission.

That's a cleverly abusive system our country has rigged up. For richer, for poorer was no joke.

Countless times, I discovered collection bills for weird stores or new credit cards ordered in my name. In his name as well, though the amounts were minimal since his financial records were deplorable. And of course, more stuff of his uncle's, too, so it was never-ending. Each month offered up a new surprise in our mailbox that I had to investigate and never learn the truth about. Blake denied everything.

"What are you talking about? I don't know where this bill came from. It has your name on it, not mine. What would I need with a new dress? Seriously, Em, does that sound like my style?"

"Someone must have opened this account, Blake," I accused, wishing for once he would just come clean about his financial indiscretions. It had to be him, though he'd fight tooth and nail against the inference that he was behind the illicit use of my credit.

"For crying out loud, instead of blaming me, why don't you just call this place and report it as fraud instead of hounding my ass about it. I actually think you get off on condemning me for anything that goes wrong in our life."

I don't know why I even tried to uncover the origins of all these mishaps. Thankfully, I'd catch the new cards and collections and be able to rectify them before they affected my credit report. It was challenging, for sure, to keep bailing us out of this buy-and-ignore addiction Blake seemed to refute having. I was afraid my mom was right that things would one day escalate out of control.

But then Blake surprised me. After one too many disagreements, he finally showed interest in wanting to help with the bills and offered to be responsible for paying the rent each month. He didn't want me to take on so much of the burden anymore and realized that he'd never understand our financial situation until he took part in it. Nervously, I agreed, willing to give him the benefit of the doubt that he was trying to make a change; a change my mother thought would be innately impossible.

I disagreed, though. Maybe him being involved in the financial planning and budgeting might actually help him see how dire things got when he created a money snafu. I thought it was a good idea for me to control things less and let him experience that monthly pain more.

Nope. I'd still get a call that the rent was late somehow. How was that even possible when I literally gave Blake the cash to walk over to our landlord that same morning?

"I knew I should have gotten a receipt. The old man is going senile—I gave him that money two days ago." But Mr. Edwards insisted he was never paid, and so I'd have to dig up the rent and double pay for the month.

Like with every inconsistency Blake was challenged with, there was always an excuse. A dramatic, cockamamie one, too. Designed to elicit pity from me and ultimately, repetitive forgiveness and understanding. And it worked like a charm.

"I called the IRS and found out they confiscated our refund because they confused me with Uncle Blake again. This stuff always happens to me. You know my bad luck. It will be months before we see it, they said."

"I don't know who set this account up in your name. I think someone got a hold of your social security number. It wasn't me."

"I'm so lonely and depressed and tired of living like paupers. I just wanted something nice to remind me that I'm not a loser. Can you blame me for wanting to feel like a man again?"

No, I couldn't blame him for wanting that—just the way he went about it. Between his marital money embezzlement and lack of steady employment, things were becoming progressively worse around the Denton household.

So, I had to be the one, once again, to pick up the financial slack. What else could I do to survive? I had to hold on to our home, car—everything. I couldn't just let it drop because Blake was unsuccessful in securing a job. Forgetting that we were in a partnership, I had to make sure that *I* was taken care of. I was not going to allow myself to become homeless. I had to do whatever it took to ensure our security.

Work for me became intense, and I'd find myself more of a workaholic than a wife once again, despite my vow to be a more attentive spouse. I was determined to keep proving myself as an overlooked up-and-coming executive at Parks, waiting for the day I'd get my big break, which left me little time to take off anymore to go with Blake on his increasing number of conventions as he tried to win his career back.

For so many weekends, we were separated instead of together, and so my job became front and center. When Blake was actually present, he pouted his constant reminders that I was bleeding myself dry for a company that didn't appreciate my true gifts like he did. He didn't get that what I was doing, I was doing for *us.*

Even though he hated my hours, he did at least encourage me to stay put, as it was better than the alternative of dealing with the same bullshit in a new company—and the money was damn good. I just had to sacrifice a little less of myself to the poachers, he cautioned.

"As long as you keep giving to them, they are going to take from you. Fuck them," he said bitterly one day when I was venting frustration over an unfair assignment. "Don't work more than you need to. Let them pay you and just do the bare minimum. You're worth more than that—they just can't see you like I can."

"I know. You're right. Maybe I should just look for another job," I relented.

"You won't find a better one out there, Em. All companies are the same. Even though everyone treats you like shit there, at least you know them at Parks. You know they'll pay you and don't want to lose you because you're a loyal workhorse. They just have to remind you that you are replaceable every now and then so it doesn't go to your head. Just don't believe them when they turn around and swear to you how great you are—they're just telling you what you want to hear."

"So you keep telling me." I was growing tired of the reminders that I wasn't good enough. I was beginning to believe all my professors and intern managers were blowing smoke up my ass every time they proclaimed I was going to be someone special. They probably said that to all hopeful students.

"Sorry, babe. It's just how the real world works."

"I just wish that they would give me a chance. Alex tells me all the time how impressed he is by me, and yet, Mindy says that there's nothing available for me to grow into at the moment. It's so hard to work with her sometimes, like I'm being held back. I thought she was a mentor, but I don't feel like she's doing anything to help me anymore."

"Mindy is a complete bitch. You know she's jealous of you and is going to keep trying to make you miserable so that you'll leave. She wants to be the star again. I think you should go above her head and report directly to the Vice President so you can be on equal ground with her. I bet you Alex would find a way to make it happen just so he can keep you on since you know he's not a big fan of hers. You can be persuasive and present your case to him. Give her a taste of her own medicine and make your own name for yourself."

"You think so?"

"Worth a try. You'll never get anywhere if you just let her keep walking all over you. You deserve better for all the hours you work."

I considered it, then gladly took his advice when I had enough of her double standards. I betrayed my old relationship with Mindy in favor of becoming her equal. Alex did, in fact, take me under his wing, and I ended up having an even better work situation as a result. Now the executives could see for themselves what I had to offer, and I was ready to rise to the top.

Unfortunately, that seemed to backfire at home and feed into Blake's jealousy, both as a husband and as a failed professional.

I don't think my successful outcome was what Blake expected when he suggested his little plan. He thought it would get us more money and make me complain less, but he wasn't prepared for my skyrocketing recognition and position of power. He seemed more dismayed than supportive of my mini promotion, which confused me because I thought he wanted me to thrive there. Maybe it made him too uncomfortable to think of me as our breadwinner; maybe it was more than his ego could take.

That's when Blake came up with the crazy idea to move out of state and start over. I looked at him like he was nuts. After all his insight into why I should keep my job and then finally advancing within the company, he wanted me to give it up and move away? I knew he was feeling depressed and aching for a life change, but this wasn't the right time to make such a drastic decision. Request denied.

***

Well, since I said "no" to the move, he had to take

a different approach to make himself feel better: disappearing more.

I didn't understand why he always had to be at the Little League office when they shut down the business months ago.

"Why do you still have an office if you're not doing Little League anymore?" I asked.

According to Blake, the guys decided to finish out the lease instead of forfeiting it because the landlord was a dick and wouldn't let them prematurely cancel. It still didn't explain why he would have to physically be there, and I'd press him for a more logical explanation.

"Why are you so paranoid? I told you I had to go down to the office to fix Eddie's fuckup with the bills as part of closing down the business. Just because I'm not some goody-goody economics major who you don't trust with our finances, doesn't mean I'm an incompetent idiot. But yeah, it does mean I'd be there quite a few hours to get things done and that I'd be home late. Or would you like to see me fail at this the way I failed at photography?"

Always throwing that back in my face. It was starting to get old.

Then there were days he'd be gone from morning until night. He said it was because he was interviewing, and when I'd gently ask if he was having any luck, he'd snarl his frustrated "no" back at me before heading into our home office to spend the night researching new opportunities online. I wanted to help him, but I couldn't even make a suggestion without him defensively biting my head off.

"I'm trying as hard as I can. It's not my fault I can't

find a job that pays as well as yours. I told you before we got married that I am a loser. Now maybe you'll believe me."

I felt guilty for pressuring him, but all I asked him to do was find any job—just something that he enjoyed doing that would help offset some of our bills. It didn't even have to be permanent. I had no expectations or demands on what that looked like or how much he earned.

But my insistence on him being employed emasculated him and made him feel even more depressed than he already was. I was destroying his self-esteem every time I wished for him to work and contribute in some—*any*—way. It was like he was giving up completely, and yet his misery continued to be my fault. And so, I'd be the one to pick up the extra job to make ends meet; anything to not make him feel worse about himself.

I didn't know how much longer I could suppress my own aggravations and keep up my nice, supportive façade. It just became an automatic reflex to apologize and do or say whatever I needed to in order to keep the peace between us. I could feel it taking a toll on me: the constant steamrolling, the walking on eggshells, the overlooking blatant problems.

But it was just another day in our life, and I was used to it. Someone had to fight to keep us alive.

I ignored my mother's repeated comments about my progressively stressful and unbalanced married life. I couldn't give her the satisfaction of knowing she was right, and so I'd staunchly defend that I was handling it. I convinced myself I didn't have a choice but to be the dutiful wife I pledged to be. Life was not a fairytale, and I was finally cured of that childhood illusion.

Blake was my husband, and I promised to support him in whatever he needed to reboot his photography career. I had to repair the damage I caused, as he often reminded me. That meant understanding his persistent desire to train and network. Sadly, even though some new conventions popped up and Blake was away increasingly more, nothing much ever came from them.

Blake had hit a really bad dry spell—and it continued to hit us in our pockets.

The money bombs grew more severe over time. No one ever knew how truly unbearable it had gotten.

The worst of it came to a head when he took a cash advance out on one of my personal cards for a few thousand dollars. When confronted, he broke down crying and confessed that he was in trouble; he had been taking pain killers for his inflamed back injury from that car accident a few years back, and since his doctor would no longer prescribe the pills, he had to obtain them illegally.

"If I don't give these guys their money, they are going to come after us."

"What are you saying, Blake?" I asked in cold, bone-chilling fear. Did he mean as in, like, mob men who would order a hit if their debts weren't paid? I thought that only happened to characters in my beloved soap operas. Was this really happening, or was my mind doing its silly wandering and overreacting again?

"I'm saying I fucked up really bad, Em. *Really* bad. I'm afraid they will go after you to get back at me. Maybe even kill you," he whispered with worry before begging me to fix this inconceivable mess he had gotten himself—and me—into. "I just need the money to pay them off, and they'll leave us alone. I'm so sorry. It will never happen again."

I didn't know what to say, how to respond, or how to feel. Numbness took over from head to toe. I simply nodded and murmured that he could keep the cash and never spoke another word about it again. I couldn't; I had to push it down, way, way down into the recesses of the "this is not real" relationship files I had been unknowingly compiling since the day we met.

As I internalized the gravity of the situation—he was on drugs, and I didn't have the slightest clue; he was dealing with murderous criminals behind my back; he put *my* physical life in danger and tried to hide this all from me as if I'd never find out he cashed my credit card—he stood there profusely apologizing and professing that this was the last time he'd ever get mixed up with people like that. He didn't want to put me at risk like that ever again.

How nice of him to be concerned about me *now*, I thought indignantly.

Who the fuck was this man I married?

I swirled in disbelief. I barely acknowledged Blake as he pathetically promised that he would go to a legitimate doctor to help him with pain management, as he vowed not to cash out my cards anymore without telling me. He could have sworn a few other oaths, but by that point, I had blocked out the sound of his voice. I didn't want to hear anymore and retreated into the solace of my bedroom to sleep an eternity.

I hoped to God he kept whatever promises he made this time. This was not some Uncle Blake mix-up. A legitimate drug lord could target me at any time to get back at my husband. I still get chills whenever I think about it. It took a long time before I stopped looking over my shoulder in public or locking my doors and windows and hiding behind darkened blinds when home alone, wondering if someone would get to me before Blake was able to forewarn me about his latest disaster.

I wanted so badly to kick him out of the house in that moment, to rid myself of this sickness once and for all, but I was too afraid to be alone. I needed him.

Who else would protect me from the monsters?

***

Life was on the edge of explosion—and to make matters worse, the people in our lives seemed to be falling further away. His family was becoming even more distant, with Camille getting married and moving across the country to Utah and Joey ending up in and out of a rehab facility. At least he had the courage to fix his problems, I thought bitterly to myself when I heard Joey checked himself in.

His parents became an ongoing source of contention. Never having a good relationship with them, he really didn't want much to do with them anymore as all they would ever do was berate Blake for his inability to provide like a man. Even though I wished myself that Blake would be a better supporter, I felt really sorry for him that they could be so outright cruel about it. I eventually stopped encouraging him to be the better person and build a bond with them. I could see it was a lost cause, and so, we rarely enjoyed family dinners with the Dentons anymore.

I thought I could at least count on my family to remain strong, but even they were falling apart at the seams. What used to be a close-knit connection began to unravel once my dad left, and it trickled into our relationship with my sister and mother. Instead of being a support system, their presence in our lives was complicating our marriage further.

In fact, Kerry was making career matters worse by acting inappropriately at the conventions Blake would invite her to. I was horrified as he told me how she took two men up to her room at once at their most recent event in Florida.

"I was humiliated, Em. You know I love her, but it's an embarrassment to have her drunk and hanging all over my colleagues, and then sleeping with several different men in one night. She can't come with me anymore. I'm sorry."

I absolutely understood how it was mortifying to him professionally, and I supported his decision to forbid her from attending future conventions. Her utter lack of professionalism was impacting Blake's already strained reputation in the industry. And that made my life more difficult since I had to carry the extra load for his declining job offers as a result.

I was so angry that I couldn't bear to confront my sister about her illicit behavior. Instead, I just quietly removed myself more from her life until I thought she was mature enough to act like an adult. I had lost so much respect for her for putting my husband, and by extension me, in such a compromising position. We drifted apart, only seeing each other at the obligatory birthday parties and holidays that my mother insisted on having.

Speaking of my mother, she took a more active, unwelcome role in my marital woes, pestering me to push Blake to see someone about his depression, with the ultimate intention of him finding a job to help support us. She badgered me endlessly about his money mishaps as if I were a little child who couldn't handle her own life. She claimed she was tired of watching her daughter juggling overtime and taking on second gigs as a cashier to make ends meet.

I knew she meant well, but it got to the point where she would even tell Blake to his face that he needed to step up as a husband, which didn't fare well with him at all.

Admittedly, the situation with my mother was getting out of control. Funny, that same word seemed to keep coming up in all conversations with Blake that referenced my mother, I noticed. Once again, he saw people better than I did.

"She can't control anything in her own life, so she is trying to control yours."

"She needs to back off and stop telling me to get a job. She might control you, but she won't control me. Our life is none of her business."

"Why are you always caving into her? Why are you always doing what she wants? She shouldn't try to control you like this, babe. You're a grown woman and she needs to accept that."

Like Pavlov's dog, my bell was the word "control," and the action was to distance.

Mom became upset when she found out I once

talked behind her back with Julie about something private in her life, and she tried to forbid me from seeing my cousin ever again. Blake felt guilty after our fight as he was the one who urged me to confess what was said to my mother to clear the air and release the heaviness in my heart over the conversation. He knew the history of conflict between the two women, but he had hoped for a better outcome. But alas, I lost contact with one of my favorite people in the whole world in deference to my loyalty to my mother.

More and more, her control became obvious.

My mother kept trying to control me into thinking that because Blake didn't have a suitable job, he was not good enough to ever be the husband and provider I needed.

She kept controlling the conversation about whether or not we were going to have children because she was lonely and wanted grandkids.

She controlled who we saw for the holidays and when; how I should decorate my home; what would be acceptable, non-extravagant vacations. You name it, she tried to control it.

Our ultimate response to this insane amount of motherly control? Moving away from everyone and everything. Just like Blake wanted to do when he felt jilted by my job. This time, I didn't say no. In fact, I was the one who suggested it.

11. DESPAIR

One single, weak moment of frustration was all it took to convince me to jump the New Jersey ship and set sail for North Carolina. I remember the moment clear as crystal—one long, hard, unappreciative workday, combined with a fight with my mother over something so insignificant, and I flippantly said to Blake that I wanted to get the hell out of this place and move far away.

I wanted to stop fighting about money, and it was cheaper there. I wanted to stop feeling overwhelmed by family, and North Carolina was close enough to visit for holidays, but far enough away to not see them every weekend. I wanted to start fresh with him, and we'd be able to build our own home from scratch with the little money we miraculously had in savings.

The answer to my suggestion was such a resounding "yes" that we made plans that very weekend to meet with a developer and get the home-building process underway. Blake wasn't going to waste a single moment of time—not when he knew I was prone to change my mind once I told others about our big news and listened to their unsolicited advice.

"Let's not tell anyone about this just yet. This is about you and me. I want to do this one thing on our own, Princess. Let's build our dream castle without anyone ruining this for us."

How could I resist that plea? I felt a twinge of hope that we could finally escape back to the life I always imagined we'd have. Even more—he ignited a spark of excitement when we selected a four-bedroom home so we could fill it with our children.

"Once we are able to live our own life, Em, we can finally have a baby. We'll be free to raise him or her our way. I think that's why I've been hesitating. But now, I feel like I'll be ready."

Well, once he uttered those words, there was no way I was turning back on our decision to move.

Everything fell into place. We researched the best school districts, found the perfect plot of land, and selected our house design. He supported my idea to present a proposal to Alex to remain employed with Parks remotely from out-of-state—and it worked. He accepted my offer, and a weight had been lifted off of our shoulders. It meant a break in our financial stress, and sitting pretty looked nice on us for a change.

It was a dream come true. We'd have a lower cost of living and our own home that we could build ourselves—plus, we'd be miles away from meddling family members. I didn't know why I resisted the idea for so long, but I was glad I came to my senses. We finally had something to look forward to in our future.

"This is going to be amazing, Em. I can already see our kids running around the place," he said as we both stood within the partially constructed frame in joyful anticipation. "Can't you?"

"I know! How adorable will their giggles be as they jump on their beds or snuggle into our arms to read a bedtime story?"

"Or the moment they take their first steps right there in the living room." I couldn't help but beam with so much love for this man and what we envisioned together. It had been a long time since we connected like this, and I was loving every minute of it.

"Oh, Blake, I've missed being this close to you. I love that we are building this brand-new future together. Just you and me."

"Me too," he said with a smile, hugging me from behind and holding me close. When we realized that we were in the very spot where our master bedroom would be, a mischievous glint appeared in his eyes as he seductively brushed his hands over my breasts and down to the front of my pants, igniting long-sleeping sensations. "Shall we?"

"Right here? Now?" I laughed, taken aback by his renewed sexuality and oddly spontaneous suggestion. It was unlike Blake to be so bold and daring, to want to make love in the semi-public outdoors and risk being seen. I felt the shot of ecstatic adrenaline rush through me as I realized he was serious. I didn't second guess his offer for long; I let him sweep me up into his arms to pre-christen our future, and perhaps plant the seed for the family we were ready to bring into our world.

It was one of the few times when we really had a chance to bond again. We continued having a blast picking out paint colors for the different rooms, buying new furniture, and designing every last detail of this unique structure we'd call ours. Our home was absolutely beautiful, and I thought this glimmer of hope and reconnection would reawaken our marriage and bring us closer. Everything seemed perfect once again.

Until moving into the new house coincided with an impromptu, yet promising, two-month program in Milan that threatened to put our reinvigorated life on pause.

This particular opportunity was different from the annual convention we used to attend together in Milan. It was an educational retreat, sort of like a crash college curriculum, where Blake would come away with a certification in digital photography. It was exactly what he needed to be considered a serious travel photographer again.

I wasn't thrilled about the prospect of being on my own without him for that long—especially in a new state where I didn't know anyone. But considering everything he had sacrificed for me to make my dreams a reality over the years, I wasn't going to deny him this second chance. Not when we were finally getting our marriage back on track. We could always start on our family planning again after he returned. What was another two months?

It all happened faster than I expected. His leaving for Milan was so abrupt, departing after only two days' notice and only a few weeks after we had set up house. Wanting so badly to support him, I scrambled to order him a credit card as a joint owner on one of my accounts just so he could have access to money while he was there. I'd figure out the logistics later—even if it meant remortgaging the house to pay it all back. With the change in the cost of living, we had the wiggle room to make it work now.

I knew the training opportunity would be worth

it, especially with all the possibilities it presented for a much more secure future based on Blake's passion. And I wanted that more than anything for my husband.

Even though our financial situation had improved slightly, he understood that he had to live on a very restrictive budget while away—grocery food instead of dining out, metros instead of taxis. I figured that it wouldn't be an issue anyway, considering he'd be on some kind of campus with a kitchen, so there wouldn't be much need to travel, except to maybe a local grocery store. As a former struggling college student myself, I was able to give him all the tips and tricks of living successfully on limited means.

But once he landed in Italy, the charges kept piling on for restaurants, bars, and other entertainment, to my astonishment. What in the world was going on over there? Great—we're an ocean apart, and I had to prepare for an age-old battle that I was not looking forward to.

"Blake, we talked about this before you left. We don't have the money to cover these extra charges, and we're going to end up in debt that we can't recover from. We just got back on our feet here, and I want to keep our savings strong for when we have a baby."

"Em, you don't understand. I am in class all day long. I am sick of 99-cent frozen meals. I need a break. So, when the guys ask me to join the group for a drink, I can't exactly turn them down. You have no idea what it's like to be away like this."

"You're right, I can't imagine how difficult this is for you. I know you are working so hard for this—for us. Okay, how about we compromise, and you go out only one night a week?"

"I can try," he offered, executing it unsuccessfully. "I'm sorry, I'm just so miserable here, and I miss being home."

I missed him so much, too. I didn't realize how challenging it would be to live without him for so long—and yet, there was something oddly comforting about being alone sometimes, too. A vision of living a simpler life without Blake flashed before my eyes, but I dismissed my selfish notions and instead concentrated on figuring out a way to make life easier on him while he was stuck in Milan.

So, I thought I would book him a flight home halfway through his time there, during a planned break. Well, that ended up being a disaster. The retreat director had decided to schedule a midterm examination during that week instead of having a full break—so Blake had not only missed the required test but was now in serious threat of not passing the course at all.

"I can't get through to this guy," he explained in utter frustration as I drove him home from the airport. "He just hates me. *Hates* me. He's thrilled he gets the opportunity to fuck me over by giving me a zero on this midterm."

"I'm so sorry, Blake. If I had known, I would have never booked the flight. I just missed you so much."

"I know. But I told you coming home would be a mistake. It's just really bad timing. And now all of this has been a waste," he sulked off, not interested in my attempts to lift his spirits or commiserate with him.

Those were a miserable few days to spend with

him; he was still so angry over the situation that he pretty much ignored me, stayed on his phone, and watched television until the day he was able to fly back. All I wanted was some time to talk, cuddle, make love, and enjoy our new home for a brief moment in time. Blake had no interest in any of that, obsessing over what he could do to salvage his midterm mistake instead.

When he returned to Milan, he was met with resistance, as expected, from his professor. He was refused the opportunity to take the exam at all, denied a chance for extra credit, and ultimately, failed the program. He would now come away with nothing but bitterness over a disastrous final chance at his dream career.

I couldn't sleep for days over that, consumed with guilt. I was just trying to do something nice for him, but I ruined everything for Blake—again—and now he was stuck in a program he was already committed to for three more weeks, knowing that there was nothing he could do to change the outcome.

I offered to speak to someone in authority to explain the situation, but he said it was no use. I told him he should just pack up and come home, but he insisted he couldn't. He'd just have to stick it out and maybe make some network connections that could help with his future.

Three weeks more he labored in Milan in a crushing depression, and I didn't have a way of reaching him—they didn't allow international mail where he was staying, so I couldn't even send him a care package to remind him he was loved. We couldn't afford cross-Atlantic cell service at the time, and since there was no campus phone either, I had to wait for him to call me collect from some public place just to talk to him when he wasn't studying. It hurt not being able to comfort him when he was so isolated under unspeakable, disheartening conditions.

This was not the fresh start I had envisioned for us.

When he finally came home, I could feel the walls closing in on us. My selfish need to see him instead of just waiting two months obliterated his very last shot at becoming a successful photographer. I didn't think he would ever forgive me—and I felt his distance spiral further away as evidence of my culpability.

I tried to make it up to him by booking us a return trip to the blue shores of the Bahamas, but I never felt more like a stranger to my own husband than I did that week. He was checked out and distraught. Neither of us could find the joy in our time away together.

Nor could we find it at home in North Carolina.

The bickering escalated to ridiculous levels. Blake was testier than normal in the days that followed his return. No matter how I asked for his help—whether kindly, nagging, begging—I was shot down as if I had no consideration whatsoever of what he was going through.

"I'll get around to cleaning up the outside when I feel up to it. My back is still hurting from the flight home. You know I can't exactly take pain pills or I'll be fighting an addiction again—and that would lead to stupid decisions like calling those thugs when my prescription runs out. I just have to suffer through this until the pain goes away."

This was a frequent line to get me off his case. In no way did I want to exacerbate his pain, which was intolerable at times, nor trigger his need to contact psychopath drug lords. Though funny how he was still able to go out bowling later that night with his new buddies—which didn't go over well when I hinted at that minor hypocrisy.

Then there were my *as-subtle-and-kind-as-possible* reminders that he needed to find some sort of steady employment to help offset the charges he racked up in Milan. Oversensitivity bombs went off.

"I'm no longer getting travel assignments. I'm not fighting anymore to get back into the business. I gave up my dream so I could be here with you, and all you do is complain that I don't work as much. I thought you'd be happy that we could spend more time together."

Never mind that his extra free time was dedicated to doing anything other than spending it with me. I actually don't know what he was doing half the time while I worked in my home office.

There came a point when I just no longer cared.

***

My light started to go out. I became a hermit and never ventured out, except to the local stores. Being new to the state, I still had no friends. Recalling my difficulty as a teen, it wasn't exactly my forte to make easy connections. Houses were far away from each other, so I didn't even have the closeness of waving to a next-door neighbor.

Worse than seclusion from society, I had to

accept Blake's constant absence day in, day out as he finally found the motivation to hit the pavement and interview for prospective jobs. Without a soul to interact with, all I focused on was work, finding creative ways to make ends meet, and trying to figure out how to make my husband happy again.

I thought his happiness would be the key to unlocking mine.

That meant no more talking about how well I was doing at my job—which wasn't hard, considering the big promotion I was set to receive before the big move was now off the table. Family was a sore spot because they gave us a difficult time about moving, and their lack of support drove a wedge between all of us, one that Blake watered with his words of aggravation.

We could have lived luxuriously, but his increase in spending while abroad sucked our finances dry and forced a second loan on the house. Shame kept me from talking to anyone about what was really going on—how I had threatened so many times that I had enough of the lies and money issues but then forgave and went back.

I always went back.

I knew what people would think of me if they realized how many fucking times I went back.

Trying to find any sense of joy in life beyond work, I had considered taking a college course in fashion design. But that was instantly shut down.

"I am still fighting to get my foot back in the door—the one that you helped to close—and you want to take the money that you claim we don't have and go back to school? Tell me, Emily. How is it fair that you get to always pursue your dreams, but it's okay if mine fail?"

Acquiescing that he had a point, I walked away from my passion once again.

Instead of pursuing school, I thought I could spend some time exploring our new little state to see all the wonders it held. I heard so many interesting things about North Carolina and was itching to check out all its little hotspots. I missed traveling since money was often so tight and the last few months kept us—well, me—homebound. I thought if maybe I went on a little local adventure, I could acclimate better to our new surroundings.

"Em, you know we only have one car. What am I supposed to do if I get a call for a job interview? You can't be driving all over the place. Do you want me to get a job or not?"

So, I shelved the exploration idea. And the free community library cooking class idea for the same reason. But I was able to borrow books and watch television. Getting lost in someone else's much better life stories became the only pastime I could muster anyway.

My energy was depleted. I was gaining weight left and right because food became my best friend. Even the fulfillment I once felt with my job no longer existed behind a stream of tedious desktop tasks and endless conference calls. There were no more date nights. No more snuggling on the same couch watching a movie. No more anything at all.

Just running an empty household that held no life—because I didn't have one.

The worst part was that Blake was never even present. I'm not just talking physically. I mean existentially—as in, he sat in the recliner just opposite me and ate at the same dinner table, but he might as well have not even been there.

Once upon a time, we talked so much that we'd end up staying on the phone just to watch the same sunrise together. We couldn't get enough of each other's touch as we'd make love for hours without coming up for air. We'd spend our evenings wrapped up in each other like blankets and fall asleep to the sound of our breath which was full of loving communication even in its explicit silence.

This was not that same silence. This was dead air. How could we not find something—*anything*—to talk about? What was so important on his phone that he could find something to say to that person but not to me, his wife? Was there nothing about his day or life that he thought I would find vaguely interesting, and vice versa?

It was cold in that house. In the middle of summer, I was trapped under a sheet of ice, trying to pound my way through to the surface of a better life. And Blake just stared at me through the thin layer, watching me struggle, and laughing at my trapped reflection as if he didn't give a fuck.

Sex was definitely off the table by that point. He was so completely dejected that anything more than a quick kiss hello or goodbye was all he could offer. No matter how I tried to seduce my husband, I'd be denied the smallest token of affection or sexual touch. The excuses reminded me of when he'd rebuff my attempts to go on a first date.

"I'm sorry, but I had a long day going from place to place being rejected on interviews. Raincheck?"

Yeah, sure.

"My back is acting up pretty bad right now. I'm just going to go upstairs and do a little more research. Maybe some other night." Not likely.

"Something's wrong with me. It's not you. I just don't really want to have sex—or at least, *he* doesn't," he confessed, alluding to a potential dysfunction of his penis. "I'm so ashamed, I don't want to talk about it. I think it's because I'm so depressed. I'm just an all-around failure."

I spent countless hours trying to boost his ego or help figure out what the problem could be; what I could have done to turn him off so much. Could it be my increasing weight gain? My incessant nagging? The fact that I had only slept with one man—*him*—making me so dull in the bedroom that I couldn't pleasure him properly?

Looking back, it had been this way since the moment I first broke his heart—this detachment from intimacy. I thought maybe it was just a slow period as we reconnected after our very first separation, or something he'd warm back up to after he had a clean bill of health, or a bond we'd naturally return to after coming down from our newlywed bliss. No matter the circumstance, I was always left wondering what went wrong.

I even wondered if our lack of married sex life was my punishment for breaking up with him or kissing that guy Michael all those years ago, but I pushed those silly thoughts to the side. He'd never use sex as a weapon of retaliation—that would be denying himself! No, it had to be something deeper that was bothering him, and I couldn't make it all about me.

Besides, that was so many years ago, and if he held that kind of a grudge against me, he would have never walked down the aisle in the first place.

As I considered his most recent reasons for not wanting to make love, they seemed completely legitimate, and who was I to make him feel bad about it? I didn't want him to ever feel like less than a man. I already emasculated him with the money situation, and with single-handedly dismantling his career, I wasn't about to make him feel like a failure in the bedroom, too. And so, I rode it out, hoping that one day it would resolve itself when he was feeling better.

But it never did get better; in fact, sex became even less frequent than I thought possible—as in, completely non-existent. I had zero shot of ever becoming a mother at this rate, I mused. Plus, he reneged on wanting that kind of responsibility, even after pledging that our big house was designed to be filled with our children, so there wasn't even a need to have basic sex for procreation.

I thought that was all there was to it. Some natural lack of interest in the idea of sex in general. That was the man I had married, and I had years to accept that fact. It's just who he was.

But I was wrong. I learned that the hard way when I found out the truth about his "virginity."

I kept replaying our lifetime of conversations over and over in my head, from the very first time we talked about sex. He told me repeatedly how his grandmother taught him to wait for the right person— for marriage; that making love was sacred and only to be shared with the woman you would spend the rest of your life with.

Based on that repeated conversation, I wrongfully assumed that he was a virgin when we first met. Years went by with me believing that theory, until one drunken night, during an awful fight, he let the truth slip out. Devastation cannot even begin to describe the humiliation I felt as he revealed what I never realized.

I can't even remember what the actual fight was about—probably about not having any sex—but I do remember saying to him that when we both lost our virginity to each other, I felt that it was a hallowed bond we'd always share for the rest of our lives.

Blake looked at me oddly before confessing, "What are you talking about? You weren't my first."

A sledgehammer pounded into my stomach and heart all at once. The room closed in all around me until I could barely gasp for air.

I wasn't his first?! Did I just hear him correctly?

"What? I don't understand. You told me that your grandmother taught you to wait for marriage."

"Yeah, but I never said I took her advice," he said, dumbstruck by my naivety. He stared at me, finally comprehending the depths of my gullibility. "Are you really that fucking stupid to think that I was a virgin when we met? Uh, hello, remember Brittany cheated on me—do you think it was with her *lips?*"

Then he laughed at my pain of betrayal like it was no big deal; no big deal that I was duped into giving up my virginity to someone I believed was saving himself for marriage. I foolishly believed that I would be this sensitive, upstanding man's one and only. He dismissed my shock as some silly little misunderstanding and went to bed as if he didn't just shatter every sense of trust and faith I once had.

I stood there lifeless, unable to figure out how I could have misjudged and assumed something so profoundly wrong all these years. Blake had sex *before* he met me; *before* we made love.

Everything began to make more sense in that department as the pieces of the puzzle thrust themselves together in front of my now-opened eyes.

No wonder why he knew exactly what to do that first night we were together. How smooth and skilled he was. How he knew where to find and rub my clitoris and put a condom on correctly and ease into me so that it didn't hurt as badly. He wasn't awkward in the least bit—that experienced son of a bitch who made me wait so long out of respect for his values, who shamed me for being sexual with other men before we met.

Anger fueled within me as the days that followed brought about even more inner revelations. I let his "innocence" be an excuse for why he wasn't more creative in the bedroom when I wanted to explore new things. For why he was against masturbating when he was in a relationship. For why he didn't like to go down on me.

For why in over ten years of being together, not once did he ever put in the effort to bring me to orgasm.

Did he ever go down on someone else and bring *her* to orgasm? If that were the case, then I couldn't fathom why he couldn't do these things for me.

Here I thought it was all because he was inexperienced and embarrassed that he didn't know what to do. Or that maybe it was because of his religious beliefs, where sex was not talked about and was only really practiced for procreation. I respected that about him and never pushed. I loved him, orgasm-inducing or not.

I reflected back on our early years of marriage and how sex with Blake was not what I had dreamed it would be—certainly not the passionate spark that brought us together. It was downright dull. Very rarely did we change from the missionary position. We once tried anal, but even that didn't seem to appeal to him—for which I was grateful.

At one point, he suggested toys, but I was uncomfortable with the idea of plastic replacing his own penis when I got very little attention from that part of him to begin with. I feared he gave up trying to do anything interesting with me after that as he had an increasing lack of desire in being intimate with me.

As much as I would try to seduce him and get him in the mood, I just couldn't. I blamed it on my increasing body size. I was no longer attractive, so I forgave him for not wanting me. I blamed it on my being a controlling nag with the money and expectations. Why would he want to make love to someone who was always reprimanding him like a child?

So, by the time it was revealed that he was not a virgin when we met and made love, I was already taking the culpability for disappointing him sexually and him not wanting to touch me anymore.

Now knowing he had one or more sexual experiences before me, I finally understood exactly why he didn't want to have sex with me. I couldn't please him. My inexperience disappointed him. He was now living a married life with no sex, and I comprehended why it made him so depressed. I transitioned from anger to shame.

I was a terrible wife.

That was the story I repeatedly told myself as our relationship dwindled down the abyss of horrors.

But then I recalled the enormous amount of contrition I felt for that single kiss I had with Michael, and how I betrayed Blake by not telling him I went to an innocent basketball game with him. Lie by omission, he claimed—but yet, it was okay to let me believe that he was untouched when we met? All the fucking while, he'd been with Brittany before—and possibly others?

I fumed over the double standard, which by the way, wasn't even in the same league of betrayal. I never slept with Michael.

The more I thought about it, the more this major disclosure started to send off little chimes of awareness in my head. If I misunderstood his virginity and values, what else did I not know or falsely believe?

I started to make some interesting observations as I head-explored all of his other sex-related incidents I had previously accepted were someone else's fantasies wrongly surfacing as his. Those girlie magazines under the bed that he claimed were Joey's. The hotel bills that would have XXX movies charged on them, which he alleged were his convention roommate's doing while he went down to the bar for a few drinks. The browsing history of porn sites on his computer that were courtesy of poor little Joey, the sex fanatic, at it again.

He'd repeatedly tell me that he thought the idea of masturbation was gross and that he couldn't bring himself to pleasure his own body.

"I don't like to touch myself. It's too weird, and I feel like it would be a sin."

Crusted towels and socks under the bed suggested otherwise, especially toward the latter part of our relationship, but I never caught on that they were from his frequent ejaculations. He'd spend hours up in the bedroom or bathroom on the phone or computer with the door closed while I watched television downstairs and could have sworn that I heard escaped moans—but he claimed he was just struggling to take a shit or working out.

If I took a moment to consider those were *his* magazines, *his* hotel movie charges, and *his* browsing history, I'd shudder to realize how much masturbating he truly did—which isn't necessarily a bad thing, but when you opt for that instead of having sex with your very willing wife, something had to be off. And it grieved me to learn that I was not the inspiration behind any of his orgasms.

Desperate to bring the intimate connection back to our relationship one night after his reveal, telling myself I could look past it, I broke down and bought sexy lingerie that hid my body flaws and set up a romantic evening. I prayed he would be pleased with my effort to spice things up. But he just looked at me, shook his head, and smirked, his face and fingers focused on whatever conversation he was having on the phone instead of the ready and available woman in front of him.

He couldn't find a single word to even try to make

up an excuse for why he wasn't going to have sex with me this time. The dejection I felt was excruciating. In a home that I shared with the love of my life, I was alone, facing a lifetime without intimate touch ever again. And I wasn't even thirty years old.

He withdrew further away after that. Leaving me to my own devices, he'd continue to go in search of a job that ended up taking six more months to find. He finally secured one, but it required so much training that it took him away on multiple overnights, and I barely saw him. When I did, he became nothing but the passing shadow of a man I used to know who barely spoke a word to me.

His self-diagnosed depression loomed over our happy new life together, yet he refused therapy—individual or couples. My own finally realized depression provided the wick for our marital dynamite stick.

What was supposed to be a fresh new start was leading to the ultimate destruction.

At times, I just couldn't take the stress and anxiety of trying to make ends meet or getting him to pitch in and do his share around the house, and I'd resort to threats, like I had done so many times over the years when I was pushed to my limit. He'd make his pleas, excuses, or nasty remarks in return, calling my bluff every single time.

But forgiveness became my norm after a threat to leave, and he counted on that.

I never followed through and instead wished the pain away by creating an escape for us—anything to bring back our magic. One that made us laugh, have fun, and not deal with reality.

And so, I'd find a way to pay bills and put some money aside to do something that would remind us about how it used to be—like how we fell in love in London, how we were the power couple at a convention, or how we were known to throw the best house parties.

Whenever we escaped our reality before, life was perfect.

I could make this work again, if only I'd try harder.

If only I could convince Blake to escape once more—into a vacation, into creative lovemaking, into parenthood—perhaps we could escape back into our perfect life.

If only…

Oh, how desperately I tried to hold on to the last few "if only" crumbs of all that was good. I took the blame as much as I could to ease his burden, but I still needed him to help me. I still needed him to support me. I still needed him to love me.

I prayed with all my heart that it was not too late to fix what we had broken.

12. EPIPHANY

But we were more than broken; we were shattered. I wasn't sure what I could possibly do to put us back together anymore. The funny thing is, I saw the signs all along and ignored them, convinced that true love can outlast any obstacle thrown our way.

And I said that to Blake, repeatedly. I forgave the explained-away lies, accepted an asexual relationship, and tolerated his inability to keep his hands out of our collective money jar. I told him the only thing that would make me leave would be if he cheated on me, and I knew he would never do that, especially being raised under such upstanding morals.

Well, at least I believed he meant to follow that particular moral of faithfulness, even if he lied about his virginity. We did take vows, after all. And vows made before God surely mattered to him, right?

Right. Well, one day, I was cleaning out our SUV before taking it to the car wash, when I happened upon an unexpected, handwritten little note tucked under an empty disposable coffee cup.

"Thanks for the Christmas kiss, Santa. Xo."

I paled at the sight of the cute and curvy penmanship and had to read it three times before

I absorbed the words. Spidey senses were activated and instantly, I brought the note into the house to confront him about it.

"Blake, what is this?" I asked as calmly as I could, telling myself that overdramatizing without having all the facts would not bode well for me in our precarious, emotionally disconnected state.

"That? Oh, it's just some joke from a girl at work. They had me dress up as Santa at the holiday party and hand out gifts, and a co-worker was just being funny. It's nothing."

He was so nonchalant about it, barely looking up from his phone to make eye contact with me. It sounded like a plausible story; still, it was a little on the peculiar side to be just a joke. Wouldn't someone sign it "LOL" instead of "Xo" if that were the case?

"Are you sure? It sounds like a little more than nothing to me. There's a heart above the 'i' in kiss," I pointed out, feeling more unsettled with each new detail I noticed. This time he looked up at me long enough to tilt his head back and roll his eyes in a "here we go again" motion.

"There you go, running away with your imagination. What would you like me to tell you? It's an innocent little note from some chick like thirteen years younger than me. They write like that now, I guess. It's a joke, Em."

"Then why is it in your car? Why didn't you just throw it out?"

"Same reason I didn't throw out the coffee cup. I forgot. Why are you making such a big deal about this? Jeez, Emily, this is exactly why I don't bother talking to you anymore. You blow the littlest things out of proportion. You're impossible, you know that?"

I might be impossible, but something about his story didn't make sense. He had become a habitual slob, true—a far cry from that first date, sexy cologne, new car, elixir of love scent, and a spotless interior. But how did he remember there was an empty coffee cup with a note in the car that he somehow forgot to throw away? Sensing there was nothing more he was willing to add to the conversation, I let it drop and made excuses to appease his perception of my overreacting. It's all I ever did these days to keep the peace.

"I'm sorry, Blake. I guess I'm just upset because you are training so much, and I never see you anymore."

"Doesn't feel good to be married to a workaholic, does it?"

The zing. That one nailed me right in the stomach. Touché, Blake. Is this how he felt all that time when I'd work for hours on end? Did he feel the same pangs of jealousy whenever I'd talk about my male boss, who was so perfect and "like a brother" to me? Could he be telling the truth, and some young, innocent twenty-something was just messing around with him?

I decided to table my doubt for the moment and take Blake at his word. Still, I was uncannily distraught, and this internal nagging that something wasn't adding up wouldn't let up. So, when he left for another 15-hour, late-night shift, I did something that I rarely did anymore: I called my mother to talk it through.

I will never forget that moment, in the middle of recounting my story of all that was going on—

between the overnight training, him wearing brand-new cologne to work, his non-stop obsession with texting on his phone, and receipts for two-person dinner charges with his boss—when the lightbulb irrevocably went off.

"Oh my God, Mom. He is cheating on me," I finally grasped, breaking down into sobs that could not be comforted over the phone from miles away. I was actually heaving and losing my breath over the magnitude of an epiphany a long time in the making. The oxygen known as Blake was just sucked out of my life, and I couldn't find my mask. He did it—he called my ultimate bluff.

"Oh, my baby girl," she responded with a mother's devastation. "I'm so sorry. I wish I could be there with you right now. What can I do, honey?"

"I don't know if there is anything anyone can do, Mom. I just have to figure this out on my own," I answered, dejectedly.

"Emily, sweetheart, you are not alone. I have all day, and I will sit here for as long as you need me to. Please don't shut me out and internalize this. Talk to me, baby. Tell me everything. I promise I won't say a word or judge. I will just listen," she pleaded, and the little girl inside of me felt so comforted to hear her maternal voice offer me emotional safety.

Crushed, abandoned, unsure of anything in life, I finally surrendered a decade of pressure that I had been holding back, ready to free myself of the mental private ping pong game I had been playing for so long without allowing in the love and support I needed to guide me. I took on way too much on my own, and I couldn't do it any longer.

This volcano was erupting and nothing I could do would keep the untamed lava from oozing out the pain and suffering any longer.

Four hours I spent on the phone with my mother connecting the dots of the last ten years. All her warnings. All the weird looks from my friends when I'd casually mention something I should be alarmed about in my marriage. All the incongruencies, lies, and manipulations. The missing money. The unusual charges on my card. The long hours and trips away from home. The sexual disconnect.

My mother, who I had tried to push away so many times before for her obtrusive meddling, became my source of strength—my savior. She made me feel safe to explore every part of this heartbreaking revelation. She was ready to hear it all with an open heart and an open ear, without judgment, advice, or anger— and so, I just let the diatribe of insights flow to my attentive sounding board as I pieced together what I closed my eyes to for so long.

Starting from the very first moment Blake and I met, his charm spelled me, and I never looked past that charismatic mask to see the con artist that lived behind it.

I didn't notice the little white lies in the beginning. So subtle, so undetectable.

How could I? I completely and instantly opened my virtuous little heart, and with that came automatic trust; so, I'd always given Blake the benefit of the doubt that every word he spoke was the truth.

Besides, how harmless could a few tiny fibs be? After all, don't we all tell little white lies every now and then? That's what I kept telling myself as I walked down the slippery slope of blind faith.

Looking back, the number of downright outrageous lies was more than I could probably count on an abacus. Being so crafty in their story development to speak to my empathetic heart, the fabrications would grow a little bigger over time, all the while I was cluelessly unaware that I was being fed any kind of bullshit.

In fact, I was even able to convince myself over and over and over again that the oddest stories were plausible because the circumstances that surrounded them seemed "just so Blake!"

Obviously, Blake's tall tales served as an appetizer of where his deception would manifest in our lives until it became the main course. How had I never noticed the intricacy of them before?

Those very first excuses for breaking our dates— his dead cousin, brother-punched wall, and cancerous cat—and how he persuaded me to believe those memories were shamefully based on a relationship with another man were just a taste of what was to come: the slow descension into a web of madness that blinded me to any semblance of truth or reality.

There they were, right in front of me: these blatant red flags waving in surrender at every turn, and I chose to ignore them. Whenever I caught Blake in an outright untruth that he couldn't weasel out of, he apologized profusely with a false promise that it would never happen again. Like the con's mark I was crafted to be, I convinced myself that it would end; that he'd learn from his mistakes and stop.

But he never did. Worse—it grew to be much more than minor little dishonesties here and there.

They were purposeful and manipulative and creatively cunning. They consumed my life in every possible way. I had no idea how ignoring all these red flags would unfold into my worst nightmare.

His childhood abuse. His self-cured heroin addiction. His virginity rouse. His polycystic kidney disease and impending death. His two-month certification training in Milan. His mobster threat ploy for needing drug cash. Too many more to list— and now, this "joke" of an innocent co-worker note.

None of it was the truth, I realized in utter horror as I recounted each one in detail, and my mother unwearyingly listened to and agreed with my honest assessment of his duplicity. I was grateful she didn't follow up her gasps of shock with her opinion over so many seedy events she never knew about and kept her promise to let me continue my mental discovery.

"Go on, baby. I'm right here. What else, honey?"

It wasn't just his lies, though, I told her. There were so many layers weaved into this relationship of manipulation that I needed to expose them one by one before I could see the big picture unveiling itself in front of me. My analytical mind needed to follow a progression to even begin understanding the depths of my own naivete. I *had* to unveil these intricate layers.

Guilt was one such layer.

Guilt is one of those things that creeps up on you because it's instilled in you as a child; well, at least it was in my household. You know the guilt I'm talking about—like how *I* had to be the one to go to college to make my family proud instead of following my dreams.

Thankfully, Mom didn't take offense to anything I was saying in the heat of the moment. Steadfast in her attention and loyalty, she remained respectfully quiet as I confessed that guilt had always been the norm in my life.

Since it was so natural for me, how could I have ever known it had no place in a loving partnership?

And it's not like it started up right away. I was so enamored from the get-go that I displayed all the attention, love, and support Blake could ever require. Guilt had no need to rear its head during the early stages of our courtship. It only took shape as we became more comfortable with each other, and I exerted a desire for some boundaries when my studies and friendships started to be affected; when I desperately needed some solitude and time to process my own thoughts and emotions.

He needed to use guilt to keep me hooked then.

Like when that nightmare about his grandmother forced me to cut my trip to Julie's short.

And how he frequently played the abuse card to earn my sympathies—the more he could convince me of his horrible childhood, the more compassionate and invested I'd become in our relationship.

Whenever I would doubt our relationship, in came the big guns: threats of leaving me for Leyla; fears that I would cheat on him like Brittany did; reminders of my betrayal with Michael, including the unfinished taste of sex meant to teach me a lesson; and hints that I was lucky he chose me or took me back. They all worked. I felt guilty, and I reconsidered my commitment to him.

Throughout our marriage, the guilt would

continue to find its way into our fights.

He repeatedly complained about being a loser who didn't deserve me, so I eased his ego by downplaying my success and smarts so that he wouldn't feel emasculated by his failures.

I needed to turn myself inside out to make up for costing him his career because of that damn wedding.

On and on the guilt traps were laid with that oh-so-delicious and tempting cheese of promised love in return for assuaging his insecurities. Like an innocent little mouse, they worked like magic on me. He would present his case, and I would condemn myself—for being a nag, for being unsupportive, for working too much, for not understanding his pain, for kissing another man when we were on a break, for being financially stingy with his allowance, for anything possibly imperfect about me that affected the quality of *his* life.

I was the reason for so much of his suffering, and so I was deservedly punished for it. Guilt trip, party of one, had a permanent reservation at Blake's table.

"Sadly, none of this surprises me, baby. I've seen bits and pieces of this behavior, but never imagined it had gotten this bad. I wish I had seen or said something sooner," she said with regret.

"Let's be honest, Mom. It's not like I would have heard you or believed you," I admitted, finally seeing the great wall of defense I had built against anyone who had dared to challenge my faith in the most wonderful man in the entire universe.

"True. It was very difficult to talk to you rationally about anything concerning Blake," she opened up cautiously. "The first time I started doubting the validity of Blake's words was when he was diagnosed with that kidney disease, and then wasn't. But you loved him, and nothing I could say was going to remove those rose-colored glasses of yours," she said with a slight hint of her motherly disappointment, but I didn't mind this time. She was on target, and I needed to hear it.

"I wish I had more common sense," I half-laughed in exasperation.

"Believe me, me too," she joined in the jest. "I couldn't believe how trusting you were so many times, and oh, how I wanted to shake you by the shoulders when you really thought Milan was a training program, but you would have never listened. Especially not to me," she said quietly.

"I'm so sorry, Mom."

"There is nothing for you to apologize for, my sweet girl. I love you with all my heart and just want to be here for you to help you get through this. But I don't want to lose focus right now. As painful as it all is, I want you to get it all out in the open. I can feel so much more from you, Emily, that wants to come out. Keep going, honey. I won't say anything more."

I took a moment, closed my eyes, and inhaled deeply. It was time for me to bravely address our biggest marital controversy: his money messes. Where do I even begin with the intricate labyrinth of deceit that kept me bumping into dead ends while all paths led to my empty wallet?

In the beginning, when he was an up-and-coming travel photographer, the money flowed, and it brought us such amazing experiences. As a struggling college student who came from a family with little means, Blake had no issue laying out the cash to wine and dine me through these extravagant dates until I had found my own cushy job after graduation.

And yet, I never realized the disease that existed as early as the abundant days. Now, I can connect those dots and admit my suspicions.

Camille never asked him to use his address for her phone; he used her information to get a phone for *himself* after he defaulted on the last one. Uncle Blake wasn't the one who purposely mixed up their almost identical names for financial gains; that would be Blake's mastermind. None of his clients stiffed him on payments; he just took the money so I wouldn't question what he was spending it on.

His applications for cards in my name, cash advances, and frequent savings withdrawals were not for expensive gifts of love for me—well, maybe sometimes, but not as often as I was led to believe. Most of the time, I traced them back to traveling, electronic toys, and my personal favorite: random clothes, entertainment, and hotel stays. Well, perhaps now it makes sense if they were for his mistress—or God forbid, mistresses.

Lord, I couldn't go down that rabbit hole of thought just yet.

But sex was another red flag that waved its banner yet could never get my attention until now. Reflecting on our intimate relationship was the hardest reality pill to swallow, and not normally the most comfortable topic to talk to my mother about, but I felt at ease as I vulnerably disclosed the shame behind our closed doors.

I gave him my innocence, my complete trust, and

my vow that he would be the only man who would ever touch me in that way. It ended up being nothing but a joke to him.

As my first sexual partner, and allegedly being his, I figured we were both navigating the world of intimacy together and didn't really know much about going from missionary position to something more exciting. I accepted his bland approach to making love and assumed this was how it really was supposed to be—not all hot and heavy like in the movies. That was before that horrible night he revealed he wasn't a virgin after all when we met.

If he could hide that fact for over ten years and was potentially cheating on me right now, what else was yet to be revealed about his sexual secrets?

He would continuously tell me that he didn't like to touch himself; that he only liked it when I did. My mother was stupefied by that confession and gently informed me that she never met a single man who didn't like to pleasure himself at one time or another. I had thought that at one point as well, but Blake stayed firm to his declaration, so I never questioned his personal choice.

Then I remembered when I caught him with those magazines. When I first saw them and thought they were Blake's, I immediately feared that maybe I wasn't good in bed or beautiful enough for him anymore and that he needed inspiration to get off in secret, despite his masturbation protests.

I easily believed—*no, had to believe*—they were Joey's. The thought of Blake admiring big-breasted blonde women over me, when he'd swear that he was not that kind of a guy, would have shattered my soul at the time. Now I know better.

Then there was the refusal to go down on me; the failure to ever bring me to orgasm; the lack of interest in experimentation or even sex in general. It had become painfully clear that there was nothing I could do to entice him to make love to me anymore. By the time I tried to salvage our sex life, it had been too late. Years too late; maybe a whole relationship too late.

This layer of pain was too hard for me to continue analyzing in that moment. I'd have to circle back to it when I had more information about this assumed affair and the strength to dive in deeper. I had no doubt there were more bombshells waiting to blow my faith in my intimate connection with Blake apart.

"Take a deep breath, Em," I heard my mother say as I felt the lightheadedness of reality come on. It was too much to take. So much being unraveled at once, like a tornado blowing through every room of my emotional house. "Maybe you should rest for a bit. Do you want to lie down and call me back later?"

"No, I'm okay," I responded, bringing myself back to clarity with a few deep breaths. "If I don't get this all out now, Mom, I'm afraid I never will."

Acknowledging my need to continue this massive expulsion in the name of releasing my pent-up pain, my mother sympathetically pointed out yet another layer: how Blake worked to isolate me away from the people who cared for me the most.

He was so damn shrewd that I never even knew he was detaching me from the very people I needed to keep me safe from him. *They* became the liars, manipulators, and negative energies that were trying to take me down by belittling our love.

And so, I followed his lead as one by one, like his coveted bowling pins, they were knocked down and swept out of my life. Into the gutter, as I fell down a dark chasm of a relationship that brought me into total and complete human isolation.

Isolation from my friends. This was the easiest, and where it all started. First with Marcus, then with Jess. He was bloody brilliant at twisting those friendships into sordid abusers without me ever realizing what he was doing. Of course, once the "big guns" were out of the picture, less important friends fell away a lot easier.

It wasn't difficult, either, because as I was losing them, he was replacing my friends with his friends. I stepped into his world and left mine behind. I never noticed the difference, until he started pulling away from them, too. I was getting too close to Melinda, and she would tell me unusual stories, like Eddie's version of Blake's accident: Blake was drunk driving and smacked into that tree. Of course, Blake had an entirely different story, saying Eddie only meant that it *looked* as if he was drunk driving, but that someone else really did veer into him and force him off the road.

I bought it that time, but now I see how continued conversations like this with Melinda would have been way too easy for me to quickly piece together tangible warning signs from within his inner circle who knew the truth better than I did.

Holy shit—the Little League business. I paled at my newest eye-opener. No, he couldn't have—could he? Yes, he could absolutely have orchestrated

Eddie's downfall for his own benefit. Wow, now I was curious to look into that as one of many stories I felt compelled to investigate after I hung up the phone. Within me, I could feel a power rising up that I had not felt in a very long time.

"Em, I unfortunately think there's a lot more you will be discovering about your husband after this. This is so awful. Part of me wishes that we're both just making up our own stories to paint Blake as the bad guy, but I'm afraid this is the first time imagination sounds more like reality than what we have been told all this time," she suggested.

"Yeah, and all because I let him shelter me away into an emotional cage," I agreed bitterly. "It was so much more than destroying my friendships, Mom. He attacked so many good things in my life."

Like my beloved carcer. He attempted to isolate me from my job and the people who supported me there. Truth be told, since his dreams were going to shit, he had to remind me that I was an ordinary human being, as if my ego got too puffed up with importance. My intelligence made him feel smaller, so he would capitalize on shrinking my success to make us "more equal." However, he was clever enough not to encourage me to actually leave the company— that would mean losing my affluent income he had become accustomed to.

Instead, he just destroyed my trust in mankind; in people I thought of like family. It worked to a certain extent, like with Mindy, but I gratefully still maintained a good relationship with Alex and the rest of the family, even from far away. That was one thing he wasn't able to take away from me completely, though the lack of close proximately helped to maintain a safe enough emotional distance.

Isolation from my actual family was a whole different level. I have to hand it to Blake: his attempt to get me away from them was quite the genius coup. But I don't think it was part of his original intention—he was genuinely smitten with the notion that a family could love him. It behooved him to stay in their good graces. Until he wasn't.

Until my dad had a suspicion that Blake was smoking pot behind my back—Blake convinced me he must have been on drugs himself when he claimed that, and soon thereafter, my father and I were estranged.

Until my cousin Julie planted her keen observations and narcissistic-spotting experience into my curious head, and he had to make sure my mother got angry enough to denounce her niece.

Until my sister was getting too close to his business colleagues and he had to ban her from accompanying him on conventions.

It now made me wonder: what did Kerry know?

Then there was Mom, who kept questioning his unusual whereabouts. As a wife of an alcoholic, she could read the signs of lies and manipulation, and she was beginning to witness them in action. I acknowledged how she'd say some things to me to get me to see an inconsistency, but I'd tell her she was being too controlling—the keyword Blake brainwashed me with. If he didn't move me away from her, I might've started giving credence to her curiosities.

She unconditionally accepted my apology again

and reiterated her promise that she was going to help me get through this—that everyone I loved would help me through this terrible ordeal. I had a bigger support system waiting for me than I ever realized.

But I wasn't done analyzing the full extent of my seclusion. There was the big move to North Carolina that was the coup d'état. Now that I was physically away from my friends and family—really anyone who could witness his erratic, withdrawn behavior, frequent trips away, overly long errands, and ultimately, overnight training sessions—the work to dismantle the remainder of who I was began.

Once I lost who I was completely, the final phase of isolation was for me to lose him. Now that I was dependent on Blake and Blake alone, I was left to his mercy. He was the only person I could possibly turn to. No family, friends, or co-workers were within my physical sphere.

My God, the lengths he had gone to just to keep me from figuring it all out.

But there was one more aspect to his lifelong deception that I had to confront: his games and how he fucked with my mind in so many ways.

The push and pull of me chasing him for a date, him running away, and then finally "letting me" catch him. How he conveniently omitted the fact that he had sex before we got together yet belittled me for having the audacity to give blowjobs to two boys in a backseat once. Telling me I was the most beautiful woman in the world in the afterglow and then making a comment about my widening hips as I got dressed.

The intensity was kicked up a notch when we broke up, and he love-bombed me with poetry and gifts one moment then subjected me to humiliation in front of his friends the next. In between a sexually domineered rejection as payback for kissing Michael, the falsification of his kidney disease to trick me into going back to him, and this most recent denial about a suggestive Santa note, there were countless examples of mindfucks.

How I was at fault for ruining his career. How I was just a number to the company I worked for. How my mother tried to manipulate our lives.

I could go on and on about the different ways in which Blake twisted me to be whatever character he needed for his current story. Only, this wasn't some romantic, extravagant photo shoot intended to bring out the best in me; it was to set me up as the villain to cover for his heinous behavior.

The worst part about all of this? I thought I knew Blake better than I knew myself. Turns out, I didn't really know either of us at all.

After hours of rehashing my history with my patient, compassionate, supportive mother, I sunk to the floor like the Raggedy Ann doll that once consoled me as a toddler, emotionally spent. My mother, helpless to hold me physically, gave me the emotional courage I needed, nonetheless. It was the one time I finally gave in and allowed her to take the control that I no longer had, the wisdom that alluded me, and the strength I couldn't find.

She pushed me to not back down now—to let myself find out the truth once and for all and stop living in a world of denial. But I already knew the truth, without any more doubts.

Blake was fucking cheating on me.

And that was just the tip of the manipulation iceberg.

***

When I finally found the will to hang up the phone and face the actuality of my situation alone, I stood in front of my bathroom mirror and was stunned to see the woman looking back at me. When was the last time I got a flattering haircut? Or applied makeup, or put earrings through my pierced ears? My eyes were no longer a shade of dark chocolate; they were gobs of lifeless mud. My clothes looked like they could have belonged in my great-grandmother's closet, and I had no recognition of the fashionable girl I used to be.

I lost my sense of style. I lost my sparkle. I lost my *self*.

No wonder I was no longer desirable. I couldn't even bear to look at my own reflection. The tears started to trickle down my reddened, un-moisturized complexion as I stared this disgusting, weak creature down with hatred. Not even a husband should have to be forced to love what I had become, I cried to myself.

Alone in a state with no family or friends—and a philandering husband—I was left with the enormity of my grief.

But then the tears eventually stopped. I looked back up at the tired, haggard girl and surprisingly felt this enormous sense of pity and compassion for her. For all she had been through. For all the lies she told herself, all the guilt she endured, and all the blame she wrongly took on. In that very moment, I realized that I could choose to let this break me, or I could fight for my life back.

The real Emily Grace Davidson was in there somewhere, and she was resilient as all hell. I just had to remember that.

Grief and sadness rapidly transformed into anger and awareness.

I was not going to be defeated.

After all, I did have another ten hours before Blake would return home from "work," and that was more than ample time for me to put on my big girl pants and wake the fuck up to my reality.

Blake was fucking cheating on me, I repeated to myself to anchor in that devastating fact.

But this time, I was not going to roll over and heel like the obedient little puppy I was trained to be.

Now that my eyes were open, I called my family, friends, co-workers—almost anyone who knew him but who I could trust not to tip him off to my inquiries. I needed to talk to the ones who for years had tried to give me subtle—and not-so-subtle—warnings about his behavior. Like a mad reporter with a deadline, I just had to keep filling in the missing pieces of ten years of blind deception.

They finally were free to share the concerns they had about his stories and my blatant disregard of the truth. Alarms my closest friends tiptoed around when I confided some of our private problems. Things I would have never believed in a million years he was doing not only behind my back—*but right in front of my face.* Some that I had come to realize or suspect on my marathon call with my mom, and others that I had yet to probe deeper into.

How did I not see that he still had a drug problem and was high on painkillers or other substances all the time?

How did I not realize that when he went out to get dinner and came back two hours later, he was busy having dessert with a woman that wasn't his wife?

How did I not realize that he used Kerry's "promiscuity" at his conventions as a reason to remove her from the equation, because she almost caught him in the act of cheating himself?

How did I not piece together that he had ulterior motives for being away in Milan for two months and didn't have an address or come back with the certification he promised?

How did I not just know from working in business myself that overnight training was not a real thing?

How could I forgive him over and over for stealing my financial identity and almost losing everything I had built?

How could so many clients cheat him out of money and then blacklist him from future job opportunities because of one wedding?

How could he be on a kidney transplant list one day and have only stones the next?

How could I think it was okay to have sex only once a year and believe he was asexual instead of the sex addict he really might be?

How did I not consider that after dropping a bomb on me one night that he wasn't a virgin when we got married that there might have been many, many others besides me?

How could I believe those porn magazines and bags of drugs in his own home were conveniently not his?

Didn't I think it was odd how he'd stay up all night on the computer instead of going to bed with me?

Where did I think all the money that disappeared was going to?

Here's a hint, Emily: drugs and women.

When all was said and done, when all the layers of deceit were pieced together, that was what the big picture came down to. I was funding Blake's every addiction and pleasure while he bled my very soul dry.

13. BUSTED

Those hours between calling loved ones and waiting for Blake to return home were excruciatingly exhausting. My brain was overloaded with information and emotion. I didn't have much time left to come up with a plan of action, but I knew I needed to pull myself together first.

So, my mind did what it always does in an emotional situation—think, analyze, piece together, and then let the feelings have their moment. Yes, logic first. I already wept intensely, and no doubt would weep some more. But now was the time to use my God-given intellect to think my way out of hell.

I was more desperate for answers than understanding. When? Where? How? Who? Why? I was determined to get to the bottom of Blake's ultimate duplicity.

Little by little, it all started to make sense—and the more I searched, the more I found.

Receipts. Addresses. Names. Proof.

It was so easy for him to hide his affair from me because I wasn't tech-savvy during those early phases of social media and the flip phone. I barely texted on my archaic cell, and I wasn't on the computer except for work, so he was able to carry on with his infidelity knowing that I would never, ever catch on.

Knowing that I wouldn't think to look at his phone messages. Knowing that I didn't make it a habit of conducting computer history searches. Knowing that I would believe every word about overnight training sessions for as long as he told the story.

Forgetting that once I figured something out, I was a goddamn genius.

And *that* gave me my advantage. Well, that, and the illusion of continued gullibility, because what I needed to do would take more than ten hours, and I was not going to give him any inkling that I was on to him until I had every last piece of information I could get my hands on.

Operation Bust Blake was set in motion.

I rallied my troops—the ones I had pushed away to be consumed by Blake under the guise of saving our marriage. I was so unbelievably grateful for the instant forgiveness and support I received from family and friends, and the allies who helped me gather my intel. I had no idea how truly loved I was by the people in my life until that moment when my whole world came crashing down.

All hands were on deck to stop the bastard and help me take my life back.

Blake did make it kind of easy on us when I found a business card in his pile of unwashed pants with a woman's name on it matching the first name signed on a much longer love—or rather, fuck me—letter I found in the trunk when he was in the shower one morning. Bingo!

Within an hour of that find, my trustworthy bestie confirmed they worked together, found out where she went to college, and even obtained her campus address. He wasn't lying about her being young at least! I won't even ask how Kayla came to learn this Bianca girl was actually a foreign exchange student from Milan. More lightbulbs illuminated. I had to file that one away for another day, but I vowed to dive into that ocean of deception later. *Focus, Em. Where are we at?*

Oh, yes. Step one achieved: identity of the mistress revealed.

Step two involved finding more proof of their indiscretion—as if the love notes weren't enough. I tried to stay strong as I read her recounts of their lovemaking in great detail—details of which I had never experienced with Blake in the bedroom in all our years together.

A knife twisted in my gut as I read how he tied her up to the bed and licked her until she exploded. How she had taken my husband's penis into her mouth and sucked him off before riding him until dawn. How they fucked in the steamy shower with suds dripping down their bodies and how he bit her nipples while he drove hard into her until she came multiple times in rapid succession. Reading that transported me to a twilight zone; this couldn't possibly be the Blake Denton I knew that she was practically creaming about on paper.

My Blake Denton was vanilla, liked only missionary positions, and wouldn't dare use handcuffs or put his tongue in a vagina. And yet, I couldn't erase the tainted images of Blake being like one of those erotic porn stars performing all kinds of sexual fantasies on a young, Italian, college girl. The thought of what he was capable of—what pleasure he denied me for over ten years—swirled into endless pools of belly bile, anger, and resentment.

Asexual, my ass.

So many times I wanted to break down and punch him in his scheming face whenever he smoothly lied about working late or attending another overnight training, but I found the courage to resist, reminding myself that acting in stealth mode right now would be the best course of action for me to take. I needed to pace myself until the time was right. Until then, I dutifully continued to make him dinner, do his laundry, and sleep beside him, even knowing he was touching himself while texting her. I somehow forced myself to play the convincing role of stupid, unsuspecting wife.

Honestly, I don't know where my fortitude came from—it was militant and focused, and for that, I was grateful. It helped to know that I had so many on standby to call after he left the house, giving me that protected space to completely break down and regain my composure before he returned to live our fake married life.

By this time, I gathered that he was too much of a coward to end our marriage himself and that these love letters, mysterious two-person dinner receipts, and other hints of betrayal were left way too exposed, where he hoped I would eventually find them on purpose. Once my naiveté was shattered, I was onto his every single move and manipulation and could predict his lies before he told them. He just didn't know that I had discovered them yet.

I learned quickly how to become tech-savvy and uncovered his browser history, which led me to a popular social media site where he secretly had an account and interacted with this Bianca girl publicly. *Publicly,* for anyone to see! How daft I must have been that he was able to be so evident and open about it, secure that I'd never have a clue.

I couldn't help but stalk her profile now that I had a picture to put with the name. *She wasn't all that pretty with that weird misshapen nose of hers,* I snarked to myself, but I guess being young and thin with big breasts was all he needed to be satisfied. I obsessively scrolled through her photos, memorizing every feature of the hussy homewrecker who warmed my husband's bed. Her face fueled me to keep going until I was ready for the eventual confrontation.

My digging also unearthed the innumerable nights he spent watching hardcore porn. I certainly found a new source of sexual education, that was for sure.

Being as though I had always squelched my own eccentric fantasies, I found myself utterly aroused and captivated as I glimpsed through these different porn search histories. But I couldn't believe that the boring-in-bed man I was married to for so long secretly worshipped what most of his Catholic-bred society would consider forms of sexual deviancy. Grandma Wilma would be rolling over in her grave if she knew what her darling *knuddelbär* was really like.

"I hope that you will always look inside to see his heart, even when he's not very good at showing it."

I cringed when I thought of an old promise asked of a genuinely kind woman. Sorry, Grandma Wilma. Not this time. Your darling grandson must have traded his heart for a virile penis because I can't find even a drop of loving blood left within him anymore.

I fully relieved myself of my obligation to seek out the man we once both loved.

None of the continued evidence I found of his con artistry phased me any longer. Perhaps I was too numb to have any emotions or to process how deeply disturbing this all was. If I did, I would fall apart at the seams. No, I had to operate on a business-like autopilot, spending my hours researching, compiling, and analyzing as if I were getting ready for a major client presentation.

I didn't have time to break down or think about how my insides were destroyed or how this betrayal was the death of life as I knew it. I needed to stay focused on the task at hand: exposing every last detail of his sordid affair so that for once, I actually had tangible proof of his unfathomable deception.

My determination paid off, and I struck gold: I found the instant messaging system they used, including the away messages they left for each other.

I created my own private, discreet accounts so I could monitor their ongoing communications—I knew when they were together and where they would be at all times. Idiots. Print screen and document. This was too easy.

He had no idea I was on to him and his games— yet. Is this what it felt like to play someone who lived in the dark? No wonder he got off on the rush of my stupidity for so long. I shamefully enjoyed the twisted role reversal, laughing as the ignorant twit thought he was getting away with his manipulations.

The puppet master had now become the puppet, and this sick sense of power was sometimes the only thing that kept me from completely drowning in the despair that haunted my every waking moment.

It drove me to maddening research, and I'd squeal with glee every time I found another piece of damning information. I was able to order a copy of detailed phone bills that itemized the number of texts sent back and forth with not only Bianca's number—but a history of different repeated numbers in a similar pattern, dating back quite a few years. That was a tough pill to swallow—the idea that there could have been other women before her—but that possibility was something I needed to shelve for later.

One betrayal at a time was all I could digest. At the end of all this, I was sure to have an ulcer.

I then found his old phone—the one he swore he lost and the reason I had to buy him a newly-upgraded one a few weeks ago—hidden in a sock underneath his dresser. The raunchy texts were still intact, as were the naked photos that brutally burned into my consciousness. I copied those as well for my ever-growing detective file, which I smartly gathered and left in a new bank deposit box I decided to rent.

Oh yes, I had risen above his level. Hidden socks weren't secure enough for *my* secret operation.

I used my own rookie gumshoe skills to download a copy of his credit report, which I could legally do as his wife, just as he used my credit for his gain. Although it shouldn't have shocked me, I found that one of his listed residences was a rental in Milan during the two months he was away! Circling back to the fact that Bianca was originally from Milan, the mathematician in me finally started to add it all up. And all this time, I thought the campus he had to stay on for the photography program didn't have a mailing address.

Because there was no fucking campus. And there was no special training program.

Fuck, me. The lengths to which I was easily bamboozled still left me both flabbergasted and impressed. I was the perfect target for deception, and it frightened me to think about how trusting I had been for so many years. From the first moment we met, he primed me, intentionally or not, to be his greatest victim.

I shook my head, then reaffirmed to myself that I was no longer that sucker. And I was ready to prove it. With all my documented information in place and friends and family willing to travel to North Carolina to help me tail him, I was finally ready for step three: the confrontation that would end the game forever.

No longer was he going to pass "Go" and collect $200 each time from my accounts—or my heart.

Today would be Blake's day of reckoning.

But being the saccharinely nostalgic person that I am, I still ached for one more moment with him. Part of me still wished I could catch a glimpse of that man I loved so much, who I thought loved me to the ends of the Earth. I wanted him to show me that I was crazy; that I was wrong; that everything I had found out was a lie and not our whole life together.

It was a fool's hope, I know. As hardened as I let myself become over those last few weeks, I couldn't fully accept that Blake was this sociopathic liar without a heart. He had to love me even a little, didn't he?

And so, on that decisive day, I needed to say goodbye to my marriage in my own backward way, even though I knew I wouldn't get the final exchange of love I was yearning for. He would never be the man he tricked me into believing he was, yet I needed a final tender memory before I detonated the bomb. Before I finally allowed myself to dismiss logic and let myself *feel*.

It was a Thursday night—his regular night for "overnight training"—and so I begged him to please go into work late that day so we could spend some quality time together. He begrudgingly relented, allowing me a meager two hours of his undisturbed time. He even agreed to put his phone away.

I thought it was what I wanted, to be held by the love of my life for one last blissful moment, but as I laid in his arms on our favorite couch, watching a movie that once meant so much to us, I held back both the tears and the puke that wanted to surface. I couldn't wait for the movie to end. I no longer wanted to touch or be touched by this insidious man. This shell of a great love. This traitor of life.

As I looked into his eyes one last time, I found the ultimate strength to lean in and give him one final kiss on the lips. I held my gaze, miraculously forbidding my eyes to even water or give me away.

"Goodbye, Blake."

"Okay..." he paused, taken aback by my sudden romantic gesture and soft-spoken words. But they fell on deaf ears. I had lost him a long time ago, and I knew right then and there: no amount of love I had to give was ever going to save us, even if I wanted to overlook everything and give it another try. To take him back just one more time. This time, there was no doubt it was over. "I have to go, I'm late. See you tomorrow."

I smiled bravely as I closed the door behind him and gave the saddened signal to my friends to put our plan into action. It was time for me to stop the intrigues and face the hardened certainty of my future.

A future without Blake Denton.

He was oblivious to the fact that Kayla and Linda followed him to the nearest grocery store, where they saw him go inside with a garbage bag and come out with a different, more casual outfit on, tossing the bag back into his trunk. He drove off down a few main roads, leading them to his work office.

Then, predictably, he met this young, sexily-dressed, busty, exotic, jet black-haired girl outside of the building—matching the picture of Bianca I gave them—and she got into his car. You can guess what their next destination was: a cheap, local hotel that, undoubtedly, would be charged to one of my credit cards used for his "training expenses."

An hour later, the lovers emerged holding hands and sneaking cheek kisses, unaware that Kayla and Linda were snapping a few pictures of proof on their phones as they unabashedly waited by their car which was parked only two spots away from his.

Blake was finally busted.

But instead of being a man and owning up to his misdeeds, he tried to lie his way out of it. And why wouldn't he? I had given him permission to lie to me for years, and it always worked. *It always worked.*

Not this time. Once I was awake, I was *awake.* I'd never be duped again.

He refused to acknowledge my friends, instead

engaging them in a reckless car chase and eventually losing them when he blew through a red light. Thankfully, no one was hurt, and they made their way back to my house to give me a full, gut-wrenching report of what I wished was a nightmare I could wake up from. They didn't need to tail him any longer—I heard enough.

There was no more living in denial. It didn't get any more real or black and white than this. Now, all I could do was nervously wait for the downfall.

About an hour later came the phone call that I was dreading.

"What's going on, Emily?"

"What do you mean, Blake?" I asked innocently.

"What are Kayla and Linda doing in North Carolina?"

"I don't know what you are talking about."

"Don't play dumb with me. Why were your friends following me?"

"I have a better question, Blake. Who is Bianca Esposito?"

"What?"

"Did I stutter?"

"What kind of game are you playing?"

"I'm not the one playing the game, Blake. You are. And it's over."

"Whatever, Em. I have to get to work. I don't have time for this."

"Oh shut it, asshole. You're not going to work. I know all about your affair with Bianca. I know she works with you. I know she goes to Greensboro. I know she is from Milan and that you used to live there with her for those two months. I've seen your love letters, texts, and online love messages. Don't even try to deny it."

"You are out of your mind. Something is wrong with you. She is just some co-worker that was bringing me dinner before my training tonight since I forgot to pack one. We'll talk about this when I get home tomorrow. If I'm late, you'll be putting another job of mine in jeopardy. Is that what you want?"

"Don't bother coming home. I told you that cheating was the only thing that would break up our marriage. Congratulations, you broke it. We're done."

"You're fucking crazy. I'm not cheating on you. That's your story. It's not mine."

"Well, I'm rewriting this damn story. And it doesn't end with our happily ever after. Goodbye, Blake."

I hung up before he could utter another rebuttal or before I lost my strength. Knowing I was home safe with my girlfriends, I hurled into a rush of sobs that needed to be released now that I exposed myself—now that I saw firsthand how easily he lied to me; how skillfully and effortlessly he twisted a situation. I painfully winced at the thought of myself buying these manipulations time after time. The years of treachery unfolded layer after layer as I cried for hours.

He had done it—Blake had repaid me for breaking his heart so long ago. It took a decade, but he checkmated me so hard that I didn't know what to do next.

I knew the absolute, undeniable truth now. I knew he was having an affair. I knew I would not stay in this marriage. I knew I had to get out. I knew I would never look back. I couldn't turn a blind eye, forgive, and ignorantly go on with our defective life any longer. This was it for me. I just didn't know how I would actually do it; how I would finally walk away.

Where do I go from here?

Gratefully, Kayla, Linda, Kerry, and my mom rallied around like superheroes and gave me the strength and wisdom I needed to lawyer up, quickly shut down or transfer my money accounts, find a real estate agent, and make a plan for moving myself back to my loved ones in New Jersey.

No longer would I be charmed by Blake. No longer would I ever believe a lie. No longer would he guilt me into staying or feeling sorry for him as if I were the one who did something wrong. No longer would he touch my hard-earned money to spend on his mistresses. No longer would he use sex as a weapon to degrade me. No longer would I be kept away from my loving support system of family and friends. No longer would he fuck with my mind and manipulate the situation to make it all my fault.

By the time I had a plan together—all while he continued his evening uninterrupted with Miss Bianca—I was ready to face the fallout.

True to his word for once, he showed up at home the next day, ready to talk. He stuck to his tale that he *really was* in overnight training and that Bianca was just some co-worker; nothing was going on between them.

Trust destroyed forever, I didn't believe a single word he said, and he was beginning to see that. He buckled in fear that I was not backing down, remembering the existence of a powerfully strong side to me that he had not seen in a very long time.

Blake paled as he saw that Emily rise up from the ashes, fortified in her decision to break free from him.

And so, to further the game, he had to up the ante to get me to fracture my sense of resilience.

Only a really good abuser can master the art of the mindfuck—assaulting a person's thought process, belief system, and foundation of trust through the clever manipulation of words. I had come to quickly learn that Blake was one of the best. There wasn't a single moment in our relationship that I wasn't mindfucked by Blake Denton, and he was ready to double down.

Now that he knew—and she knew—that I was on to them and watching them online, Bianca would purposefully leave away messages on her profiles that taunted me. Or he'd purposefully leave his phone out on the counter during his shower, knowing I couldn't resist looking at it and seeing her suggestive incoming texts, perfectly timed.

Admittedly, I was a glutton for emotional punishment by subjecting myself to this mental torture, but I couldn't help it. Whatever the crazy reason was for waiting to see what they'd say next was beyond my own rational comprehension, and something I would later work out in therapy.

Of all the times he played games with my head, these blatant mindfucks of his "non-affair" were the most difficult to bear. Because before now, I was an oblivious victim without awareness. I didn't know what he was doing. I didn't know it was gaslighting. I didn't see the cruelty, per se.

I felt it. I allowed it. I repressed it. But I never

accepted it or saw it for what it was. I kept remembering the romantic man who danced with me in the middle of an exclusive restaurant and staged a photo shoot to convince me of my own beauty. I excused all his trespasses because *my* Blake was that man who adored me to the point of obsession. No one would ever love me the way he did, he repeated ad nauseum until I was brainwashed into believing that I'd never be lovable enough for anyone else.

Now, experiencing his mockery of me at face value brought the pain of betrayal to a whole new level. And yet, I let the words they exchanged keep hammering into my wounded heart.

Sometimes it would empower me to take action—like when I saw the away message of where they would be on Valentine's Day. He swore Bianca's post was about someone else, stating that he *really was* going to get a drink with a guy friend because he was so devastated that I insisted on getting a divorce.

"Out with my babe at our fave restaurant, Luigi's. I'm so in love."

I welcomed him back home that evening with paperwork confirming I put our perfect, custom-built North Carolina house up for sale.

Sometimes the words they exchanged would slaughter the very last essence of my being with their sexual overtones and outright flaunting of their affair.

"FMLYHM, baby. Are you here yet?"

FMLYHM. An anagram for *Fuck Me Like You Hate Me*, which I figured out easily enough because I liked that song from Seether, too. I cried myself to sleep knowing he was touching someone else in a way he never wanted to touch me.

Sometimes these words were directed right at me after Blake and I would have another fight about co-existing temporarily in the same house.

"So much drama. Like, get over yourself, loser."

I wanted so badly to respond to her, but I wouldn't give them the satisfaction of affirming that I monitored them still. Hard as it was, I tried to preserve some level of dignity.

Sometimes it would make me roll my eyes, both at him and at myself, for previously falling for these kinds of games, and then I'd finally have the courage to call him out right on the spot. Like when he ridiculously claimed he wanted us to work on our marriage. That one wasn't posted; I had the pleasure of that mindfuck presented in person.

"You seem to think that you are the only one who can make decisions for us. What about what I want? What if I don't want a divorce?"

"Okay. Let's say for shits and giggles that you didn't cheat on me and you actually did have a say. What would you want, Blake?"

"Well, I think we should wait a year before rushing into this. We both need help. I think we should get individual therapy and couples therapy, and if that doesn't work out, then we can discuss divorce. But I'd like to try to fix this instead of just give up."

"Oh, I see. So, you want us to stay together so you can still have access to my money and take your girlfriend out on expensive dates while we 'work on ourselves?' Yeah, that's not happening, Blake. Nice try, though."

"I keep telling you, I didn't sleep with her. I can't

believe you don't even want to try to make this work. Didn't I mean anything to you, Emily?"

"Of course, you did. But that ended the moment you inserted your penis into another woman. I told you that would be the only thing to make me leave you. I'm not coming back this time. I'm never going to forgive and forget this for as long as I live."

"I always told you I wasn't good enough for you. Now maybe you'll believe me."

"You are right about that, Blake. You've finally said the one thing that I can actually believe."

"But no one will ever love you the way I do," he half pleaded, half threatened with those words that used to actually mean something to me.

"God, I hope not," was my final response before I walked away toward my dignity.

***

Bianca and Blake's verbally vindictive torment lasted indefinitely over a few months, until the day came that one of their ill-timed taunts backfired on them. That was the day my lawyer called to say the divorce papers were ready. I will never forget this deep pull from within me—an angelic voice that urgently whispered, "Go. If you do not go now, this will never end, and you will regret it."

I received that sign clear as day and trusted it. Obeying my intuition, I knew I needed to act quickly. I called a taxi to pick up the papers and then headed over to their "fave restaurant"—which, thanks to her previous childish taunts, I knew exactly where to locate them: Luigi's.

Lo and behold, I found them just in time, walking out toward their separate cars. While she scurried away to her vehicle, I approached Blake calmly, asking him to simply sign the papers right then and there. He refused, so I went up to Bianca's car window and knocked on it like the newly empowered bitch-ex-wife-to-be I was.

"Excuse me, Bianca?" I asked sweetly, showing her no animosity whatsoever. "Could you please explain to me if he loves you so much, why he won't just sign these divorce papers? I don't want him anymore. I'm not contesting a divorce. He's all yours. Can you please tell him not to drag this out and just sign the damn things, and then he can be free to be with you? Thanks so much." And quietly, I walked away with papers in hand and a huge smirk on my face.

My turn for checkmate.

One hour later, he showed up at the house and signed the documents, knowing that if he didn't, his little girlfriend was going to give him one hell of a fight, and so was I.

That day changed my life forever. Had I not acted on that divinely guided impulse, it could have been drawn out into one nasty financial fight. But I had one hell of a smart lawyer and an even smarter internal navigation system that, now activated, saved me from any more manipulation. I was finally safe.

I had no choice but to play by his rules in the end; it's the only way I knew how to win when the tables were turned. And by win, I mean: it's how I found my way out of the world of abuse once and for all.

The only thing left to do was to pick up the pieces of my shattered life and move on—without Blake.

14. REFLECTION

After digesting the enormity of my abusive relationship, I came to realize there were many elements that made up a great con: charm, lies, guilt, money mysteries, misuse of sex or power, isolation, and mindfucks. Blake used every one of these ingredients in his master recipe of narcissistic control.

The worst part? He was so subtle, I never even saw it coming.

Finally empowered with clear hindsight, I could literally see, hear, and feel every single deception that played out over the entirety of our relationship—the depths to which the lies spread and grew rampant like black mold throughout my soul.

They say black mold can only grow in an environment of darkness and constant moisture; my endless tears and depression turned me into the perfect petri dish for Blake's manipulation experiment.

You've witnessed my love for him blossom and die, you've read snippets of experiences in which our relationship was unhealthy, and you viewed this all through my lenses of legitimate denial—the ones I lived with for too many years.

Looking back, I now understand how people could judge me as I naively lived through this experience. How could such a smart girl be so dumb? I've wondered the same thing. I still do. Sadly, it had very little to do with smarts and more to do with hearts, and the trauma they endure and repress.

Now, in my hour of freedom and self-reflection, it's time that I face all that I repressed. All that I ignored. All that I subjected myself to as I took the path of transformation into a lifeless, abused victim of emotional distress. And all that I uncovered once I stepped back to truly see the man behind the curtain.

It was his irresistible charm that allowed him to tell me so many believable and far-fetched stories to explain away the strangest discrepancies and misunderstandings. It was indeed one of his greatest gifts that made him a master of manipulation. Yes, Blake had charm in spades—spades that were sharp and ultimately cut so deeply sometimes, I wondered if the scars they sliced would ever heal.

Luckily, once I knew how to unravel the carefully woven web of dishonesty, I was able to uncover the many layers of successful strategies that had trapped me into his sticky tarp without warning. It took me quite a while and a windfall of epiphanies, but eventually, I did it. I got out of my emotionally abusive relationship, and I never looked back.

***

I am woman enough to admit that there are two sides to every story, and every human being holds a responsibility to own his or her part in the failure of any relationship. I certainly was no saint and am acutely aware of my shortcomings and the pain and heartache I projected onto Blake during our ten-plus years together.

I own that my fears of commitment and abandonment, spurred by deep-rooted "daddy issues," kept Blake at a distance and ultimately broke his heart on quite a few occasions.

I own that I learned and exhibited a controlling nature with high expectations of perfection that were difficult to live with.

I own that I was too serious and uptight for my own good and that I acted more like a parent and less like a spouse when we faced challenging times.

I own that I told my share of lies, the biggest one being kissing and not telling, which broke a foundation of trust that was not easily repaired.

I own that I was a workaholic. That I acted better than him sometimes because of my professional status. That I mirrored our families' condescension of his lack of willingness to gain employment.

I own that in ignoring my internal warning signals and multiple red flags, I enabled a state of denial for both of us to live in, staying in a marriage in which the love had died a long time ago.

For all of the above, I was truly remorseful and actually shared that with Blake in a post-divorce letter, which remains unanswered. I felt it was only right for me to admit that I played a role in our unhappily ever after as part of the closure process.

But unlike my darling ex-husband, here is what I did not do:

I did not make up extravagant stories to win him back just for cruel revenge.

I did not use guilt to make him want to love me

or stay with me.

I did not use sex as a weapon; I was not an adulterer, nor did I ever deny him access to my willing body.

I did not fuck around with money; instead, I repeatedly saved his troubled ass time and time again.

I did not isolate him from his family and friends—in fact, I brought him closer to his parents and tried to help him heal those wounds of the past while encouraging him to go out with friends more.

I did not gaslight him. Even in my doubtful days, I was as honest as I could be about my feelings, and any dishonesty was not delivered with the intention of harming, manipulating, or controlling the emotions of another human being.

Maybe I didn't handle every situation correctly, but never once did I play a sick game with his heart.

Did I have flaws? Clearly. Did I offer up some verbal attacks of my own and commit some pretty hurtful actions? Yes. Was I a shitty wife? Some days I can argue yes, and other days an emphatic no.

Here's the core difference: I didn't blame *Blake* for my kissing another man. I didn't blame *him* for my temper tantrum about getting passed over for a promotion. I didn't make him feel like *he* was at fault for my own undesirable behaviors or failures.

In fact, I owned my weaknesses so much that I allowed myself to take the blame over and over for Blake's behavior as if *I* were the one who deserved to be punished.

Conversely, Blake turned all my flaws against me as the reason for *his* behaviors. I was the cause, and he was the effect. And that's where his narcissistic disease distorted the problem.

"A man doesn't cheat on his wife unless she gives him a reason to."

That was his mother's response to our impending divorce and his affair. I realized where he learned his callous tendencies from the moment the words flew viciously out of her tiny, dry puckered lips. That was the final source of battering that I was willing to take before I realized that I was so very wrong in accepting the blame for countless years of emotional abuse.

I repeat: I will accept responsibility for my actions. However, I will no longer believe that anything I did or did not do was a legitimate justification for being on the receiving end of Blake's distorted emotional beatings.

I will not accept blame for being so gullible that I was the perfect target for lies and manipulation.

I will not accept blame for willingly wanting to please my husband in the name of guilt.

I will not accept blame for being stolen from just because my hard work provided me with the means for financial stability.

I will not accept blame for repeatedly being sexually rejected and humiliated because of my innocence and inexperience.

I will not accept blame for trusting a man I loved with my heart, mind, and soul in such a way that I believed he was protecting me from people who did not have my best interests at heart, like he so often claimed.

I will not accept blame for breaking his heart as the reason for the malicious mental, emotional, and psychological games that ensued once he won me back.

I *will* accept that I was a victim, but that I have the power to choose to change that narrative and become a survivor.

Say what you want about my behavior, my mistakes, my personality flaws—I did not deserve the abuse that was served up cold to me from the moment he knew he had me in his web.

There is not a human being on this Earth who could ever do anything to warrant such a blatant violation of love, trust, and faith. Not even Blake. And certainly not *me*.

EPILOGUE: FREEDOM

*"I am not what happened to me.
I am what I choose to become."* — CG Jung

The path to freedom was not an easy one.

There were no apologies—just continued accusations of my insanity and delusion as if *I* were the one destroying the vows we made before God in the name of for better or for worse.

There were no retributions—just continued attempts to access my money until a finalized divorce turned those attempts from united marital access to criminal activity; a threat he finally realized I could *and would* make good on.

There was no remorse—just continued denials of an affair until he impregnated his mistress and married her within six months of our divorce.

There were, however, new details that continued to unravel as the divorce moved forward.

Turns out, there were many other women he had sex with over the course of our entire relationship, I came to discover. There had hypocritically been women during our break when I was away at college and kissed Michael—Leyla, at the very least. Women on his travel photography trips. Women at work.

More women than my heart could ever bear to learn. An ironic, undiscovered sex addiction when he

BEAT ME WITH YOUR WORDS

would only have sex with me once or twice a year. I finally knew that his detached marital connection had absolutely nothing to do with me and everything to do with an out-of-control erotic compulsion stemming from unhealed wounds.

Never having children with this man was the biggest blessing God could have given me.

The money mysteries also continued to reveal themselves. Sadly, I wasn't the only victim of his illicit money problems—nor was his uncle, sister, or any other family member he used for his financial maneuverings.

Right after the divorce, I happened to randomly run into Eddie's girlfriend-turned-wife, Melinda, at a local coffee shop, and we had quite an interesting conversation about the old days. It turned out she had reason to believe Blake was really the one behind the money theft. I nodded my head, unsurprised—knowing Blake much better now since the divorce, all signs pointed to his successful manipulation of his dear friends for his financial gain with Eddie merely being collateral damage.

He set Eddie up to take the fall for his money addiction. A man he claimed was his best friend. Although it saddened me to hear of this betrayal, a part of me felt a sense of relief that I wasn't his only casualty; that other good people were easily duped as well. That this was bigger than me; it was an actual sickness.

Oh, and that beautiful two-thousand-dollar emerald and diamond pendant he bought me as a wedding present out of love? When I went to a pawn shop to sell it for a security deposit on a new post-divorce apartment, the shop owner looked at me questioningly and said the "diamonds" were actually cubic zirconia, and the emerald was lab-created. It couldn't have been worth more than a few hundred bucks brand new.

All I could do at that point was laugh until my stomach hurt.

Although I knew in my heart that our relationship was over and I would never look back, I still yearned to see an inkling of the kindness and compassion that once made up the man I fell in love with. There had to be so much more to his heart than deceit. There had to be.

But there wasn't. The Blake Denton I knew was gone, and I couldn't save him.

So, I finally made the choice to save myself.

With my financial assets locked down and protected, I made the difficult decision to foreclose on the North Carolina house, as I was the only deed holder anyway, and moved back to New Jersey to be with my loved ones. Since Blake had no desire to take anything in the house other than his personal belongings, and he relinquished ownership as such in our papers, I sold our furniture for cash to secure the funds I needed for a fresh start.

Come hell or high water, I was going to claim my life back.

My rental home was the perfect space to begin a new life. I had a fantastic landlord who gave me carte blanche to paint and decorate however I wanted, reintroducing me to the world of creativity. I tapped into my inner seamstress to make my own curtains and bedding ensemble, and it was the first step toward remembering who I was.

The second was ditching the granny clothes and getting a fantastic wardrobe that complimented my newly svelte body. It was amazing how stress worked in my physical favor when I wasn't depressively binge eating. Makeup and jewelry returned to my life, and my hair was revitalized with highlights and a stylish cut. I was ready to rock my thirties.

Once I started to feel better about myself, I was able to focus on rebuilding my relationships. Not surprisingly, there were a lot of casualties over the years with Blake. Some are gone forever, like my childhood best friend, Jess, and my cousin, Julie. I will never be able to repair that damage—and I tried. I really did, but it was too late, and I mourn those relationships to this day.

Other connections I was gratefully able to mend, like the bonds with my family.

Even though my parents were still divorced, my path to reconciliation helped to bridge a previously delicate interaction between them and began to heal old wounds. My dad, who I found the courage to reach out to, had been through a rehab program and was showing signs of turning his life around, and we were all so proud of him. I forgave him, and he is now back in my life in a healthy way.

Mom found her calling by volunteering at nursing homes, giving her a sense of purpose and happiness. Kerry was thriving in the photography world where she met and became engaged to a wonderful man that we adored. Home was as it should be once again.

I made time for friends and found myself enjoying a wonderfully fulfilling social life—though I was gun-shy about meeting new men. For the time being, I was content with dancing, shopping, and movie nights with the girls. I didn't realize how much I missed the concept of friendship until they embraced me back into their lives.

My job—my wonderful work family—also welcomed me back with open arms, including the "no-longer-evil" Mindy. I was grateful for her acceptance of my apology with a promise to start over. Within six months of being back in the office, Alex promoted me to the position I had left behind when it was vacated by a flaky new hire. The most amazing part of the reconciliation at Parks was the realization that they never considered me "just a number"—I was as much an important part of their family and culture as I was the day I joined the team.

Turns out, I *am* someone special after all.

As I reconnected with so many people I loved, I realized that withdrawal was the worst thing I could have possibly done to myself. I pledged then and there, no matter what happened in my life, that I would never live in isolation again.

Love was a much more powerful support system than independence could ever be.

It was strange how once I no longer had Blake tapping into our resources, I had the financial abundance to manage my bills and still have enough to enjoy life comfortably. Money was no longer an issue for me. I was able to help my family, contribute to causes that touched my heart, and enjoy solo vacations to wherever I desired.

Knowing the indelible mark that Blake left on my psyche, I invested in years of therapy and soul healing to undo the damage. I confronted my childhood issues as well as worked through the whys, hows, and no mores of surviving emotional abuse at the hands of a narcissist. I learned what love was supposed to look like—and it started with how much I was willing to love and forgive myself. It was the only way to move forward.

And move forward I did. Since I had done such a kickass job at work and saved a hefty amount of money, I was able to take a leave of absence for a year to finally pursue my dreams of fashion and world traveling. I enrolled in the Paris College of Art, where I studied haute couture and technology—learning skills that took me way beyond my humble Barbie boudoir beginnings.

Paris was every bit as splendid as I remembered, and I journeyed straight to heaven when I participated in the famous Couture Fashion Week. As interns, we had the fortune of first dibs on some very exclusive designs that were set to become worldwide trends. I was destined to become the best-dressed economics major of all time.

I dined in the French cafés along Les Champs-Élysées while studying and spent my breaks touring long-awaited European hotspots. I explored the waters of Mallorca, the isles of Greece, the Olympic port of Barcelona, the biergartens of Germany, the ruins of Rome, and so much more.

I openly found peace when I went to Milan— thanking the beautiful city for birthing Bianca and sending her as the blessed catalyst to remove the toxic situation with Blake from my life. I no longer resented her, him, or my experience. I even found the compassion to pray for Bianca, hoping that the young girl didn't end up on the same abusive path I traveled with Blake. The ultimate "revenge" would be my happiness and freedom, and for that, I felt blessed. I'd let karma take care of the rest.

I returned home to New Jersey with my dream degree, deeper cultural wisdom, and the opportunity of a lifetime as a fashion stylist for an up-and-coming global conglomerate based in New York City. I was finally living my dream come true.

I even met a special man during my time in Paris—a man who taught me what love was truly supposed to be like. Dante is a kind gentleman who has restored my faith in love, trust, and partnership. It was not hard to believe in him or his love as his words, actions, and behaviors aligned with his overall values and character. No, there were no red flags where this generous lover was concerned. He was the man I finally deserved and very much worth the wait.

Only a few years after my fallout with Blake, I am able to look in the mirror with wonder at all I have accomplished and attracted into my life since releasing the chains and healing the scars: a master's degree in fashion; scoring a fancy job of my dreams; owning a beautiful home; spending quality time with family and friends; jet-setting to romantic destinations; and having a fantasy wedding on Waikiki Beach. Now, Dante and I are expecting our first child, and I couldn't be happier with the life I have made for myself.

But I couldn't have done it without Blake. I couldn't have risen so high if I hadn't fallen so low and confronted my own demons and self-sabotaging behaviors.

In a way, being emotionally abused was the greatest blessing of my life. It taught me so much about myself and forced me to step out of my innocent bubble. Because of my experience, I am no longer frightened about the world and what it can do to me—I've already proven that I am a survivor. I can look back to where I was and see how I've transformed into a stronger, wiser, more loving woman who can steer clear of the signs of abuse.

No More Lies.

I've learned to trust myself and my inner radar. I refuse to believe that everyone is automatically a liar. However, I'm a pretty good judge now when I come across a shady character and know how to disengage instead of provoke when those red flags fly high. A good story is now just that—a story and not the truth.

No More Guilt.

I worked hard to allow myself to be vulnerable again. In my quest for self-love, I realized that it is important to establish and enforce boundaries. And although compromise is a natural part of a relationship, guilt is not. I either oblige lovingly, or decline lovingly, without fear of retribution or abandonment. Because real love does neither—it works through differences instead of manipulating them.

Financial Freedom.

I think this was one of my easiest lessons and rewards. I have more money now than I ever did because no one is stealing from me, and I am grateful for everything that I have. I am generous with my abundance and protect it with smart investments, courtesy of my own background. Okay, I also use it to travel and otherwise indulge in pleasurable entertainment, like Broadway shows, dinner cruises, and yes, even gambling trips to Atlantic City. The irony isn't lost on me—I'm just in a place of trusted responsibility with no fear of lack. I'm no one's clean-up crew anymore, and it's fantastically liberating.

A Healthy Sex Life.

Good Lord, what I was missing out on all this time! I had no qualms as I allowed myself to explore the world of men and sexual fantasies. Now that I was out of my virginal cage, I learned how erotic and fun masturbating, toys, and even a little soft porn could be. The best part was that I finally had an orgasm (!) and learned that real men have no issues going down on a woman. How divine to finally experience this exquisite gift. And Dante has shown me multiple times that great sex and deep intimacy—physical *and* emotional—are very much a healthy focus in a honeymoon and marriage. I am one lucky woman.

No More Isolation.

After my friends and family rightfully slapped me upside the head with their loving, but much-deserved "I told you so" and "what the hell was wrong with you" statements, I opened my heart up to let them love me again. I let them support me through this most awful recovery of my life and refused to be alone ever again. Now, I am able to be the friend and supporter they need in return; the steady rock that holds space for their dark times and tears. My days of abandoning people who truly care about me are over. Love was the answer all along.

No More Mindfucks.

I see right through it all now. Even in the rare

instances in which I have to contact Blake for something regarding the divorce or past paperwork, I know what I am walking into and can expect. Nothing is the truth. I either laugh, research the lie, or call the bluff. But I usually just laugh and let it roll off me. It's amusing to see him try to manipulate me now, still somehow not grasping that he lost his control, or the fact that I really don't believe a word he says anymore; his charming spell has been forever broken.

I'm no longer the hushed, manipulated, naïve, conned, desperate-for-love little girl anymore. Blake will never have that power over me again.

Nobody ever will.

A NOTE
FROM THE AUTHOR

A ll is not what it appears to be.

That is the monstrous malady behind emotional abuse and this novel's exposé.

Beat Me With Your Words is a work of fiction that came to me with an urgent message that this story must be told. It reflects some of my personal experiences in multiple relationships I've had over my lifetime; stories I've sat and listened to while holding a friend's hand; hours of research; and a bit of imagination to make the novel richer. There is no one Emily Davidson, and no one Blake Denton.

Whatever its ingredients, the recipe is simply and profoundly a story of emotional abuse and gaslighting.

As a society, we cannot hide from the havoc this travesty wreaks in equal devastation to physical abuse. The time has come to shine a light on this ironically silent shadow of violence against another human being. The criticism-laced shamers, nay-sayers, good-meaning advisors, and abusive fearmongers will no longer beat me with *their* words.

We must bring emotional exploitation out of the darkness so that we can put a stop to the mental madness that quietly rips lives apart.

It's an "innocent" story of a great love gone

wrong, as seen through those famous rose-colored glasses of denial. As time evolves and awareness creeps in, the ingénue, Emily, dives deeper into the hidden (and blatant) red flags that were present the entire relationship; clues that were missed behind the promising curtain of forever. You'll witness the inner workings of emotional degradation and its casual consumption of a full life, and the "a-ha" after the survival.

If you see yourself in Emily's eyes, be empowered to recognize it, and get the help and healing you need and deserve. This in no way represents any kind of medical or psychological advisement, nor do I claim to be an expert on emotional abuse. I think the typical disclaimer is that this is "for entertainment purposes only;" however, I am sure you will find the narrative far from entertaining and much more gut-wrenching.

Read it for what it is: an inspirational journey that reflects the plight of too many Emily Davidsons in this world. This is *her* story. Yet, sadly, it's also the story of parts of you, me, and everyone else who has suffered any kind of emotional cruelty in life.

This is *our* story.

This is for every daughter who was told she wasn't good enough to reach for her dreams. Yes, you are. Get out there, follow your heart, and prove them wrong. You truly can be *anything.*

This is for every student whose teacher implied she wouldn't amount to much just because she wasn't as smart as others or didn't behave in a specific way. Who made that teacher God? You are perfect, flaws and all, so go share your unique talents with the world. We're waiting to see you soar.

This is for every friend whose "bestie" kept reminding her how she kept her around because she took pity on her—and never let her forget it. This isn't high school anymore, and she's not a friend. Fuck her and go find your tribe. The perfect weirdos will embrace you for being your authentic self.

This is for every female employee degraded by her male boss simply for having a vagina. He's just intimidated by your potential. Take your vagina and "Care Bear Stare" your fucking magical power out of it. Either shine without regrets or move on to better pastures. It's just a job—you deserve a legacy.

This is for every boy and man who has been subjected to the belittling of an insecure, abusive woman (or man). I see you. This book is written from a woman's perspective, but you are equally acknowledged for your pain and suffering. You *are* a good man—a better man than they will ever know. Time to ignore those voices and step into your pure masculine greatness.

This is for every girlfriend, wife, and partner who shrunk herself gradually into a shell of who she really was at the words of an abuser. Whether (s)he is your "soulmate," or you simply fear him/her, get the fuck out NOW.

Yes, it will be hard. Yes, it will be heartbreaking, and perhaps the most challenging thing you will ever do in your life. No, it will not be a smooth transition to safety.

But yes, you will be okay. Yes, you will heal and be whole again. Yes, you can even find genuine love one day.

First, you must choose yourself, and fight back. Leave. Get therapy—a lot of it. Take up a new hobby. Get rid of old photos and mementos. Talk to other abused women or men. Share your story. Step into the power of who you really are when stripped of the abuse and its scars. Find your happily ever after the abuse. Be brazen, not battered.

It is my wish that Emily's journey inspires you to take the next step, whatever that may be for you. Love yourself more than your abuser. And be FREE.

In love, admiration, and sisterhood,

Jenny

ACKNOWLEDGMENTS

I never thought my writer's journey would lead me here, to author a book about such a serious and important matter as emotional abuse. I hope within these words someone finds awareness, wisdom, or strength. I wrote this for you.

There are so many people I want to thank, but because of the nature of this genre and to honor the privacy of certain contributors, some shall remain nameless. You know who you are; the fearless women who shared your stories with me as I researched emotional abuse and the impact it had on your lives. Too many of you are within my sphere. Thank you for your bravery in sharing. I hope I honored your experiences in my work.

Thank you to my beta readers, who helped me to redefine my structure for a much better, richer story than I originally envisioned. (I'm looking at you, SL.) Your feedback was magical. Thank you also to my advanced reviewers; your honest, critical insight is appreciated more than you know.

Thank you to my amazing editors, Leslie and Abby, for catching what I could not and for steering me in the right direction. You ladies are rock stars! Thank you to Paul and Stacey, without whom I'd be lost in this self-publishing world. Your wisdom was exactly the guidance I needed.

Thank you as always to my family and closest friends for the unending support as I embarked on this very emotional, cathartic journey. Laura, Pam, Kristen, Molly, and Brenna in particular: thank you for holding my hand through some dark emotions and encouraging me always to keep going without judgment. Love to my mom and sisters, who have been a foundation I can always depend on. Family forever.

Thank you to my kids for putting up with my endless nights of "be right there" as I'd get lost in a whirlwind of inspiration that had to be captured. I only hope it taught you to work hard and have faith in the big picture of your dreams.

Thank you to all of the authors out their whose work inspired me to bravely take on such a triggering topic. Wounds come in all shapes and sizes, and together, I feel like we can heal through our words.

I could not have done this without you all. I am deeply grateful for every person who has played a role as the wind beneath my wings. Thank you for helping me to soar.

ALSO BY JENNY DEE

The Lost Heritage Trilogy

Call of the Celts
A Tuscan Treasure
The Catalan Key

Independent Titles

A Cali Christmas

Autobiographical Memoirs

Butterfly Travels
Butterfly Travels 2

The Cosmic Kids Club Series

Meet the Z Team
Planet Personalities
Stars Live in Houses, Too
Cosmic Kids Astrology
Numerology for Kids

ABOUT JENNY DEE

An avid writer since childhood, my career in professional writing anchored my passion and encouraged my dream to become an author—my first book, *Butterfly Travels,* was published in 2014. Since then, my world has opened up to unimaginable imagination. I love what I do.

I've never been a "one size fits all" type of girl. I like to connect to all kinds of people and share my stories and experiences in hopes that they touch a life. I don't ever want my inspiration to be limited to a single genre, so it is with a great love for writing that I offer a multitude of styles to strike your fancy, from travel memoirs and children's books to empowered women's romance and this introduction to my *Brazen Not Battered* collection of abuse survivor stories. And I have many more to tell.

To learn more about me or to subscribe to my publications, you can find me at www.jennydeeauthor.com, www.brazennotbattered.com, or simply scan this QR code.

~ Find Yourself in a Character ~